https://www.brindlebooks.co.uk

WELLINGTON'S DRAGOON 6:

# BURGOS AND BEYOND

## BY

## DAVID J. BLACKMORE

Brindle Books Ltd

Copyright © 2025 by David J Blackmore

This edition published by
Brindle Books Ltd
Wakefield
United Kingdom

Copyright © Brindle Books Ltd 2025

The right of David J Blackmore to be identified as author of this
work has been asserted by him in accordance with the
Copyright, Designs and Patents Act 1988.
ISBN 978-1-915631-27-5

# Acknowledgements

As ever I have to thank Gillian Caldicott and Neil Hinchliffe for reading my drafts and helping me see the wood despite the trees. Janet McKay continues to make useful plot suggestions and stimulate my thinking. Despite the absence of a horse from the cover, Mark Atkinson continues to help simply by keeping me riding two or three times a week. I have to thank Matthew Howarth and Buxton Crescent Heritage Trust for making the cover image possible by giving us access to Buxton's magnificent Assembly Room and Gabby Monet for making such a wonderful Elizabeth.

Finally, my thanks to Emma Garbett for the cover photography and design, and Richard Hinchliffe of Brindle books who does all the boring but essential stuff that keeps the books coming.

# Introduction

It is a little unusual, but I must start this with a health and safety warning. Please do not try any experiments with flour and candles. There are plenty of videos online if you want to see what can happen. You have been warned.

The retreat from Burgos was reckoned, by those who endured both, to be worse than Moore's retreat to Corunna. The suffering and the losses were horrendous. They are dealt with admirably in Carol Divall, Wellington's Worst Scrape, The Burgos Campaign, 1812 (Barnsley, 2012). It is, perhaps understandably, somewhat eclipsed by Napoleon's retreat from Moscow when the Grand Armée was destroyed in the Russian winter. That event had its impact on the Peninsular War, as you will read.

During the Burgos campaign, Michael Roberts finds himself the subject of unwelcome scrutiny by a senior officer and not only experiences the retreat from Burgos, but finds himself briefly in command of B Troop of the 16th Light Dragoons, who formed part of Wellington's rearguard. There is hard fighting, atrocious weather, stubborn determination and gross incompetence at the highest level.

It is not long, however, before he finds himself back in Lisbon, engaged in a deadly game with Renard's agents, one that has surprising results.

There are old friends, new friends and possibly even the love that Michael longs for as the story takes him from Spain to Lisbon, to London and back again.

# Burgos and Beyond

# Chapter 1

It was just after dawn, the sky blue and cloudless, and the full heat of the sun was still a few hours away. The road from Madrid to Valencia, rutted and baked hard under the August sun, rose gently from the banks of the river Tajuna, and headed steadily southwest, through rough brush and occasional olive groves. Since passing through the outlying British cavalry pickets the road had been deserted. Lieutenant Lapointe of the French Fifteenth Dragoons urged his horse on and up the slope. It was old, in dreadful condition, but it only had to carry him for the five days it would take to reach the French army at Valencia.

The road crested a low ridge and began to curve around an olive grove, it would hide the river from sight. Lapointe reined in the horse and turned it so he could look back the way he had come. Half a mile away he could see the two British light dragoons, sitting on their horses on the far side of the bridge over the river. Unconsciously his hand went to the breast of his coat, to the reassuring feel of his parole and his letter of safe conduct that should get him safely past any Spanish guerillas he might meet, signed by Wellington no less. He fervently hoped it wouldn't be needed. The two light dragoons remained, motionless. After a moment he turned his horse back towards Valencia and rode on.

Down at the riverside, Captain Michael Roberts of the Sixteenth Light Dragoons had watched Lapointe riding away from them.

"I suppose that old nag will make it to Valencia."

Corporal Emyr Lloyd turned his gaze away from the Frenchman towards his captain. "Aye, sir," he chuckled, paused and then went on. "It's strange thing, sir, but I wish him well."

Michael glanced briefly at Lloyd. "So do I Lloyd, so do I." He reached forward and rubbed the neck of his horse, Johnny.

They watched in silence as the Frenchman got further away.

"I certainly wish him luck when he gives my message to Renard."

"Yes, sir, I don't envy him that." Lloyd paused, thoughtful. "His men thought a lot of him, sir."

"Did they?"

"Yes, sir, when I rode with them back to our lines I managed a few words with their sergeant. He was worried about the Lieutenant."

In the distance Lapointe had halted briefly, turned to look back for a moment and then disappeared from view. Michael sat, watching the empty road for a minute, then spoke to Lloyd.

"Well, Lloyd, for good or evil, he's on his way now. Let's get back to Madrid."

The two men turned their horses and rode up, out of the valley. At the top of the slope they passed a picket of Portuguese cavalry, and Michael returned the salute of the officer in charge. It was a half day's easy ride back to Madrid and Michael saw no reason to hurry.

Michael was thoughtful as he rode, relaxed, occasionally wiping a bead of sweat from his face as the day got hotter. He was thinking about Lieutenant Lapointe. It had been a strange experience, sitting and eating and drinking with a French cavalry officer. They had mostly talked about horses and found much in common. It struck him that the young French officer was no different from the young officers of his own regiment. He was doing what he saw as his duty for his country. He was glad that he had saved him from death at the hands of Sanchez's lancers. But he could also understand Sanchez and his men. He had seen plenty of the cruelty and brutality that the French had inflicted on civilians. The farm outside Almoster, the dead family, the tortured father. He wondered what had happened to the young girl they had rescued. He recalled the cold, killing rage that had swept over him. Recollections of other killings passed through his mind. Too many, he asked himself? At the time they had all seemed necessary, still did. Which made him all the more pleased to have saved Lapointe and his men. Renard, however, was different matter, Michael would kill him without hesitation and with no regrets, just deep satisfaction.

Madrid was quiet in the midday heat and the sound of the horse's hooved echoed back as they rode through deserted streets. At the stables of the Royal Palace, Michael's dragoon servant, Hall, was waiting. Michael dismounted and handed him Johnny's reins.

"Everything well, Hall?"

"Yes, sir, but there's rumours we'm a moving, perhaps tomorrow or the day after." Hall's Dorset accent was as thick as Lloyd's Welsh. With his groom Bradley's Yorkshire and his servant Marcello's Spanish it was sometimes confusing.

"Very good, I'll see what I can find out, you can leave Johnny to Bradley and then you and Marcello had better start a bit of packing just in case."

The Royal Palace in Madrid had been occupied by Wellington and his staff and Michael made his way up marble staircases and along high ceilinged corridors to the rooms being used as offices. He was in luck and saw Colonel Lord Somerset, Wellington's military secretary, walking towards him. He saluted and Somerset greeted him.

"Roberts! Seen your fellow on his way?"

"Yes, sir."

"Good, I don't suppose you've heard, but we are off north, day after tomorrow, march at daybreak. Hill's staying here with four divisions and a couple of brigades of cavalry. The rest of us are marching, including you. His Lordship was quite specific about that." He paused and looked quickly around. He dropped his voice and went on. "Do try and avoid Colonel Gordon, His Lordship don't trust our new Quartermaster General. Between you and me he's too close to the government's opposition, writes them letters. I wouldn't mention it, normally, Captain, but if some of your, err, invaluable work became known about in London there could some embarrassment for the government, to say nothing of his Lordship. D'ye understand?"

"Yes, sir, of course."

"Yes, well, it's a shame we don't still have Murray as Quartermaster General, but there we are. Captain Campbell will try to keep you quartered away from Gordon. It's all a damned nuisance. Now, best make yourself scarce until we march, I expect you have things to do, eh?"

"Yes, sir, I believe I do."

"Oh, one other thing, Roberts, there's a post leaving tomorrow morning, if you've any letters you need to send."

"Thank you, sir."

Once he was back in his quarters, Michael confirmed to Hall that they would be leaving and told him to finish packing and to let Bradley and Lloyd know. Then he sat down to write some overdue letters. The first was to Mister Musgrave, head of the Aliens Office in London, in effect Britain's secret service. It was brief, but took some time to write as he had to put it into code. He wrote that, so far as Michael knew, Renard, head of the French secret service in Spain, was with King Joseph in Valencia. More importantly he enclosed sketches of Renard made by an artist in Madrid as studies for a portrait. The portrait he kept for himself.

The second letter was to his grandfather, the Reverend Isles, at his parish near Falmouth. It too was brief, there was little to tell that hadn't appeared in the English newspapers, but he hadn't written since his brief note after the battle at Salamanca to say that he was well. He was also able to tell his grandfather that Mrs Lloyd had been delivered of a baby girl at his house in Lisbon.

His letter writing finished, he turned his thoughts to his intelligence work, there was something he needed to do before leaving Madrid. He called out to Hall in the next room. "Hall, I shall be out for an hour or so."

A short walk from the Palace brought him to the grand house that was home to Señora Ortega. She was part of an intelligence collecting network of correspondents set up by Father Curtis of the Irish College in Salamanca and Michael had met her soon after arriving in Madrid. She covered her activities under the guise of one of Madrid's leading social figures, equally comfortable entertaining French or British senior figures. He knocked at the door and moments later he was face to face with the lady in her drawing room. In his hand was a rolled up canvas.

Michael bowed over her proffered hand. "Thank you for seeing me, Señora, it is good of you."

"My dear Captain, I am not going to turn away a handsome young cavalry officer!" She turned to the footman who has shown Michael in. "Iced lemonade, I think." He left on his errand. "Now, Captain, to what do I owe this visit?" She waved Michael into a nearby chair.

"Señora, do you remember, on my first visit to you, that I asked if you knew a Monsieur Renard, a civilian with Joseph's court?"

"Indeed I do, Captain."

"You told me you did not know him, and the business of the traitor priest Lopez rather pushed that matter into the background." The Señora raised an eyebrow quizzically, there was clearly more to come. "He is a person of more than a little interest, to myself, to Ambassador Stuart in Lisbon, indeed, to many people with an interest in, ah, intelligence matters."

The door to the drawing room opened and a footman entered with the lemonade. They sat in silence while the cold drink was served and the man left. Señora Ortega spoke first.

"You have intrigued me, Captain."

"Señora, Renard is the head of the French secret service in Spain."

The Señora's eyes opened wide with surprise and she muttered something Michael did not quite catch, but it sounded obscene. Michael carried on, pretending he had heard nothing.

"He was here, in Madrid and I have no doubt that if Joseph returns, so will Renard. Given the way you have helped, I thought you should be aware of this, in case the French should, err, return some day."

"But the English army is here!" she protested.

"Yes, Señora, but the day after tomorrow half of it is marching north, including myself. It is possible that Joseph will march from Valencia and attempt to recover Madrid, and he might succeed." The Señora sat silent, thoughtful and Michael took the opportunity to unroll the canvas, the portrait of Renard. "This is a portrait of Renard. I thought it might be a good thing for you to know what he looks like, it will help you to be on your guard."

Señora Ortega looked hard at the painting, the portrait of a man of about fifty, greying hair, grey eyes, clean shaven, unremarkable. "I shall certainly try to remember that face." She lifted her eyes to Michael's. "I think," she spoke slowly, weighing her words, "that, should he come to Madrid, he might be a useful source of information. If, of course, I can make his acquaintance. I certainly didn't come across him socially when the French were here, but then he looks so," she sought for the right word, "so ordinary one could easily overlook him."

"Señora, please, I came to warn you, not to ask you to take risks!"

She smiled winningly at him. "Captain, so gallant! And I am grateful, but you will allow me to decide what I risk for my country."

Michael gave her a bow. "Of course, Señora. May I make a suggestion, however?"

"Of course."

"I believe that, during the French occupation, you were able to communicate with Lisbon as well as Father Curtis in Salamanca?"

"Yes."

"Then may I ask that, should you learn anything, that you communicate it to Ambassador Stuart in Lisbon? It may be easier than trying to reach the good Father, particularly if we should be forced to give up Salamanca."

"Do you think that likely?"

"Señora, I have no idea, but in war..." He shrugged and left his sentence unfinished. "But, Señora, please be careful."

"Thank you, Captain. I have my little, what do you call it, network? And you may be assured that should the French return to Madrid it will return to work." She smiled. "And I shall be careful."

It was still dark, two days later, when Wellington led his staff out of the stable yard of the Royal Palace. As usual it was a long cavalcade, but, also as usual, Wellington pressed ahead and soon left behind the slow moving mules and baggage, Hall, Bradley, Marcelo and Michael's spare horses with them. Michael, had decided to ride Robbie, and with Lloyd next to him, hung back at the rear of the party with Wellington. As the dawn broke, he realised, with some disquiet, that only a few yards away was Colonel Gordon. Michael and Lloyd stood out in their blue coats and Tarletons amongst the red coated staff, and it wasn't long before Gordon noticed them. He saw him give them a long, quizzical look and then he pushed his horse forward, away from them. Michael was relieved, but not for long.

At a brief pause to water the horses and snatch a drink themselves, Colonel De Lancey walked over to Michael. They exchanged salutes and De Lancey looked around before speaking quietly.

"Look, Roberts, Gordon has just been asking me who you are."

"Oh!"

"Yes, quite. Now I know very well the sort of work you've been doing, but Gordon doesn't. The Peer, " he used Wellington's nickname, "has made it quite clear that he ain't to, either. Fellow's incompetent and supports the opposition at home, been sending them letters." He paused, "And that's indiscreet of me." He smiled, "But I am sure I can count on your discretion?"

"Of course, sir. Lord Somerset said something similar."

"Has he? Good. Anyway, I told Gordon you were one of Sir Stapleton's staff, with us in Sir Stapleton's absence and generally liaising with the Spanish guerillas. Look, I am going to try to have a quiet word with The Peer, or perhaps Somerset, see if we can't get you away, Sanchez is out in front of us somewhere. I think you might be better off with him."

"Yes, sir, thank you."

That evening Michael was in the stables, or rather the old barn that was doing duty as stables for some of the staff horses. His quarters were in a very run down and dilapidated hovel on the edge of the small village. Bradley and Marcello were going to stay with the horses. He, Lloyd and Hall would squeeze into the single room with a roof still on it. Hall was endeavouring to make it habitable. Leaving the stables on his own, Michael was surprised by figure standing nearby, a cigar glowing in the dark.

"Roberts, isn't it?" There was a hint of a Scottish burr in the voice. With a sinking heart he realised it was Colonel Gordon.

Michael saluted and saw the glowing cigar end waved in reply. "Yes, sir."

"Tell me, Roberts, what are you doing on Lord Wellington's staff?"

"Begging your pardon, Colonel, but I'm not, I'm on Sir Stapleton's staff."

"So what are you doing here and not with Colonel Bock?" There was a note of irritation in Gordon's voice. "I believe I am correct in saying that he has command of the cavalry in Sir Stapleton's absence?"

"Err..." Michael hesitated in the face of Gordon's blunt demand.

"Come on, Captain, what are your orders, what are you doing, what do you do?"

"I, err, I usually act as liaison with the Spanish irregulars, sir, such as Sanchez."

"And Sanchz is a day ahead of us, Captain Roberts, why are you not with him? And I am given to believe that you were in Madrid while he was up around Salamanca? So, what were you doing in Madrid, eh? Is there any good reason for your presence? Perhaps you should be sent home, eh?"

"Ah, Roberts, there you are! Evenin' Colonel Gordon."

"Lord Somerset, and good evening to you."

Michael saluted as the two Colonels exchanged pleasantries. He was relieved at Somerset's appearance, but Somerset was only a Lieutenant Colonel while Gordon was a full Colonel. Gordon could simply wait out Somerset and then return to his cross examination of Michael. He need not have worried.

"I'm sorry, Colonel," Somerset apologised, "but I am going to have to take Roberts away from you. His

Lordship wants to speak to him before he goes on his way in the morning."

"What? Oh, very well." Gordon turned to Michael. "I expect we shall have another occasion to talk, Roberts." With that he turned and strode off into the darkness.

"That was awkward." Somerset muttered as he watched Gordon go. He turned back to Michael. "Come along, quickly, we need to find Lord Wellington."

As they set off together, Michael asked, "Where am I going, sir, I've had no orders?"

"I know, dammit, so we need to ensure you get some, and Wellington hasn't asked to see you either. I heard some of what Gordon was asking you, and the sooner we get you away, the better."

They reached Wellington's quarters and passed in. Somerset saw one of Wellington's servants who told him His Lordship was in the first room on the right and on his own.

Somerset addressed Michael. "Now, just you wait here while I go and explain things."

A few minutes later, Somerset stuck his head out of the room and beckoned Michael in. Michael had removed his Tarleton and came to attention in front of Wellington who was sitting at a small table, writing by the light of a single candle. He looked up.

"Roberts, I hear that Colonel Gordon has been asking awkward questions?"

"My Lord."

"It's alright, Roberts, Somerset has explained things to me, and I agree that it would be best to send you away." He smiled. "Back to your old friend Don Julian."

"Yes, My Lord, thank you."

Wellington waved dismissively. "Somerset will write your orders now. You had better leave before daylight, Don Julian is a good day ahead of us. You can stay with him until Sir Stapleton returns. Frankly, Roberts, the last thing I want is you called home and subjected to damned awkward questions. And I want you out here where you can do the most good. That's all."

"Yes, My lord, thank you."

Michael and his small party left an hour before dawn. To his relief he didn't see Gordon again. For the first day he pushed on hard. He didn't want the embarrassment of being caught up with by Wellington, who was known to ride hard. He hoped The Peer's pace would be held down by the relatively slow marching infantry. They pushed on for as long as there was daylight and halted for the night in a small, walled olive grove, high in the Sierra de Guadarrama. The horses were tired, but there was grass in the grove and the walls were sound, so they let them graze. Michael, Lloyd and Hall took it in turns to stand guard, Hall last and he roused them at the first hint of dawn.

Another long day, at an easier pace, found them riding towards the small town of Villa Castin just as dusk came on. No sooner had they caught sight of the massive church dominating the town, than they were challenged by Sanchez's pickets. Then they were recognised, they were greeted with smiles and one of the lancers rode with them to lead them to Sanchez's quarters.

Sanchez had occupied the large civic building in the main plaza. As they rode towards it, Sanchez appeared on the balcony.

"Is that Captain Roberts I see? Hola, Captain." Sanchez turned and shouted behind him, "Strenuwitz! Captain Roberts has come to visit us!" He disappeared into the building to emerge into the plaza as Michael and his party were dismounting. "Come in, Captain, come in and tell me why you are here? You," he called out to one of his men standing nearby, "show the Captain's men to the stables where my horses are." He turned to Michael, "There is plenty of room in this wonderful old town, and that's without invading the Convent." He laughed. "You and your men can stay in this grand building and you are just in time for dinner. Now, come in, come in."

Michael allowed himself to be practically swept up and carried into the building. In a large dining room he found the Bohemian Strenuwitz who greeted him with a smile and a bow. "Captain, it is good to see you again."

"And you, Major." Michael replied.

Sanchez instructed Michael, "Now, sit yourself down and tell us what brings you here?"

Strenuwitz poured wine for all of them and Michael took a good draught of it. He shrugged, "I think I have been sent to be kept out of the way." He gave a wry smile. "Someone has been asking awkward questions about my, err, role in the army."

"Ah!" Sanchez nodded gravely. "I do not know quite all that you do, but I do know, as does Strenuwitz," the Bohemian nodded, "that you are no ordinary British officer, you are Wellington's Dragoon, and that is enough for me."

"Thank you, Don Julian."

"Now, come, more wine, and tell us what you have been doing. So far as you can." Sanchez grinned mischievously. "It must be six weeks since you left us." He became serious again. "I hear that things didn't turn out well with that man you stopped me from hanging?"

"No. No it didn't. He fooled me completely." He paused before saying, "I should have let you hang him, it would have saved a lot of trouble."

"But I also hear that you did well, in the end."

Michael grunted cynically. "If you call getting a good friend killed doing well."

Sanchez sat down opposite Michael and looked at him for a moment. Then he simply said, "Tell me."

To his surprise Michael found himself doing just that. Perhaps it was the wine, perhaps it was Sanchez's obvious understanding, but tell him he did. Speaking quietly, he told Sanchez and Strenuwitz about the events in Madrid and Antonio's death. They sat in silence and listened. To his greater surprise he found himself telling them about Lapointe, which meant telling them something about Renard, just enough for them to understand. Once he had finished Michael realised that he felt better, relieved at having shared the story with Sanchez and Strenuwitz.

"That, Captain," said Sanchez, "is quite a story." Strenuwitz nodded in agreement. "Thank you for telling us." He topped up the wine glasses. "I think Lieutenant Lapointe is a very lucky man to have you for a friend." He smiled. "And now we must eat and not talk of the war. Instead, we shall talk of horses and women." He grinned. "Tell me, Captain, how is Señora Martinez?"

Michael managed a wry smile in return. "Ah, Don Julian, I have not seen her since we parted after Wellington's Ball in Salamanca, towards the end of June."

Sanchez pulled a face. "Bad luck, Captain. And how are your horses? You don't seem to have acquired any more since we saw you last?"

Michael laughed as servants came in with their dinner and the atmosphere became relaxed and convivial.

The following morning they were on the road north at dawn. Michael and his party rode quietly along just in the rear of Sanchez's main body. He had seen Lieutenant Fraile briefly, just long enough to enquire after his wife and child. There would be time aplenty for more. With no duties, Michael was happy to ride gently along, the pace steady as lancer patrols explored ahead of them. He thought about the previous evening and still wondered at his admissions to Sanchez. He recalled Sanchez's enquiry about Señora Martinez, Victoria. He wondered if he might see her again when they got to Salamanca, or thereabouts. He smiled to himself at his recollections of their time together. He also had to recognise the realism of their parting, their shared recognition that what they had was a fleeting passion. He silently harrumphed. He had to face it, any relationship he might strike up was going to be fleeting, at least until Buonaparte was defeated and he was, what? Back in England? Out of the army? Could he leave the army now? Even if the war were over? He wasn't sure he would be able to do that. His life before the regiment seemed to be that of a different person, and an unconscionable sort of existence. Dull and pointless. Life, he concluded, would be far better for him, as a soldier, if he could avoid any romantic entanglements. Another silent harrumph. He knew himself too well to have much faith in that resolution, but he could be wary, careful and, dare he think it, discriminating. He laughed at his own pomposity.

Lloyd's voice broke in on his reverie. "Captain, sir, Don Julian's coming."

As it was, Sanchez wanted nothing in particular, merely playing the conscientious host to a man he liked, so they rode along together, chatting about this and that and nothing of consequence.

A week later Michael celebrated his twenty-fourth birthday in a small village to the north of the river Pisuerga. They had found the French army at Valladolid and followed it slowly as it retreated up the Pisuerga valley. Anson's brigade, including the Sixteenth, was at the head of Wellington's army, and Sanchez with his lancers and Michael was hanging around their northern flank, up in the hills above the river, protecting them from attack. There was little for Michael to do except enjoy the daily company of

Sanchez, Strenuwitz and the rest of his men. Some of the lancers even gave Hall some lessons with the lance, as they had to Michael and Lloyd in Ciudad Rodrigo. That all seemed a long time ago.

That day the French had left the town of Duenas and Anson's brigade moved in. Michael had all but forgotten about his birthday, but Lloyd hadn't, and he had mentioned it to Strenuwitz, who had told Sanchez, and that evening there was a small but merry gathering to celebrate. Michael dined with Sanchez and half a dozen of his officers, including Fraile and the always present Strenuwitz. Michael was aware that his regiment and friends were only a few miles away and wished he could be with them.

Strenuwitz was sitting next to Michael and noticed that he had gone a little quiet. Michael caught his eye. "We are both a long way from home, Major."

"Yes, indeed we are. These are good men" Strenuwitz gave a small gesture at their fellows, "but not quite family." He smiled and nodded in the direction of Duenas, "Not even your regiment just over there is real family. I know you lost your parents, do you have any family in England?"

"My grandfather and my uncle. And you, in Bohemia?"

"I have absolutely no idea. I just hope to find out one day, when Buonaparte is defeated and we can all go home."

"I'll drink to that," said Michael.

And the two men raised their glasses to each in a silent toast.

# Chapter 2

Valencia was pleasantly warm in the mid-September sun. Renard looked out from the window of his office in the Customs House. With some fifteen thousand refugees from Madrid in the city, most of them officials and their families, room was scarce and his department was squeezed onto one quarter of the top floor. He even had to sleep in his office, it was insulting to him, a senior officer in the secret police. He knew for a fact that the military headquarters were far more spacious and comfortable. They were in a more central palace, adjacent to the palace now occupied by King Joseph. It rankled.

From his window he could look down into a large open space just inside one of the city gates. The area was full of makeshift shelters for the refugees from Madrid. It was a picture of squalor. It also stank. The location made Renard feel uncomfortable and not just because of the smell. He didn't like being located just inside the city walls, somehow it made him feel vulnerable to attack, but, he supposed, it could have been worse. At least being somewhat removed from the military and the court meant that he was largely left to get on with his business without constant interference from the military. Not that he was being particularly successful. It was proving impossible to obtain any intelligence on affairs in Lisbon or Madrid.

Nothing had come from Lisbon since midsummer, when the news reached them that Loiro, a long serving and successful agent, had simply vanished.

Renard knew that Roberts had been in Lisbon and that Loiro was trying to arrange his elimination. He was convinced that Roberts was responsible for Loiro vanishing. His frustration and anger was increased by the knowledge that one of his clerks, Faucher, had sent three agents from Madrid to Lisbon back in July. Nothing was ever heard from them. And now he could get no news from Madrid.

He took a deep breath to calm his rising temper. It was that bastard Roberts, he was sure of it. Why, oh, why could no one kill him? There was a knock at the door.

"What is it?" He snapped loudly.

The door opened and one of his junior clerks looked in.

"I beg your pardon, Monsieur, but there's a messenger here. Marshal Jourdan wishes to see you at once."

He stormed noisily out of the offices, the messenger, a young infantry corporal rushing along behind him

Faucher watched him go and heaved a sigh of relief. Perhaps they could relax for a while, although God alone knew what mood the old bastard might be in when he returned. He had been getting increasingly difficult and demanding since they had left Madrid five or so weeks ago. Faucher hoped he would be away long enough that they could legitimately slip away at the end of the working day. He was sharing a room with Lucroy, another of Renard's clerks and of an equal rank with Faucher. He was not his favourite person, a bit too much of a through and through Bonapartist to make an easy fellow lodger. He wanted to get away, alone, to the small tavern he had discovered, the one with the very pretty young girl who worked there. He watched her while he ate and drank and she scurried around clearing tables, delivering food and drink while her mother worked in the kitchen, all under the watchful gaze of her father, an ugly looking brute Faucher did not want to cross.

They had been suspicious at first of the Frenchman who spoke good Spanish. They usually got a few soldiers in who just drank too much and were a nuisance. A nuisance to Faucher because then the girl would disappear. But, gradually, they had got used to him. He paid in silver and didn't haggle. He knew it was risky, going about alone, but the city seemed quiet and subdued and it was worth it to see the girl. Occasionally she would give him a shy smile when her father wasn't watching. It reminded him of a small country tavern near where he grew up, only the language was different.

While the time passed slowly in the heat of the afternoon Faucher wondered what was happening in Russia. His younger brother and two cousins were with the Grand Armée, marching irresistibly towards Moscow and victory over Russia and the Tsar. That there would be victory, no one doubted, but that didn't stop him being concerned for his brother and cousins. He wondered if it got hot there. He snorted, at least they didn't have to contend with Renard.

Marshal Jourdan kept Renard waiting, and then he kept him standing. Renard was angered, and concerned. Jourdan was no friend. He sat behind his desk, silently observing Renard's discomfort.

"Any news for me? From Madrid? From Lisbon? About Wellington's army?"

"Marshal Jourdan, it is very difficult..."

"That's no then?" Jourdan cut him off.

"No, Excellency."

Silence fell again and Jourdan pursed his lips, frowned and drummed his fingers on the desk.

"It's not good enough, Monsieur."

Renard remained silent.

"What have you and your department been doing?" Jourdan's voice rose. "It was bad enough in Madrid, but now, when I need information more than ever you give me nothing!" He slammed his hand flat on his desk, sending papers fluttering to the floor. He took a deep breath.

"For all that I know Wellington may be marching on us at this very moment. And how much warning will I get? A day if we are lucky, perhaps half a day, Renard, half a day, and do you know why? Because that's as far as I can send patrols without them being wiped out by guerillas."

He paused, pulled a handkerchief from his sleeve and mopped his brow.

"I suppose you will blame your failure on this damned British officer, what's his name?"

"Captain Roberts, Excellency."

"Yes, him. I find it very difficult to believe that a single, low ranking, British cavalry officer is responsible for reducing a department of the Imperial secret service to complete ineffectiveness and impotency. Anyway, I thought you had taken steps to deal with him?"

"Yes, Excellency, I did, I sent men after him, to Lisbon."

"And?"

"They have all disappeared, Excellency."

Jourdan rolled his eyes in exasperation. "So, added to everything else, you can't even arrange to deal with a single, junior, British officer? No, don't try to answer. I don't want to know why you, yes, you, Monsieur Renard, have failed so abysmally in your duty to the Emperor, to his brother, King Joseph, and to me, Monsieur, to me!"

Silence fell again.

"Renard, I don't care how you do it, but I must know what is happening in Madrid, what Wellington is doing, do you understand just how important that is?"

"Yes, Excellency."

"Good. And I am going to give you some help, although God knows why I should, except," his voice rose, "I need some bloody information about what is happening in Madrid!" He took a breath and smiled coldly. "There's a woman in Madrid who seemed to know everything that was going on. She is of no great intellect or importance. Frankly, I don't think she cares who runs Spain as long as she can attend balls and give dinners and hold soirees. Which she does very well, as I can testify. Both myself and the King have been entertained at the Señora's. Ha! The way she flirted with the King... Anyway, she's probably entertaining the English now, in fact, I don't doubt it, Wellington himself, probably. Her name is Señora Ortega. I suggest that if, somehow, you can get someone into her house, her confidence even, you may well learn a lot. Damn it, even some gossip would be something!"

"Yes, Excellency, thank you."

"Now, go and do something."

Renard walked back to his office in a black mood. It was all very well for Jourdan to rant and give orders, he had no idea how difficult intelligence work was. He also didn't grasp how difficult it was to succeed and how fragile that success was, how just one man might, with a little luck, foil the work of his department. And that man was Roberts. He was sure of it. The man had killed his son and now he was killing his career. He had to get rid of him, then, he was sure, everything would be alright.

Back in his office he took a petty satisfaction by summoning his two senior clerks, Faucher and Lucroy, and treating them as Jourdan had treated him.

"Gentlemen," his voice dripped sarcasm, "I have just had the pleasure of an interview with our beloved Marshal Jourdan." He paused, and watched trepidation wash over the faces of the two men. "He is not happy, which means that I am not happy, I am not happy with you and I am not happy with the performance of this department."

Faucher groaned silently as Renard ranted at them about ineffectiveness and incompetence, demanding information, demanding action on that bloody Englishman Roberts. He had heard it all before, he didn't like it, it was grossly unfair, they did what they could. He stood there, expressionless and tried to let it all wash over him, there was nothing he could do, not stuck here in the back of beyond. He paid attention again as Renard asked a question that seemed to need an answer.

"So, what do you suggest we do to put right this unacceptable state of affairs?"

That "we" was a first thought Faucher. He took a chance to speak.

"Well, Monsieur, we did send three agents to Lisbon from Madrid, Monsieur, nearly two months ago, before we left Madrid."

"And what have we heard from them? Nothing!"

"No, Monsieur, but since we did leave Madrid, that will have made it harder for them to communicate with us, Monsieur."

"And had we heard anything before we left Madrid?"

"No, Monsieur."

"And have we heard anything from Madrid? Marshal Jourdan is very keen to know what Wellington is doing. He tells me his patrols can't go more than a day's ride from Valencia. He needs to know if Wellington is coming this way."

Lucroy chipped in. "We have sent people, Monsieur," then his face fell, "but we've not heard anything from them, Monsieur."

"And have we received anything from anyone? No, don't bother, I know the answer, nothing!"

Renard regarded them both. "Well, we will have to send more people. Oh, in his wisdom, Marshal Jourdan suggested a possible source of information in Madrid. A Señora Ortega. Do either of you know anything about her?"

Faucher and Lucroy exchanged glances.

"Err, yes, Monsieur," Lucroy began, hesitantly.

"Come on, out with it man?"

"There were rumours, Monsieur. She was said to have sympathies with the enemy, Monsieur."

"Is that it?" Renard bellowed. "Most of bloody Madrid had sympathies with the enemy!"

"We tried to investigate, Monsieur," Faucher added, "but she has powerful friends, Monsieur, like the Marshal, and the King has dined there, Monsieur. It was said he, err, was rather taken with the Señora, Monsieur. We were warned off, Monsieur."

Renard stared at him. "You didn't think to mention it to me?"

"I'm sorry, Monsieur, but they were only rumours and she seemed pretty harmless by all accounts."

Renard sighed. "Yes, I'm sure you are right, Jourdan said much the same." He brightened up. "But rumours must start somewhere, and if not her, perhaps among the guests to her balls and dinners there were those who kept their ears open and passed on what they heard? Jourdan might be her friend, but he has suggested that we must try to get someone into Madrid and into her establishment. See if they can hear anything useful. And if the Marshal suggests..." He sat, thoughtful for a moment. "Faucher, you can concentrate on Lisbon, see if you can manage to do something there. Get some more agents in there, or perhaps I should just send you?" He smirked at the look of shock on Faucher's face. Lucroy grinned, and incurred Renard's wrath. "And you, Lucroy, you can look to Madrid. Get someone in there, and into Ortega's if you can. That might keep the Marshal happy, even if they don't come up with anything. And he is right about needing more than half a day's warning of any advance by Wellington. And remember, I can send you as well! Now, both of you, get out and do something! Let's see which of you has a future in intelligence."

The two men returned to their desks without speaking or even looking at each other. Faucher was livid. He had sent the three men to Lisbon, not Lucroy. It wasn't his fault if they had then been driven out of Madrid, severing any communications with Lisbon. Well, he would try again, and was quietly confident he would be more successful than Lucroy. The man had no subtlety, was too dogmatic, too fervent in his belief in the Emperor. He would show him how to run agents, him and Renard both. He would start afresh and assume the three men already sent were dead or otherwise lost to him. He would think about the best way to achieve what he wanted, he would not be rushed.

Lieutenant Lapointe was about half a day's ride from Valencia when he came across the first French patrol. He was making his way quietly along when he was challenged by two chasseur vedettes hidden amongst trees at the roadside. They had surprised him, but it was they who seemed the more surprised. A French dragoon officer was the last thing they expected to see coming down the road from Madrid. One of them escorted him a little further along the road and handed him over to an outlying picket of a sergeant and half a dozen chasseurs. The sergeant questioned him, curiously, apologetically, then he sent him on down the road with two chasseurs as an escort. And so it went on, passed from escort to escort, until, finally, a slightly bemused staff officer knocked on a door and showed him into the presence of Marshal Jourdan.

"Well, well, who do we have here?"

Laponte saluted. "Lieutenant Lapointe, Marshal, Fifteenth Dragoons, Army of Portugal, released from Madrid on parole, Monsieur."

"You are a long way from home, Lieutenant?"

"Yes, Excellency."

"And on parole, you say?"

"Yes, Excellency." Lapointe pulled his parole from inside his coat and handed it to the Marshal.

Jourdan's eyebrows shot up in surprise. "This is signed by Wellington himself!"

"Yes, Excellency."

Jourdan indicated a chair. "Sit down, Lieutenant, and tell me how you come to be in Valencia with this parole when your regiment and the Army of Portugal are God knows where up in the north?" He addressed the staff officer, "Fetch coffee for us, I suspect this is a long story."

And Lapointe told him. Told him about how he and his escort were captured by Sanchez when carrying dispatches intended for Paris. Then Jourdan remembered.

"You came to Madrid, without your dispatches or your men, just some wild story no one believed. I seem to recall that no one believed the Spanish wouldn't have killed you if your story was true. Were you not left in the Retiro?"

"Yes, Excellency, and I was captured again when it fell. And it was a Captain Roberts who got me my parole, Monsieur, he had captured me the first time, he was with Sanchez."

"Roberts?" Jourdan exclaimed.

"Err, yes, Excellency. He saved my men and I from being killed, Monsieur. Took my surrender and then faced down Sanchez and his men to protect us."

"He did, did he? Now just why did he do that? And just why did he arrange this rather impressive parole for you?"

"He wants me to deliver a message, Excellency."

"A message? Who to?"

"A Monsieur Renard, Excellency. I understand he is something to do with intelligence?"

Jourdan laughed. "Yes, you might say that. He is the head of the secret service in Spain. Show me the message."

"It's not written, Excellency."

"No? So, what is it?"

"Excellency, my apologies, but the message is that Captain Roberts is going to kill Renard, Excellency, sorry."

Jourdan stared at Lapointe and then roared with laughter.

Lapointe was confused. "Excellency, I don't understand, why is that funny?"

Jourdan smiled. "I suppose that it isn't really a laughing matter. And it is probably better if you don't know." Jourdan looked thoughtfully at Lapointe. "I think, Lieutenant, that you should go and deliver your message. One of my staff officers can show you where Renard can be found, and make sure you get away again. Then, I think, we will find you quarters here until I decide what to do about you."

Renard was just thinking about going in search of some dinner when there was a knock at his office door. In response to his summons one of his clerks looked in.

"Begging your pardon, Monsieur, but one of Marshal Jourdan's staff officers is here to see you, with a dragoon officer, Monsieur."

Renard groaned, what new indignity was Jourdan about to inflict on him? The door was opened wider and a staff officer he knew by sight came in. He was followed by a young dragoon officer who looked more than a little the worse for wear. His green uniform was torn and patched, his boots filthy and his brass helmet, tucked under his arm, was dull and tarnished.

The staff officer spoke. "I beg your pardon, Monsieur Renard, Marshal Jourdan asked me to bring this officer to see you, and to return him to the Marshal." The odd phrase caught Renard's attention. "This is Lieutenant Lapointe, Fifteenth Dragoons, Army of Portugal, he has a message for you, Monsieur." With that the officer took a few steps back, leaving Lapointe to face Renard.

"Very well, Lieutenant, what message do you have for me from the Army of Portugal?" He held out his hand. "Be so good as to deliver it to me then you can go."

"It's a verbal message, Monsieur, from a Captain Roberts in the English army."

The staff officer could not help but smile at Renard's reaction. His eyes bulged, his face turned puce, he struggled to speak, and eventually he did.

"What the devil do you mean by this, Monsieur?" He glared at the staff officer. "Is this some sort of sick joke?"

Lapointe answered him. "No, Monsieur, not at all."

"What is it then, tell me!"

"Captain Roberts," Lapointe paused, took a deep breath and went on, "Captain Roberts says he intends to kill you, Monsieur."

There was a moments silence, and then Renard screamed. "What! How dare you come here and talk to me like that? Who do you think you are? I shall have you arrested and thrown in prison." He rang a handbell on his desk furiously and a moment later the door opened and a clerk came in. "Fetch the guards, I want this man arrested!"

The clerk made to leave, but the staff officer stopped him with a hand on his arm and a shake of his head. "No, Monsieur, my orders from Marshal Jourdan are quite clear. I am to see that Lieutenant Lapointe delivers his message and then escort him back to headquarters. Come Lieutenant, you have delivered your message, I think we can leave now." Lapointe shot out of the room followed by the clerk. The staff officer looked at Renard, standing, fuming by his desk. "Good day, Monsieur, thank you for your time." He pulled the door closed behind him and faced the outer office with a smile on his face. "That went well."

"What was that about?" Faucher asked. He and all the clerks were on their feet looking shocked.

The staff officer continued to smile. "Are you aware of an English officer, Captain Roberts?" Faucher nodded, bemused by the officer's reply. "Well, the Lieutenant here has just informed your Monsieur Renard that Captain Roberts intends to kill him." He looked around. "I should leave him until he calls for someone. Come along, Lieutenant, they will be serving dinner in our quarters shortly."

Slowly all the clerks resumed their seats, staring nervously at the door to Renard's office. They had all heard what he had shouted about arresting the dragoon officer. Lucroy was the first to break the silence.

"That officer should have been arrested, he must be working for the English, he must be a traitor."

Faucher looked at his colleague but did not respond. Renard was being more than unreasonable in his demands, he knew he had done his best, and the men he had sent to Lisbon might be dead for all he knew. Dead because he had persuaded them to go. One thing did occur to Faucher, if Roberts was in Madrid and with the English army, then he probably wasn't responsible for the disappearance of those three agents. He needed to ask Lapointe when he had been captured, but the more he thought about it, the more he thought it unlikely that Roberts had been active in Lisbon since Loiro vanished. In which case others were at work and Roberts was not solely to blame, contrary to what Renard was insisting. And if Roberts wasn't solely responsible, it was rather a waste of time going after him. Faucher began to think Renard's obsession was more to do with the death of his son than the intelligence war and that he was using the secret service to get his revenge. It was all so wrong.

Renard didn't appear for the rest of that day. No one knew what he was doing, no one was prepared to find out. No one dared leave for dinner. Instead they pretended to work until they felt they could safely slip away for the night. Faucher made his way across the city, grateful that it was still daylight. At the military headquarters he asked for Lieutenant Lapointe. The orderly sergeant on duty was about to send him on his way when he produced his papers identifying him as a member of the secret police. The effect on the sergeant was instantaneous. Within a minute he had sent a soldier off to find the newly arrived dragoon Lieutenant. Ten anxious minutes passed before he returned, followed by Lapointe. Lapointe looked at Faucher as if he vaguely remembered seeing him somewhere, then Faucher reminded him.

"My apologies for disturbing you, Lieutenant, but I wonder if I might have a few words with you. I was in the outer office when you called on Monsieur Renard."

Recognition dawned and Lapointe replied, "Yes, of course, Monsieur...?"

"Faucher, Lieutenant. There's a small tavern I know, perhaps I can buy you a glass of something?"

"I take it from your offer that you do not bring some difficult message from Renard? Or do you?"

"No, no, Lieutenant, he doesn't even know I have come to see you."

"Oh?" Lapointe paused, looking thoughtfully at Faucher, then he made up his mind. "Then lead the way, Monsieur."

Three infantrymen were sitting at a table when they walked into the tavern. At the sight of Lapointe they started to rise to leave, but Lapointe waved them back down with an easy smile. He also gave a smile to Faucher's waitress, as Faucher thought of her. Faucher ordered a jug of the local red wine. Both men remained silent until the wine was poured and they were left to themselves.

"So, Monsieur," Lapointe began, waving his hand at the wine, "to what do I owe this?"

"I should like to ask you about the English officer, Captain Roberts."

"Why? What is his connection with Renard? I don't understand why he would want to kill Renard!"

Faucher took a deep breath. "Please, Lieutenant, tell me your story, and then I shall explain."

Lapointe paused, took a mouthful of wine and repeated the story he had given to Marshal Jourdan. Faucher interrupted just once, to ask Lapointe when he had been captured. The answer told him that he was right, Roberts couldn't have been in Lisbon when the fresh agents had been sent.

When Lapointe had finished, Faucher asked him, "What did you think of Captain Roberts?"

"I thought he was a decent man, he saved the lives of myself and my men. The way he faced down Sanchez and his lancers took courage. Frankly, I don't understand why he sent that message, but he said that was why he saved us. I can only assume he has his reasons."

"He saved you?" Faucher sounded surprised.

"The Spanish guerillas don't take prisoners, Monsieur."

"Ah, yes, of course."

"Now, what can you tell me about Captain Roberts."

Faucher told him about Renard's son, Renard's subsequent attempts to have Roberts killed and how he held Roberts responsible for his intelligence set backs. He added that from what he had just heard it was not possible for Roberts to be solely responsible, but Renard had convinced himself that he was. He hinted that it was the death of his son that was driving Renard's determination to kill Roberts rather than anything to do with the intelligence war.

Lapointe refilled their glasses. "That, Monsieur is quite a story." He shook his head. "All I know is that I am alive thanks to that Englishman." He chuckled. "It is a strange thing, to be indebted to an enemy." He thought for a moment. "If he did kill Renard's son, then how and why?"

Faucher shrugged. "All I know for sure is that young Renard was on some sort of intelligence gathering mission. He didn't return."

"So it might not have been Roberts that killed him? If he is dead and isn't rotting in some prison somewhere?"

"Apparently there was a report from an agent in Lisbon that told Renard what had happened."

"Have you seen it?"

"No, it was received in Paris, before Renard came out here."

"Could you ask the agent for information?"

"No, he's dead."

"Ah!" Laponte took a drink. "All I know for sure is that I have spent time with Roberts, and he didn't strike me as a dangerous killer. In fact, I rather liked him. And, as it turned out, I could trust him."

"Why do you say that?"

"He didn't just put me on a horse to take my chances with the guerillas between here and Madrid, you know." He reached into his coat and pulled out a paper that he handed to Faucher. "He got me this"

Faucher read the paper with increasing surprise. "But this is a safe conduct signed by Wellington himself!"

"Yes, fortunately I didn't need it." He reached to take it back, but Faucher held on to it.

"Do you need it anymore, Lieutenant?"

Lapointe hesitated. "No, I suppose not. Is it useful to you?"

"I don't know, yet. But I will be grateful and do what I can to help you."

Lapointe shrugged. "Very well, but I shall hold you to that."

Unknown to the two men, they had been seen talking together. When Faucher returned to his office the following morning a smirking Lucroy informed him, "Renard wants to see you." He knocked on Renard's door and went in with Faucher.

Renard wasted no time. "What were you doing talking that dragoon Lieutenant? Don't try to deny it, Lucroy here saw you. What did he tell you? Were you plotting against me?"

My God, thought Faucher, the man is mad. "No Monsieur, of course not. It just occurred to me that he might be able to tell me something that would make it easier to eliminate Roberts. I know that has to be a priority for us!" God forgive me, he thought.

"And did you learn anything useful?"

"I am afraid not, Monsieur, the Lieutenant didn't spend much time with him."

"Ha, but well done for trying. You see Lucroy, that is using your initiative! Now, get out, both of you."

Lucroy scowled at Faucher as they left Renard's office.

The following evening, Faucher found Lapointe in the tavern and they had a late supper together. Lapointe had no money and Faucher was glad to help him. They chatted about things amiably and Lapointe speculated about what might become of him. Jourdan seemed to have forgotten all about him, he had no duties and was just kicking his heels. They began to meet regularly. Then Faucher told the Lieutenant that there was a convoy being organised to send a large number of the refugees from Madrid into France. He offered to try to get Lapointe on it, if he liked. Lapointe said yes, at least he might get back to his regiment's depot, even if he was on parole.

Lapointe's message began to have the effect Michael had hoped for as Renard fretted over it. Over the next few days he began to be more cautious, he took to locking his door at night, he stayed in after dark. He became jumpy, nervous. Then, gradually his fears subsided, until about a week later. He was out after dark, returning from a meeting at the military headquarters. As he walked through the empty streets he heard footsteps behind him. He stopped, they stopped. He turned around and peered down the dark street. He could see no one. He shrugged and went on his way, but the footsteps followed him. He began to walk faster, but the footsteps behind also got quicker. He broke into a run, sweat pouring off him. He ran around a corner and ran straight into a patrol of half a dozen infantrymen. They seized him, demanding to know his identity.

"Monsieur Renard, head of the secret service, you damned fool. Someone is after me, go and look, catch them, they're trying to kill me."

The corporal in charge sent two of his men to look. They soon returned shaking their heads. Renard was marched to a nearby guardhouse where he was able to produce his papers and prove who he was. Renard insisted on an escort to his quarters. The story soon got around, along with the corporal's belief that Renard had been scared by the echo of his own footsteps.

About the same time a large party, several thousand strong, of refugees from Madrid was marched off to France. Lapointe was amongst them, still on the old horse Michael had procured for him.

<h1 style="text-align:center">Chapter 3</h1>

The latter half of September was mild, dry and pleasant, even in the hills to the north and east of Burgos. Wellington's army had driven the French army before them, first up the valley of the Pisuerga and then the valley of the Arlanzón until it halted to lay siege to the French held citadel of Burgos, which blocked further advances after the main French army.

Anson's Brigade of three light dragoon regiments, including the Sixteenth, a battery of Horse Artillery and Sanchez's lancers were on the move away from Burgos where the siege of the castle was getting underway. They were riding up the valley of the Vena, a tributary of the Arlanzón, in the direction of the French in order to provide early warning of any advance by the French army to relieve the castle. Sanchez had joined the brigade the day before and Michael had been ordered by Anson to rejoin his staff. Anson rode at the head of his staff up the broad valley with low, rolling hills to either side. Behind came the three regiments while Sanchez and his lancers were a mile or two ahead of them.

Michael was riding Robbie and talking to Captain Weyland, also of the Sixteenth and a long time member of Anson's staff. While Michael had been in Madrid, the Sixteenth had stayed in the north and this was Michael's first chance to catch up on the Regiment's news. Major Hay was still commanding, but Lieutenant Colonel Pelley was on his way out from England to take over. Poor Alexander had finally decided soldiering was not for him and had gone home to sell out. Keating and Penrice had already gone back to England and the Regiment's depot. The Regiment, however, was short of a captain as McIntosh was sick. Consequently, Lieutenant Lockhart had taken command of one of the troops in Captain Murray's squadron. The main piece of news was that Cocks had finally got a place as a Major, and had left to join the Seventy-Ninth Foot. He was now with them at the siege. Michael, recalling events at Badajoz, did not envy him. Tomkinson, who had served as Cocks' Lieutenant since their arrival until he got his captaincy, now commanded B Troop in his place.

A few miles up the valley the road divided and so did the brigade. General Anson rode on with Sanchez's lancers still out in front and was followed by the Eleventh and Twelfth Light Dragoons, taking Weyland with him. Michael was ordered with the Sixteenth and the artillery along the other road that veered off to the right to the small village of Fresno de Rodillo, which would be the location of the brigade headquarters with the Sixteenth and the artillery acting as a reserve.

The village was not large, but it had been abandoned by its inhabitants and showed signs of French depredations. There was not a stick of furniture left in the village and many of the buildings were damaged, lacking windows and doors removed for firewood. However, it comfortably accommodated the troops now billeted on it and was an improvement on bivouacking in the open. Michael claimed a large house in the village centre as Brigade Headquarters and left the staff baggage to settle in. The best room was reserved for General Anson and Michael took a smallish room that overlooked the barn and outbuildings being used for stabling. It had the luxury of glass in the window and a complete roof. Leaving Hall to get his room ready, Michael went down to the stables. Lloyd, Bradley and Marcello were hard at work on the horses and he was not needed, so he took himself off to explore the village and locate the Sixteenth's headquarters. The artillery had posted themselves in three pairs of guns to command the approaches to the village and Michael saw pickets from the Sixteenth riding out to take post on surrounding vantage points. Elsewhere the commissary was distributing rations. It was a very familiar routine. The village was on high ground and had sweeping views all around. It would have been idyllic, were it not for the distant rumble of cannon fire that reached them from Burgos.

Anson returned just as dusk was falling and after approving of his quarters, he and Michael strolled to the Sixteenth's officer's mess where they had been invited to dine. The Regiment had made itself comfortable in the relatively luxurious surroundings of the village and the officers had commandeered a large ground floor room as a dining room. Some officers were absent on picket duty, but there were still nearly twenty at dinner.

Michael found himself sitting on an improvised bench between Captain Persse, who he knew well, and Lieutenant Crichton who had joined the regiment in July, along with three other new lieutenants and, perhaps more welcome, ninety horses. Even so, they were only able to field just over three hundred men with nearly a hundred men on the sick list. The harsh conditions of life on campaign in Spain took their toll.

Persse greeted Michael with a smile. "Hello, Roberts, how's my best corporal doing?"

"What? Oh, Lloyd, he's very well, thankee, Persse. And a father to boot."

"Another dragoon?"

"No, a young lady, but Mrs Lloyd and Miss Lloyd are safely ensconced in my house in Lisbon."

"That's good to know. I don't suppose there's any chance of getting the good corporal back?"

Michael laughed. "None at all, he's far too useful to me."

Crichton had been listening closely and Persse said, "I don't think you've met Lieutenant Crichton? Joined us in July. Crichton, this is Captain Roberts, our expert on special duties."

"Glad to meet you, sir. Err, special duties, sir?" Crichton asked, hesitantly.

Michael gave Persse a frown, then laughed and said, "I think what Captain Persse is referring to is the time I spend with our Portuguese and Spanish allies, like Don Julian Sanchez. I speak both languages, you see, makes me useful. I'm here, there, everywhere as a glorified messenger."

Persse snorted and Crichton said, "I see, sir," although he plainly didn't, which was what Michael wanted.

Michael took the opportunity to change the subject. "Tell me, Mister Crichton, what do you make of Spain so far?"

To Michael's relief that was the closest reference to the work he had done for Wellington in the intelligence war. It was not something he wanted becoming any more broadly known or suspected than it already was. The one interesting piece of gossip was a further honour for The Peer, Wellington had been made a Marquess.

After the dinner was over, Michael walked back with Anson and parted from the general to check on his horses. As he had half expected he found Lloyd, Hall, Bradley and Marcello in the stables, sitting around with a couple of bottles of wine between them. When they saw him they leapt up and the two dragoons saluted.

"At ease." Michael returned the salute. "Is all well with the horses?" As he spoke he walked over to Johnny and squeezed between him and Robbie to reach his head. He scratched the horse behind his ears, and then turned to Robbie who had given him a gentle push with his muzzle. "All right, lad, you as well."

"They're as right as rain, sir," offered Lloyd, "but how we will manage for fodder, I am not sure, there's not much around here, sir, and with winter coming it will only get worse."

"Then let's hope Burgos falls quickly and we can get into winter quarters." Michael squeezed back out from between the horses, running his hand over Johnny's back as he did so. There was a comforting warmth from all the horses and the smell of horse was always good. "I shall ride Johnny tomorrow, best be ready for daylight. Lloyd, you can come with me. Hall, you can stay here, see what you can do by way of some fresh supplies and fodder. Marcello, you help him. Bradley, just a little light exercise for the others.”

There was a chorus of understanding and Michael walked to the door.

“Begging you pardon, sir,” it was Loyd who spoke as he stood up again, “if I might have a word, sir?” His eyes flicked towards the outside.

“Of course, come outside, I’m just going to have a cigar.” Once outside Michael turned to Lloyd. “What is it?” he asked as he lit a foul smelling Spanish cigar.

“It might be nothing, sir, but some of the lads have been around asking me about what we get up to, spending so much time away from the regiment and not seen with the staff either, sir.”

“What did you tell them?”

“Said we’d been playing nurse maid to a party of Spanish guerillas, sir, trying to make proper soldiers of them. Hall and Bradley said nothing, just nodded. They’ll not say anything out of line, sir. Marcello didn’t really understand.” He paused. “I’m not sure they entirely believed me, sir, but they stopped asking.”

“Thank you for telling me. There’s not much we can do about gossip, but what you told them is true enough, although I’m not sure Don Julian would agree with the suggestion that his men aren’t proper soldiers.” The two men smiled at that. “But now we are back with the army and the brigade if not the Regiment, Monsieur Renard is at the other end of Spain and I hope we can get back to some proper soldiering. Then, perhaps, our other activities will be forgotten."

The next week passed quietly enough for Anson's Brigade. The hardest thing was keeping the horses adequately fed. The news from the siege, however, was not good. The French garrison was making a real fight of it and Wellington's lack of a proper train of siege artillery was beginning to tell. The French army, further into the mountains to the north east, was quiet and there was no contact save for reports from Sanchez's patrols who kept a very watchful eye from the hills and mountains around the valley. A routine had become established. Anson and his staff rode out every morning before dawn. As the first light of day appeared they were at Monasterio, a small village housing the Eleventh and Twelfth Light Dragoons, anxious to know if the French were advancing. It also became usual to wait until Sanchez rode in to report, and then all sit down to breakfast together.

The first time they rode into Monasterio Michael had been surprised to see the heads of horses sticking out of windows on the first floor of some houses. It was one of the strangest and funniest things he had seen. The explanation was simple. The village was built on the side of a hill, the ground floor on one side was the first floor on the other. It became a joke not to warn any newcomers about it and to enjoy their surprise.

September turned into October and the news came that Sir Stapleton Cotton had returned to resume command of the cavalry. Along with him came Lieutenant Colonel Pelly to take command of the Sixteenth and also Lieutenant Lloyd of the Sixteenth who was appointed to Anson's staff. Cotton sent along a message with Pelly ordering Michael to rejoin him and his staff at his new headquarters at Villamar. Colonel Pelly had just arrived at the Brigade headquarters and was talking to Anson when Michael walked by.

"Ah, Roberts, a moment, if you please." Pelly called out to him and then spoke to Anson, "Forgive me, sir, but I have orders for Roberts. Now that you have Lieutenant Lloyd, Sir Stapleton would like Roberts to rejoin him, he's at Villamar." He turned to Michael. "Did you hear all that?"

"Yes, sir." Michael acknowledged.

Anson spoke. "Best get on your way, Roberts, and good luck."

"Thank you, sir." Michael saluted and walked off to get his party under way.

It was a short two hour ride to Villamar and Michael arrived there in the early afternoon. He located Cotton's quarters and there he found Cotton's quartermaster, Captain Campbell, who greeted him warmly.

"Good day to you, Roberts, wasn't sure if you'd get here today. How are you?"

"Well enough, Campbell, thank you. How is Sir Stapleton?"

"Almost fully recovered, he can ride well enough, but he's damned vexed that his wound has stopped him playing his violin." He grinned. "The rest of us ain't so sorry." Michael smiled and Campbell went on. "Anyway, we've some good quarters, I'll get an orderly to show you and your men where everything is. Sir Stapleton has gone off to see the Marquess and see how the siege is going, I don't think he'll be staying there for dinner, we will be dining in a couple of hours. I, ah, think Sir Stapleton will want a word with you."

"Oh, anything in particular?"

"Err, I think he will explain." Campbell looked slightly embarrassed and Michael decided he would find out soon enough.

Sir Stapleton did return, just in time for dinner and all the staff gathered together. Apart from Sir Stapleton and Campbell, Colonel Elley was also back with Captain von der Decken and Captain White, who had all been in Salamanca with Cotton while he recovered. Cotton greeted Michael.

"Ah, Roberts, good to see you, Captain. We shall have a little talk after dinner. However," he raised his voice to address everyone, "Gentlemen, it seems that the Prince Regent has seen fit to grant me the honour of making me a Knight of the Bath." There was a chorus of congratulations, which Cotton quietened with a wave of his hands. "Thank you, gentlemen, thank you. Lord Wellington is to invest me with the order and give me a dinner the day after tomorrow, I expect that you will all come with me. Now, let us eat."

After dinner, as most left to leave, Cotton waved Michael back into his chair. Campbell also stayed put. No one spoke until the door closed behind the last of the diners and servants.

Cotton simply said, "Tell him Campbell."

"Ah, well, its like this, Roberts, I was over at Wellington's headquarters earlier today and I had some business with Colonel Gordon. It didn't take long, but then he, err, asked me about you. Was most inquisitive, wanted to know just what it is you do. I'm afraid he seems to have got wind of something. I think, at the moment, he just has questions about what you have been doing with Don Julian, but from what he said I gather he picked up a hint as he came through Lisbon to join us. He was wondering why a staff officer would spend so much time there." He gave an embarrassed little shrug. "And that's it"

"There you are, Roberts," Cotton said, "some of us know a little of the valuable work you have done on counter intelligence and we keep our council. I suspect that only you know everything and would like to keep it that way?" Michael nodded. "Yes, of course you would. My fear is that Gordon might continue poking about and discover one or two things that, whilst necessary, and I assure you that those who matter out here share that assessment, are things that some back in England might seize upon to embarrass the government and the Marquess. The crass stupidity of some of our politicians beggars belief, frankly. However, the last thing we want is anything getting into the papers and you being recalled for some sort of enquiry, or worse."

"Thank you, sir, I'm grateful for your opinion and confidence." Michael spoke slowly, hesitantly, gathering his thoughts. "If I may be frank, sir?"

Cotton nodded, as did Campbell when Michael glanced at him, adding "Ye've nothing to fear from me, Roberts. I know little, but enough to know I could nae do what ye've done, and I'm grateful you can."

"Thank you."

"Campbell's right, Roberts, those that know are damn grateful to you, those that don't know don't need to."

"Thank you, sir." Michael paused. "When I joined the Sixteenth I had no idea that I would get involved in intelligence matters. It seems to have come about through chance circumstances and my ability with Portuguese and Spanish. I did not ask for it, sir." As Cotton nodded his agreement Michael thought to himself 'and it has become personal, very personal', but that was something he kept to himself. He went on, "In many ways I would rather be with the regiment with my own troop, just ordinary soldiering, proper soldiering, sir, but it has come about and, dare I say, so far I have been successful. If it contributes to victory that is sufficient. So far as Colonel Gordon is concerned, I see little alternative to keeping out of his way and trusting to yourself and the Marquess to help with that."

"Aye, well," Cotton replied, looking thoughtful, "that's all fair enough, Roberts. Now, you'll come to this investiture and dinner. I've no doubt Gordon will be there, but I've an idea we might throw a little dust in his eyes."

The investiture was to be as grand affair as could be managed during a difficult siege, one that was not going well. Nearly all of the divisional commanders were there, as were all the cavalry brigade commanders and most of the regimental commanders. Cotton's orders to Michael were "Stick close,

Roberts, and if Gordon says anything, let me respond and just follow whatever I say."

Out of concern for Cotton's health, Wellington sent an old Spanish coach for him, drawn by four mules. Cotton looked at it and shrugged. "Very considerate of the Marquess, I'm sure. Do any of you gentlemen wish to share it with me?" There was only silence from his assembled staff, all about to mount their horses. "No, I thought not. Well, you will all make a very fine escort." Carefully he climbed into the coach and pulled the door closed behind him.

The occasion was not as grand as the one witnessed by Michael in the Cathedral at Mafra when Wellington had given the same award to Beresford. A lavish dinner preceded the investiture itself and Michael found himself seated some distance from Cotton, the guest of honour. Fortunately, Gordon was also some distance away. The dinner came to end as the light began to fade and Michael stood to one side of the room as the guests readied themselves to leave for the church just outside the town where the actual investiture was to take place. In looking out for Cotton he became a little careless, helped by the wine, which had been plentiful if not of the best quality.

A voice spoke to him from behind his shoulder. "Captain Roberts, we meet again."

Michael turned to find himself face to face with Colonel Gordon. "Yes, sir," he stammered in surprise.

"Yes, I've been hoping for another word with you Captain, concerning your duties here, in Spain and in Portugal, and most particularly Lisbon."

"Yes, sir?"

"Put simply, Captain, tell me, what is it you do with Don Julian Sanchez and why are you so frequently to be found in Lisbon for long periods when the army is in the field? Is not your place with your regiment, or Sir Stapleton's staff?"

To Michael's great relief another voice cut in as Cotton appeared behind Gordon. "Ah, Colonel Gordon! You've met Captain Roberts, I see. I'm very sorry to interrupt but I have a little errand for him." Cotton stepped forward to stand between Michael and Gordon. "Roberts, I want you to go and find some of that rather fine wine you acquired for me yesterday, a couple of dozen bottles should do."

A bemused Michael could only manage "Yes, sir, at once, excuse me, Colonel," before he made a beeline for the door and escaped.

Outside he found Captain Campbell. "Got away, did you Roberts? I've sent an orderly to fetch your horse, and then you can make yourself scarce."

Michael was back in their quarters a good hour before Cotton appeared, Campbell with him. Cotton called for a bottle of wine and led the way into the deserted dining room.

"Damn me, but I need a drink. Roberts, would you credit it, that damned coach turned over? Fortunately I landed on my good arm. A bit close, eh, Campbell?"

Campbell grinned, "Aye, a little close, sir."

A servant entered with a bottle and three glasses and the three men waited while he served the wine and left. Cotton took a healthy draft and then gave a little chuckle.

"That's better. Now, I think we might have dealt with Gordon's interest in you, Roberts, if you'll forgive me?"

"Forgive you, sir, I don't understand."

"No, well, the thing is I rather implied that you were only out here on sufferance, as a favour to General Earl Harcourt, who had asked the help of the Prince Regent, and the Earl was doing it as a favour to his old friend from the American War, your grandfather. I might have used the phrase 'sheer damned nepotism'. I may also have suggested that you were on the staff because no one dare let you anywhere near a troop. As for Lisbon, you know it well, speak the language and have been the best person to send to secure various supplies that we have needed, thus keeping you out of the way. Oh, and Mister Stuart in Lisbon has also made use of your language skills and in order to keep him happy the Marquess has been happy to send you to Lisbon." He paused to take a mouthful of wine. "I rather fear that we have destroyed any reputation you might have had, at least so far as Gordon is concerned. And Campbell here helped."

"Really?"

"Aye, Roberts, I told Sir Stapleton, while he was still talking to Gordon, that I had just seen you rush off and I hoped that you would nae get lost, again."

"Oh!"

Cotton laughed. "Don't look so downhearted, Roberts, those who matter know the truth, or a part of it at least."

"Yes, sir, I do hope so."

Two days later came news that rocked Cotton, his staff and the Sixteenth. Michael was sitting in the headquarters dining room reading a newspaper that had recently arrived from England, it was only a month old. The door opened and an ashen faced Colonel Lord Somerset came in. Michael leapt to his feet and saluted, but Somerset seemed not to notice.

"Roberts, where's Sir Stapleton?"

"I'm not sure sir, he's around here somewhere."

Somerset sank into a chair. "See if you can find him, there's a good fellow." Michael started for the door, but Somerset spoke again. "It's Major Cocks, he's dead"

Stunned, Michael went in search of Cotton. He found him near the stables chatting with Colonel Elley. Cotton saw him approaching and asked. "What's the matter Roberts, you look rather pale?"

"Colonel Somerset is in the dining room, sir, he asked me to find you for him, it's Major Cocks, sir, he's dead."

The shock reverberated around headquarters, it reached the Sixteenth and left many shattered, not least Tomkinson who had been Cocks' Lieutenant for many years before taking over his troop, B Troop. There were few who were not shocked at the loss of the highly thought of Cocks. It transpired that Cocks had been involved in repulsing an early morning sortie by the French. He was rallying his men to recover ground taken by the French when he was shot at close range, he had died instantly.

The funeral was held the following day at the camp ground of the Seventy-Ninth, close to Villamar. Wellington attended with all his staff, as did Sir Stapleton Cotton, Generals Pack and Anson and everyone of the officers of the Sixteenth and Seventy-Ninth who could be spared from duty. Troop Sergeant Major Blood of B Troop and Regimental Sergeant Major Williams were there. Wellington barely spoke to anyone, standing aside and unapproachable. It was well known that he had held the highest opinion of Cocks. Tomkinson, who had taken upon himself dealing with Cocks' personal affects, looked broken. Michael had not known Cocks as well as Tomkinson had, but he knew him well enough to feel a great loss. There was a subdued air about the cavalry that was slow to lift.

The next week was one of routine work for Cotton's staff, but Michael did receive two letters. The first came from his lawyer in Lisbon, Senhor Furtado. Michael had written to him before they had reached Madrid in August and it was only now that he got a reply. Furtado informed him that Maggie Lloyd had agreed to take on the job of Michael's housekeeper and that he had found some help for her. Most importantly he wrote that Lloyd's daughter had been christened Julietta. Michael gave a delighted laugh and hurried to the stables to find Lloyd.

"Lloyd, Lloyd," he called out as he approached, a huge smile on his face and waving Furtado's letter.

Lloyd's head appeared over the back of Rodrigo. "Yes, sir?"

"I have a letter from Senor Furtado, he sends news of Miss Julietta Lloyd!"

"Duw! Julietta!" He grinned from ear to ear. "Now that's just lovely. Julietta! Does he say how she is, sir?"

"Just that she is good health. And Mrs Lloyd has agreed to be my housekeeper and he has got her some young local girl in to help."

"Duw, now isn't that just lovely, sir, thank you."

Hall and Bradley were also beaming, while Marcello just looked confused. "Now you can toast the health of Miss Julietta, Lloyd, and I am sure Bradley and Hall will help you, and do explain to Marcello, he looks all at a loss."

Another letter soon followed, but this came from London, from Mister Musgrave of the Aliens office who had received the sketches of Renard. He expressed his gratitude to Michael, but had nothing else of any value to say, writing that nothing had been heard of Renard since the French had left Madrid.

.        .        .

Renard was busy packing. It had been announced that King Joseph and his army, reinforced by the army of Marshal Soult from Andalusia, were going to retake Madrid, now that half of Wellington's army was in the north, and more importantly, Wellington was with them. Renard had been informed that he was expected to march with the King, although most of the court and civil administration were to remain, for the time being, in Valencia. Renard decided to take Faucher and Lucroy with him, along with a few junior clerks and servants, leaving the bulk of his department behind for the moment.

Renard was eager to return to Madrid, he wanted to know what had been going on, he wanted to reestablish a network in Lisbon. Despite his best efforts and frequent rants at his staff for their failings, all recent attempts to gain intelligence from either city had failed. He also wanted to know about Roberts, he wanted to launch an attack on him, to kill him, finish him for once and for all. He had become more convinced than ever that Roberts was the cause of all his woes. Lucroy was wholehearted in his support of Renard and keen to strike back at the English. Renard was beginning to scare Faucher with his wild accusations against Roberts and his unpredictable behaviour. Renard was, in Faucher's private, very private opinion, becoming more than a little deranged where Roberts was concerned, to say nothing of being utterly unreasonable in his demands on his staff. Lucroy, on the other hand, was calm and thoughtful, cold even. He saw the promise of promotion and rewards if he could help Renard to succeed, and if that included his vendetta against the English cavalry officer, well, that was all meat and grist to Lucroy. He shared Renard's view that Roberts was a threat. He defended Renard's views and actions where Roberts was concerned. Faucher also knew that Lucroy had an appetite for violence.

It was a reluctant Faucher who left Valencia. He was fed up with Renard's endless demands for action, for progress, demands they could not meet despite their best efforts. He was sceptical about just how much a single English cavalry officer could be responsible for their problems. He knew he was not at all responsible for some of those problems, but Renard would not have it. He was fed up with Renard neglecting his real work while he obsessed about Roberts, dumping all his work on his clerks. Renard was also clearly drinking heavily, and Faucher was concerned for his judgement. He was also concerned for his own well being, as Renard became increasing unreasonable and irrational and Lucroy backed him up.

# Chapter 4

Little more than a week after Cocks was buried, the reinforced French advanced to  relieve Burgos. It was late afternoon and Michael, along with Cotton, Elley and von der Decken was in the middle of dinner when a horse was heard to gallop up to the headquarters and a moment later an orderly burst in followed by a dragoon of the Sixteenth, sweat stained and dusty.

"Begging you pardon, sir," the dragoon saluted as he spoke, "But the French have driven in the picket in front of Monasterio, sir, looks like a brigade of infantry."

There followed a few minutes of confusion as officers called for horses. Michael shouted to Bradley, "Get me Johnny saddled up!" To Lloyd he said, "You are with me, get Rodrigo ready." To Hall and Marcello, "Start packing and then get the other horses ready to move."

Ten minutes later Cotton led his staff out of the small village, which had become a scene of frantic activity as servants and batmen rushed around to prepare to move. The village was also the site of the cavalry's hospital and preparations were under way to evacuate them if necessary. It was about twelve miles to Monasterio and Cotton led them at a good fast trot for the first six, and then pushed into a steady canter for the second stretch. The horses were rested and had been well fed, and they covered the ground comfortably.

A couple of miles on they met the baggage of Anson's brigade hurrying towards Burgos. Cotton reined in and demanded of the officer in charge what was happening. He replied that a French infantry brigade had advanced within two miles of Monasterio and had driven in the advance picket of infantry, capturing most of them. Anson had pulled the outpost troops back and was forming his brigade next to the village. Cotton led them on again at the canter, an anxious expression on his face. Everyone was straining to hear any sounds of combat above the beat of the horses' hooves. There was nothing. The horses settled to a steady pace, eating up the miles. Then, suddenly, they saw Anson's brigade ahead of them, formed to the right of the village and facing up the valley, the Eleventh and Sixteenth in line with the Twelfth in reserve behind them. The battery of horse artillery was drawn up on a slight rise just off the road. Beyond them, beyond the village, on the valley floor and the steep hill that rose over it, nothing was visible, there was no sign of any French. There was a lessening of the tension they had felt all the way.

Cotton dropped the pace to a trot and rode to where he could see Anson, close to the guns. Anson turned at the sound of approaching horses and saluted Cotton.

"Good evening, sir."

"Evening, Anson, what's going on?"

As Anson explained and Michael could plainly see, the position was impossible for cavalry. If French artillery got on the hill it could shower rounds into its position. The steepness of the hill made it impossible for the cavalry to take and hold it, but it was perfectly accessible to French infantry. To make matters worse, the guns of the horse artillery couldn't elevate enough to fire at the hill top.

"Sir! On the left!" Michael didn't know who had shouted but like everyone, he turned to look away to the left and saw a large body of cavalry coming down from the valley side. Cotton started to order the Eleventh to wheel to face them when Michael realised who it was.

"Sir, it's Don Julian!" He shouted to Cotton.

Cotton turned and said, "Are you sure, Roberts?"

"Yes, sir!"

"Then be so good as to ask him to keep his men on the high ground and cover our flank. Ask him to join me."

"Yes, sir!"

With Lloyd beside him, Michael cantered across the gently sloping valley side towards the oncoming force. As he got closer he was reassured that he was right, it was Sanchez and his lancers. He spurred Johnny into a gallop.

Sanchez halted his men as Michael rode up and drew rein.

"Hola! Captain Roberts, do you bring orders?"

"Don Julian, yes, Sir Stapleton's complements and would you keep your men on the high ground to protect Anson's flank and would you be so good as to join him."

Sanchez turned to Strenuwitz, next to him as ever. "You heard that, Major, see to it and I will join Sir Stapleton." He turned back to speak to Michael. "I have some information that he will  want to hear."

A few minutes later Sanchez was in conversation with Cotton and telling him that, behind the brigade they knew about, the entire French army was marching down the valley towards Burgos. They spoke for a few moments and then Sanchez rode back to his men. Cotton turned and looked over his staff.

His eyes rested on Captain White.

"White, your horse fit?" he asked.

"Yes, sir!

"Then go and find Lord Wellington and tell him what's going on. Sharp now." Cotton turned to look up the valley. "Where the devil are they?" he asked no one in particular.

Night was rapidly falling and as the air grew still they heard the sound of canon fire from the direction of Burgos. The staff looked at each other. It sounded like an assault was being made. Then, a little later, the sound of a huge explosion rumbled up the valley to them. On Sir Stapleton's orders, Anson sent a patrol up the valley to see if the French were still advancing. Then they all, staff and regiments, dismounted to give some relief to the horses. The next three hours were an anxious wait, no one took the chance to sleep. Eventually, a dragoon returned from the patrol, the French were bivouacking at the small village the forward picket had been in. They had seen no sign of any cavalry or artillery. Then Captain White returned and reported to Cotton.

"Sir Stapleton, Lord Wellington's compliments. The latest assault has failed, sir, His Lordship is forming the army on this side of Burgos, General Anson is to withdraw his brigade immediately and Lord Wellington requests that you join him, sir."

Dawn found the Allied army drawn up along a ten or twelve mile front just to the north east of Burgos, occupying a line of high ground dominating the valley down which the French must advance. Wellington and Cotton, with their staffs, had taken up quarters in Rubena, just in the rear of the line and on the direct route to Burgos, some seven miles away, where a small force was keeping the French garrison bottled up. With their baggage available, Michael changed horses, giving Johnny a rest and choosing to ride Robbie.

The day began quietly with no sign of the expected French attack. Cotton passed by Anson's brigade at one point and Michael managed a quick word with Buchanan at the head of the centre squadron while Cotton spoke to Pelly. He noticed that Lieutenant Lockhart was on the flank of the squadron where Tomkinson should have been. The two captains exchanged salutes and Buchanan greeted Michael.

"Any idea what's going on?"

"No, none at all, waiting on the French to do something. The Peer was expecting them at first light. Where's Tomkinson?"

"He's sick, gone down with the fever. Sent him off yesterday to the hospital. Caught a cold at Cock's funeral and didn't look after himself. I'm afraid he's rather cut up about Cocks."

The rest of the day passed quietly and Cotton and his staff spent a nervous night in Rubena, wondering what the French were up to. Michael had done relatively little and decided to stay on Robbie. Hall woke him early with coffee and bread and then they were mounted and out before daylight, waiting to see what the dawn would bring. There were still no French. It was not until late in the afternoon that anything happened.

First of all some of Sanchez's lancers who were out in front of the line came galloping in. They rode up to where Wellington and Cotton were sitting together on a log, their staffs all around, dismounted, quietly chatting and casting frequent, worried glances up the valley. They reported that the French were advancing and were a little over a mile away. Within moments everyone was back in the saddle, all around there were shouted commands and drum beats as the army shook itself into order. Then bodies of French light infantry appeared, small black specks swarming across the valley bottom and moving straight towards Rubena. Behind them came massed bodies of infantry in columns, a good two divisions worth, perhaps ten thousand men. There were cavalry as well, a brigade of light cavalry, another six hundred men or so. There was no indication that the main body of the French army was following them.

In the centre of the Allied army was the British Seventh Division. As the French advanced, Wellington called out, "Stay here, Sir Stapleton!" and with that he rode off at speed to the left, followed by his staff. Michael watched him go, heading up the valley side at a full gallop. For a long, nervous fifteen minutes nothing happened save for the remorseless advance of the two French divisions. Their light troops started to engage the Seventh and it was only a matter of minutes before the main line would be engaged. Cotton was looking around at his cavalry, judging distances and times, ready to send them to assist the infantry. Then, over the top of the valley side came the First Division, in three lines and marching straight at the flank of the French. A moment later and the Fifth Division appeared, behind and to the left of the First. Down the valley side they rolled, an unstoppable force.

With only minutes to spare the French suddenly started to retreat. They went back in disorder, rushing to escape the trap closing on them. It was touch and go for a few long minutes, but escape they did, followed by a few long range shots from a battery of horse artillery that came up just as darkness fell and allowed them to make good their escape.

Another nervous night followed but the dawn didn't bring the French, instead a letter arrived towards midday for Wellington from General Hill commanding the troops that had been left at Madrid. He was retiring north towards Wellington in the face of an overwhelming French force. King Joseph had united all the French forces in the south and was coming northwards. Wellington and his staff immediately set about organising the withdrawal of the army back towards Portugal, giving up the attempt to take Burgos.

The rearguard, once clear of Burgos, was to be the Seventh Division with Anson's and Bock's brigades and Sanchez's lancers. The trickiest part would be marching over three divisions of infantry through Burgos and over the town's bridge without alerting the French garrison in the castle. Anson's were told off to hold the army's picket line where it had been formed for the last few days. The retreat began as soon as it was dark. Cotton stayed with Anson's. The infantry had lit camp fires before marching off, and Anson's did their best to keep them burning, throwing piles of wood onto the fires to convince the French that the army was still there. They had been told to hold the position until three in the morning.

Cotton, Anson and their staff officers were gathered around a fire in the middle of the line. Cotton pulled out his pocket watch and peered at it by the firelight.

"Three o'clock, or as near as damn it." He closed the watch and put it away. "Anson, I'll leave you here to gather up your brigade. I shall wait for you at the bridge in Ibeas, I want to be sure Bock and Sanchez have gone on their way."

"Yes, sir, the regimental commanders should be pulling their men back now. We should be at the bridge by about five o'clock."

"Good, I want to have the rearguard assembled at Buniel before daylight and that's a good two hour ride if you push on hard. Good luck."

The baggage had gone off as soon as darkness had fallen, but Michael had had time to change horses and was back on his favourite, Johnny. Now the small party with Cotton rode south east towards Ibeas and its bridge over the Arlanzon. There was little conversation as they pushed forward as fast as they dare, trusting to their horses' superior night vision. No sounds reached them and it was hard to believe that out in the darkness thousands of men, horses, cannon and wagons were on the move.

At Ibeas they found a vedette from Bock's heavy dragoons waiting for them at the bridge. The German NCO in charge of the vedette informed Cotton that Bock's were an hour ahead of them. Cotton told the German dragoons to wait for Anson and then pushed on after Bock.

As dawn broke Michael was standing at Johnny's head, letting him graze on scrubby grass. All the staff were doing the same. To his right Anson's were just dismounting, to his left Bock's were already off their horses. He stifled a yawn. He had, like everyone on the staff, now been on the go for over a day, save for an hour or so of precious sleep as they had sat on the picket line. At least the horses could get some sleep on their feet. They had crossed to the north bank of the Arlanzon and were now posted behind the bridge just outside Buniel. The morning passed slowly and quietly, men and horses dozing as they could. In the afternoon the pickets left behind galloped in saying they had been driven in by French cavalry.

Cotton walked his horse to where Anson was standing. "Post new pickets here, then move your brigade along the river. I think it's too late in the day for the French to try anything. I shall go on ahead and look for a position to hold them. Not too far, then perhaps we can get a little rest."

Cotton found his position another five miles on. He posted Anson's and Bock's behind the steep sided banks of the narrow Hormaza, a tributary of the Arlanzon. The two battalions of light infantry with the rearguard, under the command of Colonel Halkett, were spread out along the banks to either side of the bridge. Sanchez had stayed on the other bank of the

Arlanzon and was out of the reckoning as the river was unfordable. Out on the left were another band of guerillas, not well known to anyone, that of Marquinez. Marquinez himself had been killed recently and the steadiness of the guerillas was uncertain.

Once the rearguard was in position, it settled to get what rest it could, the men sleeping at their posts. The cavalry slept at the heads of their horses, reins in hand. The horses remained saddled, and cropped what grass they could reach. Michael and Lloyd both managed a few hours of deep sleep, but woke feeling stiff and cold. There was little food available. Michael and Lloyd shared a chunk of stale bread and drank water from the Hormaza.

The whole were roused an hour before dawn. In the companies and squadrons, officers and sergeants went about checking everyone's readiness. Then they waited. The sun was hidden behind clouds and the daylight came on slowly, bringing little warmth. It had been light for an hour or so when they heard distant firing. Minutes later the pickets left at the bridge at Buniel appeared, men of the Sixteenth, galloping hard for safety. A little way out in front, and not moving quite so fast was tight group of three riders. As they got closer Michael could see that in the middle was an officer who was being supported in his saddle by two dragoons. It was Lieutenant Lockhart who had been given command of the pickets. They thundered across the small bridge, closely followed by the rest of the pickets. Behind them Michael could see a squadron of French chasseurs coming on fast. At the sight of the rearguard formed behind the small stream they halted.

The pickets rejoined their troop and the surgeon rode forward to help Lockhart as he was taken to the rear of the brigade. From where he sat with Cotton's staff, a hundred yards or so away, it was clear to Michael that he was in a bad way.

Cotton spoke, tersely, "Follow me," and led his staff to where Anson was deep in conversation with Colonel Pelly. The two men turned and saluted as Cotton approached.

"Anson, Pelly," Cotton acknowledged to two officers. "How is Lockhart?"

It was Pelly who replied. "Shot through the body. It looks very bad, sir. I was just discussing with General Anson about how to replace him, he had taken command of Tomkinson's troop. There's only Crichton with the troop now, and he's too inexperienced. We are damned short of officers as it is, with McIntosh away sick as well as Tomkinson."

Cotton thought for a moment, then announced, "You had better have Roberts then. But I shall want him back." He turned to Michael. "There you are, there's your troop for you, and take Lloyd with you."

"Yes, sir, thank you."

Cotton looked across the river. The squadron of Chasseurs were being joined by what looked like an entire division of French cavalry, some two thousand men. The French were sending a few squadrons forward, looking for a crossing point, but they were soon driven back by the fire of the light infantry.

"Anson, I am going to retire the infantry. Give them as long as you can and then retire yourself. Good luck."

Michael rode with Pelly over to the Sixteenth. They were behind the other two regiments, ready to cover their retreat.

As they rode, Pelly said, "B Troop is on the left of the centre squadron under Buchanan. You go and take the left flank while I tell Buchanan."

Michael swung away towards the flank of the centre squadron where a very nervous looking Crichton was sitting on his horse, nervously fingering the grip of his sabre.

"Mister Crichton, you are relieved, take post to the rear and be so good as to inform Sar'nt Major Blood that I now have the troop."

With a hasty," Yes, sir!" Crichton wheeled his horse away to the rear.

Michael rode into the vacated post and Lloyd took up position behind him. They drew their sabres and tightened the sword knots around their wrists. In front of the squadron Pelly had finished speaking with Buchanan and turned away to ride across to the left squadron. Michael switched his attention to the French cavalry across the river, all tiredness vanquished. For the moment there was nothing to do except watch as the French across the river. And as he watched, Michael saw even more French cavalry arriving.

Halkett's light infantry withdrew from their position along the river bank and started a fast march to the rear. Within minutes of them leaving, the French cavalry were probing along the banks of the stream looking for a crossing point. A quarter of an hour passed, perhaps more and then the French found what they were looking for, a stretch of river where the banks were low enough and the water shallow enough for them cross on a squadron frontage.

The Eleventh and Twelfth went threes about and began to march after the infantry, passing on either flank of the Sixteenth. As they passed, the regiment began to advance. Pelly swung the line of advance to the left, towards where the first French squadron was already fording the river. Each of the three squadrons went right shoulders forward, swinging to the left and onto the new line, the squadrons now in echelon instead of side by side, the left squadron some fifty yards ahead. The pace increased to a trot. A second French squadron began to cross as the first drew up to face the oncoming Sixteenth.

The left squadron increased the pace to a canter, then fifty yards further on, Michael saw Buchanan go into a canter and shouted as loudly as he could "Canter March!" The line surged forward and Michael felt Johnny pulling at the reins, trying to go faster. He played lightly down the reins, steadied him and said, quietly, but firmly, "Steady lad." He glanced to his right, saw the line was bulging slightly, he called out, "Steady, lads, we'll be there soon enough," and saw a few grins, saw the line adjust.

Now the French were only a hundred yards away and he saw the left squadron go into the charge, straight at the first French squadron that stood waiting for them. The second French squadron was just climbing out of the river, trying to ready itself to receive the centre squadron's charge. With a mere fifty yards to go, Buchanan pushed his horse into a flat gallop and Michael screamed out "Charge!". He squeezed

Johnny's flanks and felt the horse surge forward under him. He gripped his sabre and then, as the gap closed to just a few yards, he, and all the front rank, began the series of cuts towards the enemy's heads that was known as The Assault. Instinctively the French defended themselves, negating the longer reach of their sabres, and then the squadron crashed into the French.

Men shouted and horses screamed as the two lines mixed. Michael caught a French Chasseur across his face, the man screaming and dropping his sabre to clutch at his face with both hands. He saw a French horse rear and try to turn away, it fell, binging down its neighbour and both riders. To his right the men of the centre squadron were hacking at the French, face to face over their horse's heads. The French line gave under the violence of the onslaught and fell back, colliding with a third squadron, which was just forming behind them. Both became disorganised, but the sheer mass of horses stopped the Sixteenth's forward movement. Michael parried a thrust, cut back, but missed. Lloyd, pushing forward, took the man with a cut to his neck. Then came shouts from the centre of the squadron, spreading to the flanks where Michael took up the shout. "Retire!"

The confusion in the French ranks allowed them to break the contact and get away, all three squadrons now galloping back up the slight incline like some mad horse race. A quarter mile ahead Michael saw the Eleventh halt and goes threes about to face them. Then they were streaming past the Eleventh, around the flanks, through the gaps between the squadrons and, as they did so, slowing their blowing horses to a trot, looking to see where they should reform.

Anson, with his staff were sitting on their horses and waiting for them, shouting at them to halt and reform. Within a few minutes the regiment was more or less back in order, facing the French. Then they were ordered "Threes about!" and they rode away.

A few miles on another stream cut across the valley to join the Arlanzon, and there they found Bock's brigade and Bull's battery of horse artillery posted behind a bridge. Halkett's two battalions of infantry had marched hard and were some distance further on. Halting some distance short of the bridge, the Sixteenth were again faced about to cover the retreat of the other two regiments.

All attention in the Sixteenth was focussed on the front as the other two regiments passed by them, making for the bridge. Then, without warning, the Spanish guerillas that had been out on the left came pouring down the hill, pursued by French Hussars, and heading straight for the Regiment's left flank. Before the left squadron could do anything, the galloping mass of Spaniards and French crashed into it. Buchanan ordered the centre squadron to "Trot march, right shoulders forward" to bring them around to face the new threat. They almost got round.

Spanish guerillas rode at breakneck speed past them, some crashed into the front rank, bringing down men and horses. The French hussars baulked at the sight of the steady squadron and tried to go around, most did, many failed and were cut down as the squadron fought desperately to hold its ground against the onrushing mass. Michael had to defend himself as the hussars came up on his left, he turned Johnny to face them and sensed rather than saw Lloyd come up on his left. Suddenly, Sar'nt Major Blood crashed in along side them on his horse, cutting at speed.

Through the confusion Michael saw the left squadron break and everyman turned for the bridge and safety. Then the centre squadron gave, and the regiment broke, turned and made for safety in one disorganised mass, Michael, Lloyd and Blood staying close together and trying to protect the exposed flank of the squadron. They cut and thrust and parried until they were suddenly clear of the enemy.

The Eleventh and Twelfth had turned to face the French and the broken Sixteenth, inextricably mixed up with Spanish guerillas, streamed past them and over the bridge, crashing into each other, men cursing and swearing, officers and NCOs simply swept along. Once across the whole mass, as if by some instinct made to the rear of Bock's brigade, waiting a few hundred yards beyond the bridge, and there they halted, shook themselves free of the Spanish, and began to reform.

The French hussars broke off at the sight of the two light dragoon regiments, formed and waiting for them. They fell back towards the main body of the French and began to reform their ranks. The Eleventh and Twelfth turned about and rode quietly over the bridge, to join the Sixteenth behind Bock's.

The confusion in the Sixteenth was increased by the absence of Colonel Pelly. In his place Major Hay had assumed responsibility for the Regiment. He rode across the front and Michael heard him call out to Buchanan that Pelly had been captured, Murray wounded and that he was going to command the Regiment from the head of the left squadron. Michael looked across at the left squadron and realised, with horror, that it had lost almost half of its men.

Further to the left, Michael could see the battery of horse artillery was in position to fire at anything crossing the bridge. He saw Hay turn the left squadron the left in threes and move off at the walk. Buchanan ordered his squadron to do likewise. As they marched towards the left Michael glanced to his right. He saw French cavalry beginning to cross the bridge and then realised that the Eleventh, closer to the rear of Bock's was marching straight across the front of the battery, preventing it firing.

The Sixteenth and Twelfth went behind the guns, but by the time the front of the guns was clear, the French, lancers leading, were pouring across the bridge. Anson's brigade was forming to the left of the guns as they finally opened fire. Away to the right, Bock's heavy dragoons started down the slope towards the French and charged home before Anson's began to move.

Anson had his three regiments in a single line, and with him at their head they began to advance slowly down the hill towards the waiting French cavalry. The horses were tired and reluctant, but as they advanced they slowly built up speed, going into the trot, the canter and then the gallop. This time, the Sixteenth did not have the same impact. The charge quickly degenerated into a struggling, heaving mass of men and horses, swords hacking and cutting.

Bock's broke away first, followed a minute or so later by Anson's. Seemingly without orders, the whole galloped away, the French letting them go as they tried to recover their own formations after the onslaught of Anson's and Bock's. Michael saw Cotton and his staff, on a slight rise, the staff spread out and waving their arms.

"There," Michael shouted," Rally there!" The retreating regiments realised what was required and the men reined in their horses, looking around for their comrades, gathering in bunches that gradually turned into squadrons in line, all facing back towards the French. The French were a good distance away, similarly recovering, and showing no sign of coming on again.

Staff officers galloped to both Anson and Bock, and the brigades were ordered to retire at speed. The regiments all went right about and the squadrons set off at a good fast trot, still in line and ready to halt and face about if threatened. Glancing back over his right shoulder, Michael could see up the valley side, and saw a large, a very large body of French dragoons riding down towards them. The pace was increased to a canter until, a mile or so further on, they passed the two battalions of light infantry, who had halted and formed squares.

Another half mile and the two brigades halted, faced about, and set about sorting their formations out. It meant they had a grandstand view as the French dragoons charged the two squares. Several times they hurled themselves at the infantry, but close range volleys emptied saddles and brought down horses. The squares stood firm and the dragoons broke against them in vain.

The valiant stand by the infantry gave Bock's and Anson's the breathing space they badly needed and they were able to get themselves into a reasonable order and present a determined sight to the French in support of Halkett's infantry. The French hesitated. Cotton got the rearguard moving and as it got dark the French let them go without further trouble. Night fell and they went from line to column, now free of any immediate threat. Michael rode at the head of B Troop, Lloyd behind him, Blood at the rear keeping everyone up.

They marched on through the dark for two hours or so before Cotton halted them and allowed a rest. Michael dismounted his troop and dropped to the ground, glad to get out of the saddle for a while. He stretched, and started walking along the troop, checking men and horses as well as he could in the dark. He took extra care to speak to Blood and the Troop's sergeants, it was his first chance since being thrust into command and he thanked them for their help, particularly Blood.

He saw Hay talking to Anson and was about to approach when Cotton walked out of the dark, leading his horse. At the same time Barra and Sar'nt Major Williams appeared to ask after B Troop's horses. Michael didn't hear the exchange as Cotton interrupted Hay "What's the damage?"

A weary Hay answered. "We've lost Colonel Pelly and Lieutenant Baker, both prisoner, with ten or so men, I think, it's difficult to be sure. Lockhart's wound is bad, sir, very bad, Murray's wounded as well, they've both gone to the rear. Sar'nt Major Williams and Mister Barra are going over the horses just now with each troop commander, but overall we seem to have lost about eight men killed and the best part of forty wounded. We've lost nearly forty horses dead, another thirty and more with various wounds and injuries. Beauchamp lost two horses but he is uninjured, somehow. Sergeant Major Blood has been a tower of strength, Baxter as well, and I am damned pleased to have got Roberts with us." He paused in his litany of dead and wounded and the state of the Regiment. "It's been a bloody awful day, sir, but we are still here. A little rest will soon put us right, sir."

There was a moments silence and then Cotton said, "I think you had better keep Roberts here, I think the Regiment's need is the greater just now." He paused, "I know everyone is tired, but I want to put more distance between us and the French while it's dark. We'll have another fifteen minutes and then resume the march."

Some hours later, Michael thought it was about two o'clock in the morning, his watch had stopped as he had forgotten to wind it, the brigade was halted and Michael ordered his troop to dismount and rest. The men simply lay down where they dismounted, reins in hand, horses still saddled and bridled, and slept. Michael did not know who was on picket duty to watch for any French advance, he was too tired to care. A drink of water, a quick walk around the troop with Sar'nt Major Blood and he wrapped himself in his cloak and fell straight into a deep sleep.

The morning saw the brigade mounted and moving before dawn. Anson's had the rearguard, but the French did not bother them. Late morning came and they crossed the river Carrion on a bridge at a small town called Villamuriel. Engineers were preparing to blow it up. There, Wellington was drawing up his army to stand off the French. The battered regiments of Anson's were marched on, past the infantry divisions and finally halted in a quiet area in a little valley with a stream running through it. There the commissary was waiting for them and, just as welcome, their baggage. To his surprise, Hall was riding Castanha.

Michael asked "Hall, where's Billy?"

He explained, "It was all just too hard for the old boy, sir. We got here, got across the river and then he just went down, sir. Vetenry said there were nowt anyone could do, so he shot 'im, sir. Thought I'd best ride Castanha, sir."

"That's quite alright, Hall, and I'm sorry about Billy."

"Thank you, sir, one o' t'ponies is a bit lame as well, sir."

Bradley was with Marcello by the two ponies. He was fretting over one of them, bending, gently feeling down a foreleg.

"Is there a problem here, Bradley?"

"Aye, sir, he's carrying isself and there's heat in this foreleg." He straightened up. "T'other pony's areyt, best if he carries most o't baggage, sir, try to give this un a bit o' a break, sir."

"Damn. Can't be helped, let's hope he gets over it. With luck we may be here a day or two. In the meantime, I want to ride Robbie, give Johnny a rest."

"Reyt tha'r, sir."

"Bradley, do you think you and Marcello could manage all the horses and the ponies without Hall?"

"Aye, sir, ah reckon as how we could. Marcello can ride Jasper and lead one o' t' ponies and I can ride tha spare and lead t'other pony."

"Good, I think we are going to need every man we can mount. Hall, you can join B Troop with me." He gave a wry smile. "It seems I have finally got my troop."

# Chapter 5

Two and a half weeks later, the army took up positions on the river Tormes, north of Salamanca. It was familiar ground, it was where they had been just before the battle fought just across the river to the south. They had been forced from the position on the Carrion where everything that could go wrong for Wellington had gone wrong. The French had forced a crossing and Wellington had retreated again, to a line on the Pisuerga centred on Valladolid. There they got two days rest, but a brave action by French light infantry seized a crossing point and the retreat went on. The army fell back to the line of the river Douro, which was held for five days before Wellington ordered a further retreat to the position at Salamanca.

The position was a strong one, and they had reached it almost unmolested by the French. Anson's brigade, Michael and the Sixteenth hadn't been in action again. But it had been a hard retreat. The weather had turned cold and wet, many men had straggled and been lost, many had died, dysentery and rheumatism became common. Michael's pony with the bad leg had collapsed and had been shot. The good news was that General Hill had successfully completed his retreat from around Madrid and joined the main army. Wellington had got as many of the troops under cover as possible and hoped to give them a long rest to recover. For Michael, the immediate consequence of quietly reaching the Tormes was that he was ordered back to Cotton's staff.

He couldn't say that he had enjoyed the brief time in command of B Troop, it had been under particularly arduous circumstances. Food and forage had been in short supply, men and horses had suffered and been lost. He had worked hard and been grateful for the support of Blood and the other NCOs. And Lloyd, who had compensated for an overworked veterinary surgeon and saved several horses, but not as many as he would have liked. For all that, however, it had felt good to be back in the Regiment, amongst friends and comrades, and engaged in proper soldiering, to have fought with them, marched with them and gone though adversity with them. The Regiment, already weakened, had been further reduced by the retreat from Burgos. But Murray had returned and Hay was confident they could manage, and so Cotton had taken him back.

.      .      .

At the same time as Michael was saying his farewells to B Troop, Renard arrived back in Madrid. He moved straight back into his old quarters and dispatched Faucher and Lucroy on various missions. Renard was impatient, he had plans of his own. That first night back in the city an impromptu ball was organised for King Joseph as the citizens endeavoured to show their support. Unusually, Renard went.

He stood unobtrusively in the shadows of the candlelit ballroom of the Royal Palace. King Joseph and Marshal Jourdan were surrounded by senior officers and courtiers. Selected citizens were allowed to approach and pay their respects. Joseph seemed to be enjoying himself, but Jourdan was stoney faced and clearly not enjoying the ball. Renard heard Señora Ortega announced. She swept, there was no other word for it, into the room and made straight for the King. No one made any effort to intercept her. Arriving in front of Joseph, she dropped a long and deep curtsey. Joseph smiled down at the decolletage on display and Jourdan gave the first smile Renard had seen him make that evening. She was clearly well known to both men. Joseph stepped forward, offered his hand and raised her up. A snap of his fingers and a servant appeared with a tray of drinks. Ortega and the King both took one and raised their glasses to each other.

Renard waited, patiently. Eventually, Joseph turned his attention to another citizen of Madrid and Ortega moved to the edge of the crowd around the King. Renard moved in and came up beside Jourdan.

"Your Excellency, I wonder if I might presume on you for an introduction to Señora Ortega?"

Jourdan turned. "Ah, Renard! Taking the advice of a simple soldier, eh?"

"No, Excellency, a Marshal of France."

"Ha! Come along, and let us see what you make of her, but be careful, very careful, there is no suggestion she is involved in spying in any way and the King is something of an admirer. No doubt he would like to be more, but..." He shrugged. "I warn you, I shall introduce you as who you are, she is too likely to hear anyway, and I think an honest approach most likely to work."

"Of course, Excellency." Renard replied while thinking Jourdan a fool. Jourdan led the way around the throng of courtiers and sycophants that crowded around the King to where Ortega stood, watching the room and fanning her face.

"Señora Ortega," Jourdan gave a small bow as the lady faced him, and she dropped a small curtsey in response. "May I present Monsieur Renard, he is the head of our intelligence services here in Spain."

Ortega's expression did not alter as she turned her gaze on Renard. He gave her a bow, she returned a curtsey and looked at him, waiting.

"Señora Ortega," Renard began, "it is a pleasure to finally make your acquaintance. I have heard of your wonderful soirees and I am saddened that I have always been too busy to seek an invitation."

Ortega raised her fan to her face as if embarrassed by Renard's declaration. "Monsieur, you flatter me."

Jourdan broke in, "Excuse me, but I think His Majesty is looking for me." He spun around and left Ortega and Renard together.

Ortega watched him go, and said, with a small, fond smile, "Such a busy man, and such a support for our dear King." Then she turned her attention fully to Renard, her expression becoming serious, "And you, Monsieur, head of intelligence services? That sounds dreadfully important and not a little exciting. Tell me, what do you do?"

Renard had been observing her closely. He could see no hint of guile, nor any apprehension at meeting him. Either she was exactly what everyone said, or she was very, very good. "I seek out the King's enemies, Señora, and learn what I can of their intentions."

"Oh, you mean like the English? But I have found them all to be perfect gentlemen, I find it difficult to imagine any of the ones that I have met dabbling in anything as squalid as spying." She blushed, and Renard was convinced of her innocence, no one could summon up a blush like that. She went on, "Oh, Monsieur, please, forgive me, I did not mean..."

Renard smiled and stopped her, "There is nothing to apologise for, Señora, spying is a dirty business, I wish it were otherwise, but the King, and the Emperor command and I must obey."

"You are too kind, Monsieur. It is good to know that the King, such a lovely man, has people like you to help him. Now, you must come to one of my soirees and if I can be of any assistance to you, you must just ask."

Renard bowed in appreciation of her offer. "Thank you, Señora, I shall." Then he paused as if struck by a sudden thought. "Tell me, Señora, when the English were here, did you ever come across a cavalry officer, a Captain Roberts? It's a matter of no great importance, he was involved in the parole of one of our officers recently." He watched her carefully.

Ortega looked thoughtful. "No, Monsieur, I don't think I did."

But Renard had caught a slight flicker in her eyes, a minute hesitation. She was lying. "No matter, Señora. Now, perhaps I may escort you for some refreshments?" He gave her his arm and as they walked his mind was full of how he might use Señora Ortega and kill Roberts. It was only later that he realised she had been the first to mention spying. Had that been an assumption on her part, or a mistake? He decided it was a mistake. Señora Ortega had become a person of more than passing interest to him.

Faucher and Lucroy had been sent out to discover what they could about the fates of Father Lopez and Montero. It didn't take them long. An informer sent them to a small taverna near the Plaza Mayor. There a waiter gave them a graphic description of the fight and the capture of Montero. From the description they were given it was clear Roberts had been involved. That one of Roberts companions had been killed was no consolation. From the taverna they went to the church where Father Lopez had worked. That Lopez had been executed was general knowledge, but an old woman in the church polishing brass added the rumour that a British cavalry officer had been involved. Faucher wasn't looking forward to telling Renard, it would only fuel the man's paranoia and obsession. Lucroy, on the other hand, was very pleased by the information and saw it as all the more reason to go after Roberts. He was almost excited by what they had learnt.

Faucher was right. In the morning they gathered in Renard's office and Lucroy eagerly told him about Lopez and Montero and Roberts' apparent role in their capture and subsequent execution. Renard listened in silence, and then he exploded. He swore and cursed, shouted so that spittle flew from his lips. Then he turned on Faucher.

"And what about that bloody muleteer you found who was supposed to go and kill Roberts? Eh? Eh? What about him? Did he? No, it would seem not. What happened to him, eh? Just vanished, I suppose? You are bloody useless, Faucher. Now, get out, both of you!"

In their adjacent office, Faucher slumped in his chair, staring at his desk. He was furious with Renard, thought the man was mad. He wondered how he could escape.

Unnoticed, Lucroy slipped out. He had an idea. He had an idea that could put him in Renard's good books and show up that feeble Faucher once and for all. He went to look for a man. A man he had been introduced to the last time he was in Madrid. He had hoped he had found a killer to go after Roberts, but Faucher had got in first with his muleteer. Then they had been forced to leave Madrid and he had lost touch with the man. Now he made his way to the maze of narrow streets that lay in the south of the city. He found the small church he was looking for and went in.

It was gloomy after the light of day, he stood for a moment and let his eyes adjust. A priest approached him and asked if he could help. Lucroy simply answered that only Diego could help. Then he left, crossed the little square outside, entered a filthy looking taverna, ordered a jug of wine with two glasses and sat down to wait.

A number of Spaniards came in, had a drink and left. Lucroy waited patiently. The man he wanted to see was very careful and would not be rushed. Lucroy had picked up rumours and it had taken a long time to meet Diego and even longer to arrive at any sort of understanding. He waited nearly an hour, and then Diego came in. At first glance he looked very ordinary, there was nothing about his outward appearance to give a clue as to just how dangerous this man was. He was clean shaven, his clothes neat and tidy, his appearance said I am no one special, look elsewhere. Diego sat with his back to the wall, poured himself a drink and raised his glass to Lucroy, who responded.

"So, Monsieur, you are back? How long for this time?"

"I have no idea. For ever?" Diego smirked at that. "A few months, weeks, days, I really have no idea."

"And what do you want with me? I thought you had a job for me, but nothing came of it and then you all ran away from the English."

"I may still have a job for you."

"May? What good is may to me?" There was an angry edge to Diego's voice and Lucroy sipped nervously at his wine.

"You must understand that it was no fault of mine. A colleague got someone else for the job, but they failed."

Diego knocked back his wine and refilled his glass. "So now you come back to me? What is the job?"

"It is an English officer."

Diego shot a quizzical glance at Lucroy. "That would be no small undertaking, Monsieur. It would cost you a lot."

"I know."

"And where is this Englishman?"

"I don't know," admitted Lucroy. "With the English army, I think."

"You don't know? Then why the Hell are you wasting my time, eh?"

"Because I simply want to know if you would be interested in such a job. Then I can tell my chief..."

Diego stopped him short as his hand shot out and grasped Lucroy's arm. "Tell him what, exactly? Tell him how to find me? Who I am? Do you want to die, Monsieur?"

"No, no, it's not like that. I would just tell him I have found a man, a very good man at what he does who can take care of this Englishman."

"Hmm. I might be interested. But not if your man is with the English army. That would be too difficult." He paused for a moment. "Very well, you can tell your chief I will do it, if he offers me enough and if the man is not with the army." He laughed. "I can't really see this happening at all." The laugh disappeared. "So I am going to leave now and not waste any more time on you or this bad wine. You will not leave for another five minutes and you will not come to find me again unless you have a definite offer for me. One I can carry out. Understand?"

"Yes, of course."

A few hours later, Lucroy nervously knocked on the door of Renard's office went in.

"What is it?" Renard growled, head down, reading.

"Monsieur, I have found a man who might be able to deal with Roberts."

Renard's head shot up and he fixed Lucroy with a piercing stare. "I do hope you are not in jest, Lucroy. You know what I think of Faucher and his muleteer."

"Yes, Monsieur, I mean no, this is not like that at all."

"Tell me."

After Lucroy fell silent, Renard sat, thoughtful for a moment. "If I have understood you correctly, you have found a real killer, a man known for his success and skill and who is willing to kill Roberts, if we pay enough and if Roberts isn't with the British army? Is that the strength of it?"

"Yes, Monsieur."

"And how do you suggest we get Roberts away from the army and to a suitable location for your man to do his work?"

"I, err, I don't know Monsieur."

"No, I didn't think you did."

Lucroy grasped at a straw. "But, Monsieur, Roberts is often in Lisbon, we know that."

"Are you suggesting we send this man to Lisbon to wait around indefinitely just in case Roberts should one day turn up? Hmm? Well?"

"No, Monsieur."

"Lucroy, stop looking like a whipped dog. You have at least shown some initiative. Keep in touch with this man. Tell him the job is his if we can locate Roberts somewhere suitable."

"Thank you, Monsieur."

"Now get out, and don't mention this to Faucher, he's had his chance."

Lucroy saw Diego again the following day and told him what Renard had said. Diego grunted and looked unimpressed.

"You know how to find me," was his only comment.

After only four days back in Madrid, the decision was taken to march north against Wellington, following Hill, and joining with the forces already in the north to bring overwhelming numbers to bear on the British. Renard, his two senior clerks and a handful of other staff went with them. The brief time in Madrid had given them no chance to try to establish communications with Lisbon, let alone find anyone to send there. Renard was furious, how, he asked himself, was he supposed to run an effective intelligence department while constantly on the move, up rooted, sent from pillar to post and back again

Had Jourdan no idea just how difficult it was to establish effective agents and lines of communication? He vented his fury on his staff, Faucher in particular.

.     .     .

The situation of Wellington's army at Salamanca remained quiet for some days. It gave everyone a chance to recover from the rigours of the retreat. For the cavalry that meant an incessant search for fodder and hard work for the farriers reshoeing most of the thousands of horses. Michael was sent hither and thither by Cotton as they strove to get the cavalry back in good order. Anson's, the Sixteenth in particular, had suffered severely during the retreat from Burgos. In the midst of all that, Michael received a letter from Furtado. He informed Michael that he had broken the news of Antonio's death to his friends and ascertained from them that Antonio left no dependents. He also wrote that he had heard, again, from Senhorita Cardoso who wanted to buy the quinta Michael had inherited when his parents died. She was unaware it was Michael's and, as Michael had suggested, Furtado had given her to believe that the owner of the quinta was in the Brazils, but might be visiting in the winter. She had written to ask if that was the case as she was anxious to acquire it.

Michael put off replying, he wasn't sure what he wanted to do. He did, however, send Marcello into Salamanca to see if Señora Martinez was at her house there. His instructions to Marcello were to tell her to leave at once for her farm, if not for Portugal, as the situation was threatening. He was gone for almost the whole day, but returned to say that the house was empty. He had asked around and no one knew for sure, but a few people had thought she was at her farm. Michael felt some relief at the news.

Once again the respite was broken as the French attacked. King Joseph and Jourdan with their forces from the south had finally linked up with Marshal Soult and with the French forces already in the north. As they had before they endeavoured to get around Wellington's flank. Their first attempt failed when they couldn't take the bridge over the Tormes at Alba. But they persevered and eventually crossed the river further upstream, threatening Wellington's flank. Wellington moved his army to face them, offering battle. A long wait in cold, drifting rain followed. They were on familiar ground, it was the battlefield of the previous July and French skeletons lay everywhere. In case a retreat should become necessary, all the baggage was ordered to make a half day's march towards Ciudad Rodrigo and Portugal.

As soon as he heard the orders, Michael sent for Bradley and Marcello. He was clear in what he wanted.

"Bradley, Marcello, I want you to take Robbie, Jasper and the baggage pony. I will ride Johnny. Marcello, show Bradley the way to Señora Martinez' farm. When you get there, tell her to leave at once. Go to Ciudad Rodrigo, you should all be safe there. If we hold our position here, come back, find the staff baggage, I won't be far away, but if we retreat and if there is the slightest indication of the French besieging Ciudad Rodrigo, get out, get well into Portugal, and take the Señora with you." He smiled at Bradley, "And Señorita Linares as well. Leave us as much food as you can, a bag for each of us, myself, Lloyd and Hall. Now, go and pack and get ready and leave as soon as you can. Good luck and I hope to see you back here or in Ciudad Rodrigo."

Bradley and Marcello rushed off and Michael turned to Lloyd and Hall. "We will have to depend on what we carry or find for a few days."

Hall grimaced and Lloyd said, "Not to worry Captain, we'll manage."

At two o'clock in the afternoon, a steady rain falling, Cotton and Wellington were together, watching the French manoeuvres, their staff mingling behind them. To Michael's relief there was no sign of Colonel Gordon who, apparently, was organising the withdrawal of the baggage and supplies. Wellington turned to address the staff.

"Gentlemen, it is clear the French are trying to get between us and Portugal. I fear we must retreat. Sir Stapleton, you and the cavalry will cover the march of the infantry. We shall direct our march on Ciudad Rodrigo." As he spoke the rain increased and it became torrential as he rode off to organise the retreat.

Cotton's staff and orderlies sat in a group in front of five brigades of cavalry that were standing ready to protect the retreating infantry. The rain ran down Michael's face, he felt the cold as it soaked through his cloak, dolman, waistcoat and shirt. He sat hunched on Johnny, who was trying to turn his head away from the rain.. Michael was not the only one doing so. At least there was some warmth coming from his horse, trapped by the large cloak that covered the horse from withers to quarters.

The last of the infantry moved clear as it was getting dark and the cavalry moved off after them. They rode slowly, the ground was heavy, the mud slippery, horses stumbled and fell in the gloom, their riders cursing. Michael was thankful he was not in the infantry. The roads were bad, the mud deep and the rain continued, cold and incessant. Cotton gave orders to the brigades in person, so there was little for the staff to do except follow him and shiver. Remarkably Cotton looked just as relaxed and flamboyant as he always did. Then Michael realised he was deliberately showing himself to the troops, saying he was suffering the conditions with them, setting an example of stoicism.

At last they forded a small river, Michael heard someone call it the Valmusa, he didn't care. What he did care about was the small village they rode into. Captain White was waiting and directed them to their billets. Wellington and his staff were also there, there was not a lot of room. There was, at least, a large barn that was crammed with horses, steaming by the light of a pair of lanterns. Michael found he was sharing a small room with Captains White, Campbell and von der Decken. It was cosy. Lloyd and Hall had found space in a hayloft, that was quickly emptied of any hay.

Lloyd had commented, "Duw, probably warmer up there, over the horses, than in that house, sir."

Michael and the other captains shared what little food they had, stale bread, cold meat and hard cheese, and then tried to get some sleep, wrapped in wet cloaks on the hard floor. Michael could hear the rain hammering on the roof and thought that, all in all, things could be worse, he could be sleeping out like most of the army.

As they mounted their horses in the darkness before dawn, it became known that there had been no issue of food to the army. It was still raining hard, and the day became a repeat of the previous one, except for increasing hunger pangs and the rain and the cold reaching everywhere. As they moved off, Michael walked Johnny alongside Lloyd and Hall.

"Lloyd, Hall, how are things with you?"

Lloyd answered, "Damn cold, sir, begging your pardon. We got through half our supplies as well, sir, and I hear there won't be any more?"

"So I have heard, but let's see."

At the midday halt they heard what had happened. Quartermaster General Gordon had sent all the supplies off by the wrong road. They were currently twenty miles or more away and they would not meet up with the army until they reached Ciudad Rodrigo, another three days away. The few scrawny bullocks still with the army were slaughtered then and there and the meat distributed, such as there was. Men began to straggle from the ranks, searching for something to eat.

Late afternoon brought the army across another watercourse, at a village called Matilla. The cavalry, bringing up the rear, found themselves pushing stragglers ahead of them. There were infantry, many shoeless, some who had fallen out to look for food, or with simple exhaustion. Then there were the women and children who followed the army. Some children were lifted on to horses, their mothers hanging to stirrup leathers. The roads were becoming marked by broken carts abandoned in the mud. There were dead horses, dead men, dead women, dead children, killed by a combination of exhaustion, starvation and the cold and wet. The rain continued, unbroken.

As darkness came on some French cavalry caught up and there was a sharp skirmish before the French were sent off with their tail between their legs. The army could still fight. All through the night more stragglers came in. There were no billets, the staff, the army, slept as and where they could. The hunger grew, it made the cold and rain harder to cope with.

Dawn brought no relief. Once again the army was on the march before daylight, the sun didn't rise so much as the day gradually got less dark. In the gloom the rain still fell. Even the smallest streams became serious obstacles to tired men and horses as they were swollen by flood waters. More were falling out, simply lying down and dying. The number of broken carts and dead horses increased until the edge of the roads seems lined with them.

Dusk brought another river, another defensible line behind which the army might get what rest it could, and could wait for the stragglers to catch up. Michael was with Cotton watching the last of the army, the Light Division, crossing the river, when the French launched an attack. Sitting on their horses in the rain, they watched as the Division hurried down the far valley side and marched quickly to the fords. Behind them a skirmish line held off the French light infantry pressing hard on them. Once across the river, the Light division, now joined by the Seventh Division, formed to oppose the expected French attack. The skirmishers fell back, running to follow the main body across the river, and a fierce firefight developed all along the river between the skirmishers of both sides. Then the gloom of the late afternoon turned to the dark of night and the fighting petered out. Both sides withdrew to the shelter of woods on the valley sides.

The retreat began again at four o'clock in the morning. Dead and dying were abandoned. Michael cast his eyes across the cavalry, there were now as many marching on foot as were mounted, such had been the loss of horses. An hour after dawn came welcome news from the pickets left behind to watch the French, they were not following. During the day the rain began to ease, but it got colder. The tracks they took were so bad that in places the troops were reduced to marching in single file. Cotton and his staff, with the cavalry at the rear, rode steadily through the detritus of the army, the carts and the dead. There were sights Michael would never forget, try as he might. He saw a small family, an infantryman, with his arm around his wife, she holding a baby, all dead. They just kept riding on. There was none of the usual chatter amongst the staff. Everyone was wrapped in their own misery. When they halted they simply tied the horses to a tree and lay down to sleep.

That night the rain finally stopped and, instead, there was a frost. The terrain was one of scrub and scattered copses of oaks. There was nothing to do in the morning except to resume the march. There was no longer any threat from the French, it had become a simple struggle against hunger, exhaustion, the cold and the mud. Where the ground was less muddy, many, Michael amongst them, had taken to dismounting and leading their tired horses, trying to give them some respite from the constant struggle of the march. There were none of the usual sounds of an army on the march, no drums, no bugles, no shouted commands or admonishments. Each man was solely concerned with his own survival.

Michael had lost count of how long they had been marching. Was it four days? Or was it five? As he climbed into Johnny's saddle in the dark, he didn't care. He was hungry, so hungry, and cold, and tired. Hall had shaken him hard to wake him. Michael was glad he had him, he was a tough as old leather, for one still young. He and Lloyd had stuck close to him and they had all watched out for each other. They had walked together, leading their horses, now tired and looking malnourished.

Captain Campbell appeared out of the dark. "Morning Roberts. Seems we should reach Ciudad Rodrigo by midday."

Michael managed a smile. "Thank God for that."

In the late morning they crested the hills overlooking the fortress city. Michael paused for a moment and stroked Johnny's nose as the horse stood next to him. Most of the staff were also on foot and leading their horses. Between them and the city was the army. Cotton had insisted on bringing up the very rear, where he had been since leaving Burgos. Just ahead was Anson's brigade, now much depleted. Somewhere along the way Michael had heard that Lockhart had died of his wound. Many men were suffering with rheumatism and dysentery. He had watched the Sixteenth walk by that morning, many bareheaded, uniforms tattered and torn, looking pale, some obviously ill. He had seen Persse call out to one of his men, Thornton, and tell him to report sick. The man had protested, insisted he was fit, until he was taken with a fit of shivers and rode quietly away in search of the surgeon. It had made Michael feel proud of his Regiment.

The afternoon was spent distributing the brigades around various villages about the city. Somehow they managed to get every man and horse under cover. Food was distributed by the long lost commissary and the regiments began the long, slow job of recovery. Eventually, Michael followed Cotton and they rode into the city. Captain White was waiting for them at the city gate.

Cotton returned White's salute. "I hope you have somewhere warm and dry for us, White?"

"Yes, sir, I think you will be pleased."

"Then lead on!"

The billet was a fine house on the Plaza Mayor, not the finest, that was where Wellington was, but it was fine enough. Michael was again sharing a room, but only with von der Decken. The stabling was good and Lloyd was happy with it, particularly as he found room over it for himself. Hall was in with the other servants. With no baggage there was little for him to do, so Michael gave him some of his small reserve of ready money and sent him out to buy what supplies he could find in the city.

Michael was sitting in his room, examining his boots and wondering if they were repairable, when Hall returned, and he was not alone.

"Begging you pardon, sir, but Mister Bradley is 'ere."

"Is he, by God, then send him up."

A moment later Bradley entered.

"Badley, how are things with you? I'm damned glad to see you!"

"Thank you, sir, ahm reyt good, sir. Young Marcello got us to the Señora's farm, sir, and we got her away reyt quick, sir. She weren't too happy, sir, but I said that you had said and she give up and away we went, sir. And now she's safe and sound in the city, sir."

"Thank God, for that. And thank you, Bradley, you've done very well, I am grateful to you."

"Thank you, sir. All the 'osses are 'ere as well, sir."

"Good, we've got good stabling here."

"Yes, sir, Mister Hall is showing Marcello where it is, sir, and the horses all be well, sir."

"Good, now, to find you a billet..."

"Err, no, sir, thankee, sir," Bradley interrupted, looking more than a little uncomfortable. "You see, sir, ah'm afraid that I must give thee mah notice, sir, immediate like, sir."

"What! What do you mean?"

"Ah'm reyt sorry, sir, but ah'm going to work for Señora Martinez." He looked embarrassed. "Señorita Linares has agreed to be mah wife, sir, and the Señora has offered me a place looking after all t'orses on her farm, sir."

"Good God!" Michael was staggered. "Well, yes, err, my congratulations, Bradley. Um, it's a long way from Yorkshire."

"Aye sir, 'appen it is." He shrugged. "But ah reckons there's a new start 'ere for me, sir." He paused. "There's nowt for me in Yorkshire anymore, sir." Sadness briefly clouded his expression. Then he went on, "And Marcello is going to stay as well, sir. Sorry, sir."

"Very well, I can understand that." Michael rose to his feet, walked over to Bradley and offered him his hand. As they shook, he said "I wish you all the very best, Bradley, every happiness. And thank you for your service. If I can ever do anything for you..."

"Aye, well, thank you, sir."

" I must settle yours and Marcello's wages. I shall need to find a paymaster, get some money from him, perhaps you and Marcello can come around here tomorrow evening?"

"Aye, sir, that will be reyt good."

The next day was taken up with the work of starting to get the cavalry back into effective order. It was going to be a long slow job, but there was the fear the French might yet attack and as much as could be done quickly was got underway. Michael was constantly around the cavalry billets, and riding from village to village on Robbie, who was in fine condition compared to poor Johnny. He managed to find a paymaster and extract some money from him. When Bradley and Marcello duly appeared he was able to settle with them in full. It was only after they had gone that he realised that he hadn't enquired as to where Victoria was lodging.

It was, he decided, just as well.

# Chapter 6

Wellington's final retreat to Ciudad Rodrigo had been half-heartedly followed by Marshal Soult and his army. Meanwhile, King Joseph and Marshal Jourdan with their army had marched to Salamanca to consider their options. With nothing to occupy him, Renard spent much of his time hanging around the King's headquarters and trying to avoid Jourdan. After two days of rest, King Joseph held a review of the French forces outside Salamanca. It was still raining and the whole thing passed off badly with nothing achieved except everyone getting soaked to the skin.

Renard watched as the King and his entourage returned from the window of a warm room, a glass of good brandy in his hand. The King arrived first and hurried inside. Renard could not supress a smile as he saw Jourdan, dripping wet, dismount from his horse. Various staff officers followed suit, handed their horses to servants and made for the dry of the headquarters. Most made for their own rooms to change, but, behind Renard, the door opened. He turned to see a dragoon Colonel come in and walk to the fire to warm himself. Renard didn't know him, guessed he was with the Army of Portugal, one of General Souham's staff. He turned back to the window, he had no wish to speak to any staff officer, but the Colonel spoke to him.

"Pardon, Monsieur, but you are Monsieur Renard?"

Directly addressed like that, Renard had no choice but to reply. He turned to face his questioner. "I am, Colonel." He was curt, almost rude. Then the Colonel surprised him.

"Forgive me, Monsieur, I have been hoping for the opportunity of a word with you in private. If I might...?" Renard nodded, his curiosity piqued. "You sent a request out some time ago, last May, I think, asking after a British officer, a Captain Roberts." It wasn't a question. Renard became very alert and watched the Colonel carefully.

The Colonel continued. "I am curious to know why he is of such interest to you that you sent out a general request for information on his whereabouts?"

Renard paused for a moment, before speaking, weighing up how to reply to him, there had been more in his voice than mere curiosity. "Yes, I did." He decided to ignore the Colonel's question. "But why is that of interest to you?"

"Because he killed my son." The statement was blunt.

Renard was stunned, momentarily speechless with surprise, but he had detected a flash of underlying anger. "I am sorry, Colonel...?"

"Delatour."

"I am sorry to hear about your son." Delatour nodded an acknowledgement, but his face was stoney. "As for Roberts, he has been a thorn in my side, he has thwarted my attempts to gather intelligence about the British and has killed several of my agents." Renard was unsure, feeling his way carefully. " I assume that, like me, you would like to see the world rid of Roberts?"

"I would, but my interest is personal, I see yours is professional."

They stood facing each other in silence, each waiting for more, both reluctant to bring the conversation to a close. Renard wondered if the Colonel might be able to help him. He was reluctant to reveal more, concerned it might further undermine his position if it became common knowledge. He realised Delatour was waiting in hope, hope that Renard might offer him something.

"I assume, Colonel, that I can rely on you to keep anything that I tell you confidential?"

"Of course, Monsieur." The hope in Delatour showed clearly.

Renard paused. "Colonel, I will admit to you that my desire to see Roberts dead is more than professional. I want him dead because he killed my son."

It was Delatour's turn to be shocked into silence.

"It occurs to me, Colonel, that as a senior officer on the staff, you have a freedom of action not open to me. On the other hand, I have access to sources of information that you do not. I do not know exactly how, but I hope that we might, together or separately, achieve vengeance for the deaths of our sons. Should I succeed, believe me, I shall take great pleasure in letting you know. I trust that you will do the same?"

"You may rely on me, Monsieur."

Solemnly, the two men shook hands. Renard turned to a table with a bottle of brandy on it, poured another glass and handed it to Delatour.

"Here's to the death of Roberts." Renard proposed the toast and the two men drank.

It was a long week before the King decided he would march south to recover Madrid, leaving Marshal Soult in the north with the bulk of the French forces. Renard was informed when Jourdan summoned Renard to his quarters in Salamanca.

"Monsieur Renard," he began, without any preamble, "We are returning to Madrid, we leave tomorrow. I suggest you use the time we will take to get there to decide what you are going to do to reestablish some sort of flow of intelligence for His Majesty. I trust that once back in Madrid you will be able to do that? It is, after all, why you are in Spain."

"Excellency, I shall of course, do all that I can."

"Make sure that you do, God knows we need some good fortune. I had hoped that war breaking out between Britain and the United States would end the American supply of flour to the British army. That would force them to retreat, even to leave, but the damned Americans like their money too much and have kept up the trade."

"Yes, Excellency, that is a shame."

"That is putting it mildly. Whatever Wellington might be planning, an end to the flour trade would blow up all his ideas!"

Renard frowned a little, unnoticed by Jourdan, the Marshal had rung a bell somewhere in the depths of Renard's memory. Jourdan went on, "so if you can do anything it would help, not to mention be surprising. Now, go, get ready, and make your plans." He waved dismissively and Renard got out quickly.

Renard was furious. He was sick to death of Jourdan's constant criticism and refusal to understand the difficulties Renard faced. It was all very well for the Marshal to carp on about how was it that a single British cavalry officer seemed to be able to repeatedly thwart a senior member of the emperor's secret police and intelligence department. He fought to control his fury, turning it to determined, constructive thought. He would show them all. He would secure some victory in his war that would leave them all stunned and in awe. And he would see Roberts dead. That above all. Then, perhaps, he might be left to get on with his work, or even return to Paris. He did not see Colonel Delatour again before marching for Madrid, but the fact there were two men intent on Roberts' destruction brought him some comfort.

The journey south was cold and wet. Renard had managed to secure a carriage, which rattled and jolted, but at least it kept him dry and blankets and rugs kept him warm. It also gave him time to think without interruption. Three days into the journey they passed through a small village and over a narrow river. By the bridge was a derelict mill. It would be, thought Renard, a long time before that mill produced any flour. And then it came to him. It was a memory from more than twenty-five years ago, he had been a very junior clerk. His job then was to keep a watch on what was happening in Italy, and he mostly did it through the Italian newspapers that he was sent regularly. It had achieved little except to improve his Italian. But he remembered a curious report, one that had caught his eye for no good reason. A flour mill, somewhere in Piedmont if he remembered correctly, had blown up. It was claimed that the very flour itself had combusted to cause the explosion. He knew that the Americans were sending thousands of barrels of flour to Portugal, through Lisbon where there were huge warehouses for it. What if, he thought, he could get them blown up? Was it even possible? Who might know?

Renard usually avoided the military, if he mixed with anyone it was the other senior civil servants of Joseph's government. That evening was an exception, but he was looking for a very specific type of soldier, he was looking for an engineer, the more senior, the better. He was in luck, so much so that he wondered if this was something that was meant to be and augured well for his idea. The man he found was a Major, a similar age to Renard and an Italian to boot. More than that, he too remembered the flour mill explosion.

"I was a young man," he laughed, "things like that interested me. I wanted to be an engineer, to blow things up as well as build them."

"So it is possible for flour to explode?"

"Not as such, but if you get a cloud of flour in the air, then that can burn, combust, and if that is in an enclosed space, then, yes, you get an explosion. Just as gunpowder will just burn in the open air, but confine it..." He shrugged and grinned. "Here, let me show you."

"Isn't it dangerous?"

"No, not with just a spoonful."

Ten minutes later the Major had a candle burning and a spoon heaped with flour. He held the spoon over the candle flame and shook a little off. A small white cloud of flour fell towards the flame and then, with a flash, it ignited. He did it again. Renard grinned.

"There you are, Monsieur, a nice little party trick, unless you are a miller."

"Yes, yes, I see." Renard thought for a moment. "Could you, say, blow up a barrel of flour?"

"What? Oh, no, Monsieur, it has to be a cloud, in the air."

"Oh!" The smile disappeared from Renard's face.

The Major thought for a moment. "I suppose," he began, haltingly, "that if you blew up the barrel first, you would get a cloud of flour, and then you might be able to set fire to that." He shrugged. "But what would be the point, the first explosion would have destroyed the barrel anyway."

"Hmm, yes, I see." Renard thought for a moment. "But what if, say, there was a source of ignition after the explosion?"

The Major's brow furrowed as he considered the question. "The best thing might be a second explosion, almost immediately after the first one, while the flour is still in a cloud. That might work."

"And what, Major, do you think the result would be if that happened in a warehouse full of barrels? Might the explosions spread?"

The Major looked hard at Renard. "Frankly, Monsieur, I have no idea. A cloud of dust in a mill is one thing, it can happen naturally, and then, if there's a candle, whoomph! But barrels in a warehouse? I really don't know. It's a long step from my party piece here." He waved the spoon at the candle.

"Hmm, yes, I see what you mean. Ah, well, never mind. Thank you, Major, that was most instructive."

"My pleasure, Monsieur."

Renard started to leave, then stopped. "Major, I wonder if you could let me have a little flour?" He smiled. "It is such an amusing trick."

Renard walked slowly back to his carriage, deep in thought. By the time he reached the carriage, he had made up his mind.

"Lucroy, Faucher, come here." He climbed into the carriage and held the door open for his two clerks. They were surprised. So far Renard had been a solitary, brooding presence in the carriage while they had been lucky to get a lift on the back of wagon carrying trunks and chests of paperwork for the King's civil service.

Renard got comfortable, facing the two men who had to perch themselves on trunks and valises. He looked at them thoughtfully for a moment.

"Do you, Messieurs, think you could carry out a plan that could win the war for us in Portugal and Spain?"

Lucroy snapped back with "Yes, Monsieur, of course!" He looked excited.

Faucher was half a second behind him, long enough for Renard to look at him and raise an eyebrow quizzically. "Yes, Monsieur, of course." He tried to look enthusiastic. Inside he was full of apprehension at what was to come.

Renard explained that he had a plan to destroy the British army's flour supplies in Lisbon, which would force them to retreat, perhaps even to leave Portugal.

He realised Faucher's worst fear when he told them the two of them would be going to Lisbon to carry out the plan. Then he explained how it would be done. He gave no hint of the uncertainty expressed by the Major of engineers.

"You will make up two explosive charges, the bigger the better, but small enough for you to carry. Two for each warehouse, however many there are. Then you will gain entry to each flour warehouse. I can't imagine there will be much of a guard on flour. There will need to be two separate explosions inside the warehouse, so the charges will need fuses accordingly. I would suggest a single fuse splitting into two, one slightly longer. The first charge will blow up a number of barrels of flour, creating a cloud of flour in the air. The second one will ignite the cloud, cause a powerful explosion and destroy the warehouse."

Lucroy looked even more excited, but Faucher exclaimed, "But flour won't explode, Monsieur!"

Renard smiled pityingly at him. "Oh, yes it will, allow me to demonstrate."

A lantern lit the carriage interior and Renard opened it and extracted the candle, still burning. "Now, let me see, Lucroy, pass me that box." He took it dripped some wax onto it and then stood the candle in the wax. "I think that will do."

Next he pulled out of his coat pocket a twist of paper containing the flour the Major had given him. He untwisted it, held it above the candle, and shook a little out, forming a small cloud as it fell. There was a small flash and the flour had gone.

A sharp intake of breath from both men told him his demonstration had worked. He suppressed a sigh of relief.

"As soon as we get to Madrid you will prepare to travel to Lisbon, you will leave as soon as possible. You will travel separately. Once there make contact with the man we sent in June, what was his name, Faucher?"

"Err, um, Vargas, Monsieur."

"Yes, good, if he is still alive. If not it will simply make matters a little more difficult for you. I am sure you will be able to manage. You will enlist his help to acquire enough gunpowder for two small charges for each warehouse. You will gain entry to the flour warehouses and detonate your charges." He gave a mirthless little smile. "I would suggest that you are well away before they explode."

Lucroy laughed, slightly hysterically. Faucher sat silent, his mind racing, full of doubts he dare not voice, questions he dare not ask.

Renard continued. "Not a word of this to anyone, no one at all. You are simply going to Lisbon to take personal charge of our operations there. Do you understand?"

Both men nodded their understanding. "Good, now go, we can talk it over again tomorrow evening."

As they walked away, Lucroy was jubilant. "What an opportunity for us, to win the war for the Emperor. It is a move of pure genius on Renard's part!" He was practically bouncing with excitement.

Faucher wasn't so sure. Renard's plan sounded like a fantasy to him. He had seen the cloud of flour flash and vanish, but that was a long way from a warehouse full of barrels of flour. He was far from convinced that it would work. Still, it seemed to have cheered Renard up a little. As for being sent to Lisbon, he was a little less concerned about that than he might have been. He reckoned it would take about three weeks to get to Lisbon from Madrid, keeping as much as possible to the mountains, following the smugglers routes. The first thing he would have to do was find a guide, someone who could be trusted. At least he could make his own arrangements, travelling separately from Lucroy. Faucher's lack of concern was due to his possession of a safe conduct pass signed by Wellington. He smiled quietly to himself. With any luck the idiot Lucroy would be caught and he could decide what to do when he got to Lisbon.

Renard was feeling pleased with himself. He had to admit, if only to himself, that he wasn't sure about his plan. There was no real evidence that it would work. True, at least one flour mill had blown up, and he had seen for himself how flour could explode. Whether or not it would work in a warehouse full of barrels of flour, who knew? There was only one way to find out. He had to do something to regain his standing in the eyes of the King and Jourdan, and if it cost him two clerks, well, he would be well rid of them. Lucroy was a sycophant and Faucher, probably the cleverer of the two, was a sceptic and he doubted his commitment.

The great shame was that Roberts clearly wasn't in Lisbon, but with the army. The damned message delivered by that dragoon officer made that obvious.

If Roberts had been in Lisbon he could have sent the man Lucroy had found after him. At least Roberts being with the army, and somewhere on the northern Portugal frontier meant he couldn't interfere with Renard's plan. Renard grunted to himself. He would rather have Roberts dead than anything else. The man had killed his son. He could put aside all the intelligence upsets Roberts had caused in the interests of winning the war, but not that, that took precedence over everything. More than anything that fuelled his hatred. Revenge for Roberts' interference in his work would just be an added bonus.

Then he had an idea. It was so devious that he grinned manically and almost laughed out loud. If the English knew about his plan they would undoubtedly send Roberts to deal with it. If he was in Lisbon, Lucroy's man could kill him. Somehow, he had to tip off the English that an operation was under way in Lisbon. He realised he might lose Faucher and Lucroy, but it would be worth it to kill Roberts. And as only he would know about the plan to get Roberts to Lisbon and kill him, if it failed no one would ever know, and if it succeeded and he got Roberts killed that would reestablish his standing in no small way. He needed to know about Lucroy's man. But he would have to be careful, he didn't want Lucroy or Faucher to realise he was prepared to sacrifice them.

The chance to speak to Lucroy came at the midday halt the next day. Faucher was nowhere to be seen.

"Lucroy, a word with you."

"Yes, Monsieur."

"Tell me about the man you found in Madrid, the one who said he would go after Roberts if he was in Lisbon? What is his name?"

"Diego, Monsieur. He has quite a reputation, the Madrid police have been after him for years, he is known to have killed quite a few people, mostly other criminals, but also one or two citizens who had upset other citizens. He is not easy to find, Monsieur. After I heard about him, it took me weeks to arrange a meeting."

"I see. Do you think he might meet me?"

"Oh, ah, err, I don't know, but I could try to arrange it, Monsieur."

"When we get back to Madrid, Lucroy, I would very much like to meet your Señor Diego. Arrange it."

"Yes, Monsieur, of course."

Standing just behind Renard's carriage Faucher overheard most of the conversation. He knew of Diego, Lucroy had boasted about finding him. Why Renard should be interested in him he didn't know. He could hazard a guess, Diego was just the sort that Renard would send after Roberts, but Roberts was with the army and not in Lisbon, he was beyond the reach of any assassin. He put it down to Renard's obsession and thought no more of it.

.    .    .

Towards the end of November it became clear that the French were not going to come after the British army, and Wellington ordered it into winter quarters. Wellington went to the remote village of Freineda where he intended to pass as much of the winter as he could hunting the local foxes with his pack of hounds. Sir Stapleton Cotton had not fully recovered from the wound he had received at Salamanca and he took the opportunity to go to England in order to complete his recovery. In his absence the cavalry would come under the command of the German, Major General Bock. Consequently, Cotton sent Michael off to join the Sixteenth for the winter.

Fortunately he didn't have far to go to join up with the Regiment. With Bradley and Marcello gone, Michael rode Johnny and led Robbie, Lloyd was on Rodrigo leading Jasper and Hall was on Castanha leading the baggage pony. He was, he realised, in need of another servant, perhaps two if he got another baggage animal. The one he had was just about managing, but he was short of supplies. Restocked for the next year's campaigning there would be a lot more to be carried.

After three days easy riding Michael caught up with the Sixteenth in the village of Freches, where they had paused on their way to winter quarters in the Mondego valley. There they had found Tomkinson, now recovered from his illness. He had resumed command of B Troop and Michael made himself useful as part of the Regiment's headquarters. Also waiting for them at Freches were new unforms for all the Regiment, officers and men. It was the new style that was replacing their Tarleton's and silver laced dolmans. The uniforms were left in their bundles and carried along to their new quarters at Olivera do Hospital, a small village in the mountains above the Mondego. Its situation gave stunning views all around. It was cold, but healthy.

The day after they arrived, the distribution of the new uniforms began. They were different. They were, admittedly, still blue coats, but there the similarity ended. Gone was all the silver lace for the officers, white for the men. Instead there were broad red lapels with silver plated or white metal buttons and epaulettes of silver for the officers, white wool for the men. The Tarleton's were replaced by shakos with silver or white decoration. As Sergeant Major Whitmore was heard to comment, "They're bloody French uniforms!" The resemblance was unmistakable and worrying. There was, at least, plenty of time for the uniforms to be fitted to the men by the few tailors in the Regiment.

It wasn't just the uniforms that were new, there were new saddles as well. They were of the type that had been used for some years by the army's hussar regiments. They were, in many ways, an improvement on the older style. They were easier to repair and, as horses grew fat or thin, their fitting could be altered by changing the folding of the blankets used under them, making them thicker or thinner to fit.

That evening the officers of the Regiment gathered for dinner, still in their old uniforms. Major Hay looked around the table. "I think, gentlemen, that we might keep the new uniforms for duty, in the mess or on other, shall we say, social occasions, I think we might keep our old uniforms, which have served us well through many campaigns and engagements." The suggestion was met with universal approval.

It soon became clear that the Sixteenth was not the only regiment to feel that way. The other regiments in the brigade shared their view, and the old uniforms became, throughout the light dragoons, the unofficial dress uniform of the officers.

Pedro Moreno and his friend Rafael Martins had been with the sixteenth as grooms cum servants since soon after the Regiment had arrived in Portugal. Now, Pedro decided he had had enough and was going home to Lisbon, back to his father's livery business. The two young men were also in a difficult position in the Regiment. They had been taken on by Captain Ashworth to help the officers of his troop, which had included Michael. None of those were any longer present with the troop. They made their living by odd payments from anyone they did anything for. It had become an uncertain, hand to mouth existence, which had, in part, influenced Pedro's decision. His friend, Rafael, didn't know what to do. He had no particular reason to return to Lisbon, but did not like the idea of carrying on in such an uncertain way without his friend. Michael heard about this from Lloyd and felt responsible as he had found them their jobs with Ashworth.

He found Rafael sitting outside the officers stables, looking disconsolate. "Rafael, I hear that Pedro is going home?"

"Yes, Senhor."

"What are you going to do?"

"I don't know, Senhor."

"Very well, I need a servant, I'll pay you two dollars a week. How does that sound?"

Rafael's face lit up. "Yes, Senhor, that s very good, thank you. I should like that very much."

"Good. That's agreed then. Go and collect your things and find Senhor Lloyd or Senhor Hall, they will find somewhere for you and you can help Hall with his duties."

Michael took advantage of the relatively quiet pace of things in winter quarters to write home to his grandfather. There wasn't a lot to say, except to assure the Reverend Isles that he was well. He wrote about Lloyd and Hall as he knew his grandfather was as interested in his domestic arrangements as he was in the course of the war, which he could follow in the newspapers. He told him about taking on Rafael, and as he wrote he realised that Rafael definitely was not going to be enough. With his spare horse, Jasper and the pony, Rafael could probably manage reasonably well, but he also wanted to get a second baggage animal. Just relying on one was too risky given all the threats to horse welfare that campaigning offered. He wrote to his grandfather that he hoped to find another servant before too long.

As the Regiment slowly recovered the condition of men and horses there was one great cause for celebration. Troop Sergeant Major Whitmore had asked to see Major Hay on a personal matter. A somewhat puzzled Adjutant knocked on the door of Major Hay's office.

"Come in! Yes, Mister Barra?"

"Beg your pardon, Major, but Sar'nt Major Whitmore would like to speak to you on a personal matter, sir."

"What? Well, best bring him in."

Barra opened the door wide and Whitmore marched smartly in and saluted the Major.

"Now, Whitmore, what's this about, eh?"

"Begging your pardon, sir, I would like your permission to marry, sir."

"Eh, what?" Hay was taken aback. "Err, well, to your Spanish Senorita, I suppose?"

"Yes, sir. We've been together a while now, sir, and through the march from Burgos, sir. I've asked her, and she's agreed, sir."

"Mister Barra, what do you say?"

"Well, sir, there's no reason why not, sir. We got Lloyd married a while back, sir."

"Yes, but his bride was a widow of the Regiment, already on the strength."

"True, sir, but we don't have the full allocation of wives with us, sir."

"We don't?"

"No, sir."

"Then I suppose it's alright then." Hay stood and came around the table serving for a desk. He offered his hand to Whitmore and said "Congratulations, Sar'nt Major."

Whitmore beamed as he shook the Major's hand. "Thank you, sir."

The wedding was the best the Regiment could manage. Regimental Sergeant Major Williams gave the bride away and the NCOs of the Regiment gave the couple a wedding breakfast. Major Hay and Mister Barra represented the officers, along with Captain Perssc, Whitmore's troop commander. It was almost Persse's last act in command as he was leaving for England the following day. Accordingly there was quite a night in the officers' mess as well as the NCOs'.

As Hay observed to Sar'nt Major Williams. "Just what the Regiment needs, eh, Sar'nt Major?"

"Yes, indeed, sir. Cheer everyone up no end, sir."

Michael watched Whitmore leave the small church with his bride and felt pleased for him, for them both. He was pleased for Lloyd with his wife and child. He wondered if he would ever be so lucky.

Persse wasn't the only departure from the army. The news went around that Colonel Gordon was going home for health reasons. No one was sorry. His carelessness on the retreat from Burgos had cost many lives unnecessarily. It was also rumoured that Colonel Murray would be returning to resume his role as Quartermaster General, a thought that put smiles on faces. Michael wondered what this might mean for him. He found out two days later when Lieutenant Barra, the adjutant, sought him out.

He found Michael in conversation with Major Hay. "Beg your pardon, Major, but orders have come in for Captain Roberts, sir."

Hay nodded and Barra passed the orders to Michael. "Looks like we will have to do without you again."

"Been expecting this since we heard about Gordon," was Hay's wry comment.

Michael quickly read the document. "Yes, sir, I am afraid so, I am ordered to headquarters at Freineda."

"It's been good to have you back with us, but I suppose His Lordship has other work for you," Hay observed. "You can leave in the morning, it's a good days ride."

At dinner that evening, Michael received the good wishes of his fellow officers and a little leg pulling about an easy life at headquarters. He drank a little more than was good for him and regretted it in the morning. Hall woke him early with a steaming cup of coffee. He rose, splashed cold water on his face and shaved, which helped. A couple of bread rolls also helped. Then as the sun was rising, he set off. He rode Robbie, Lloyd was on Rodrigo, Hall rode Castanha and led Johnny, Rafael was on Jasper and led the baggage pony.

Wellington's headquarters at Freineda was in a long building opposite the small church. The ground floor appeared to be storage, with a stone stairway leading up to a first floor, colonnaded balcony. As Michael dismounted, Major Krauchenberg appeared on the balcony and called out to him.

"Hello, Roberts! How are you, thought you might arrive today." He turned and called to someone behind him, "Tell Colonel Campbell that Roberts is here, and then show his men where the stables are and their quarters."

Another figure appeared, Major Scovell. "Hello, Roberts, good to see you." Scovell came down the steps as Krauchenberg called out, "You are just in time for dinner."

Scovell shook Michael's hand, "Glad to see you, Roberts. You must dine with my wife and I tomorrow."

"Your wife, sir?" Michael was surprised.

"Yes," Scovell smiled broadly, "she came up from Lisbon a week or so ago. I think I can promise you better than you'll find at Lord Wellington's table. I have good quarters and dine five or six most nights. But I must be off, I shall see you in the morning."

"Thank you, sir, that's kind of you."

"Nonsense, I might have deciphered those messages, but you got them for me in the first place. The Spanish still bring them in from time to time."

Michael climbed the stairs to find Krauchenberg waiting. "Come now, Captain, I must take you to see His Lordship. This way." He turned and led the way into a narrow corridor leading into the depths of the house. He stopped, knocked at a door, opened it, stuck his head in and Michael heard him say, "Captain Roberts, My Lord."

A moment later Michael found himself in the presence of the Marquess of Wellington.

"Ah, Roberts, do ye hunt?"

"Err, yes, My Lord."

"Good, takin' my hounds out tomorrow. Ye'll join me." It was not a question.

"Yes, My Lord, thank you."

"Excellent, De Lancey will tell what you need to know." He waved, dismissively. "I shall see at dinner, no doubt?"

"Yes, My Lord."

Wellington's dining room was a fine wood ceilinged room with beams and carved decoration. The table was crowded.  Michael found himself seated with Krauchenberg to his right, and to his left, the young Prince of Orange. Michael and the Prince knew each other a little, the Prince had been on Wellington's staff for some time. This was, however, the first time Michael had found himself in such close proximity. To his surprise, he found the Prince to be easy going and excellent company. Michael began to look forward to the rest of the winter at Freineda.

# Chapter 7

King Joseph, his army and Renard arrived back in Madrid in early December. Joseph and Jourdan were intent on rebuilding Joseph's grip on the kingdom, and to demonstrate his intent, the theatres were reopened, court functions were reestablished, and Joseph visited hospitals and other public institutions. Joseph and Jourdan expected Renard to play his part by the speedy provision of intelligence. They wanted to know what the Spanish were thinking, who could be trusted, who was a threat to be eliminated. They wanted to know about everything, particularly what the British were doing, They continued to put pressure on Renard to produce results.

Renard had spent most of the journey back going over and over his plan to destroy Roberts. He had given little thought to anything else. He had convinced himself that once he achieved that, all his problems would vanish like the early morning mist in summer, and he would be able to demonstrate exactly what he could do for the King and Jourdan. He would be feted, lauded, praised, given his due recognition. That was now his overwhelming priority. He piled pressure on to his clerks just as it was piled on to him. He pressed Faucher and Lucroy to organise their departure for Lisbon. The other junior clerks had everything else piled on them. Lucroy got an additional task when Renard called him into his office.

"Lucroy, on the road here we spoke someone that you had found who was willing to go after Roberts, a professional assassin, did we not?"

"Yes, Monsieur."

"What was his name again?"

"Diego, Monsieur."

"Diego, yes, that was it. I told you I want to meet him, now you can arrange it. Tell him I want to meet him."

"Err, but, Monsieur, it isn't that easy."

"What do you mean?" Renard snapped.

"He once told me that if I came to see him again without a job offer he would kill me. I believe him."

"Well, you can tell him I have a definite job for him and I will pay him well, but he must come to see me."

It was a very reluctant and rather scared Lucroy that set out to meet Diego again.

"What do you want?" Diego demanded as he dropped into a chair at Lucroy's table in the taverna.

"It's my chief, he wants to meet you, he has a job for you."

"Is it the English officer."

"I think so, he didn't tell me, but he said he would pay you well."

"Did you tell him that if this officer is with the army I am not interested?"

"Yes, Señor, I did."

"And he still wants to see me?"

"Yes."

Diego sat and thought for a moment. "Very well, let's go."

Lucroy looked panicked. "You mean now?"

"Yes, why not?"

"Err, no reason at all."

Renard looked up in surprise as his office door burst open and an ordinary looking man of middling height and build, clean shaven, neat and tidy, strode in. Lucroy was hard on his heels and calling out, "This is Señor Diego, Monsieur, he insisted on seeing you immediately. I'm sorry, Monsieur."

Diego halted in front of Renard's desk, "I believe you wanted to see me?" The ordinary looking man stood there with complete self-assurance.

Renard met the man's stare. "Get out, Lucroy."

The door closed behind a relieved Lucroy. Renard waved at a chair, "Please, Señor, take a seat."

Renard smiled slightly as Diego moved the chair so he could see both Renard and the door. The man showed promise. They looked appraisingly at each other, neither showed any indication of what they thought.

Renard broke the silence. "I believe Lucroy has told you what I want?"

"Some English officer killed. Did he tell you my conditions?"

"Yes, he did, and I believe I can arrange for the man to be in Lisbon before very long."

"How?"

"Come now, Señor, please."

Diego grunted. "How much will you pay?"

"Five hundred dollars, two hundred and fifty now, the rest when the man is dead."

Diego looked impressed. "Why so much?"

"I want him dead very badly, and I understand you are very good, and quality does not come cheaply."

Diego gave a nod of appreciation. "I can go to Lisbon, that is not difficult. From what you say, however, I assume he is not there at the moment?"

"No, I believe he is with the English army."

"Then it seems to me that you have the difficult part to play, getting this man to Lisbon."

"I know."

"Very well, I can go there and wait, for, let's say eight weeks. If this officer does not appear then I keep the two hundred and fifty and return to Madrid. But I want another hundred dollars to cover living in Lisbon for eight weeks. It is expensive to be discreet."

Renard smiled at the sheer nerve of the man. "Very well, Señor, we have an arrangement."

"Then tell me, who is this man?"

Half an hour later Diego left. Renard held his office door open for him and as he walked out he asked, "By the way, Señor, I assume you know Lisbon?"

Diego paused momentarily to reply. "You need have no fears there, Monsieur. I know it almost as well as I know Madrid."

Head down over some papers, Faucher pretended to take no interest, but what, he wondered, was that about?

Once Diego had gone, Renard settled at his desk to put the rest of his plan into operation. First he wrote a long letter to Savary, the head of the Police in Paris. He had no idea how long the letter might take to reach Paris, but he wanted to ensure that he got the credit for any success in Lisbon, and wrote accordingly. In it he said that he was sending two agents, two of his own staff due to the importance of the operation, to Lisbon and was hopeful of a significant outcome. It was, he wrote, his intention to have a devastating attack made on the British army's flour supply, which would have a huge effect on the British ability to campaign, perhaps even force them to leave Spain and Portugal. He left out the detail of the method of attack, that was so unbelievable that he didn't want to reveal it until it had succeeded. If it failed the detail of the how need never come to light. He would simply blame Faucher and Lucroy. He drafted the letter and then put it into code. He carefully addressed and sealed the coded letter, he would take it to the military headquarters himself to go in the next batch of post for Paris. The draft of the letter he carefully burnt. Then he took a fresh piece of paper and wrote the draft of another letter, also addressed to Savary in Paris, but this one would never be sent. This was the one designed to bring Roberts to Lisbon. It spoke of the intention to launch a covert attack on British army supplies using agents in Lisbon. One that could swing the course of the war in favour of the French. It made no mention of flour, referring simply to essential supplies and sending agents. He hinted that the agents were renegade Portuguese, which was something Roberts had experience with. He smirked at the thought of the paranoia that might produce. Once it was finished, he carefully folded it and put it in the pocket in the tail of his coat. Now he just needed to ensure the English got hold of it, and he thought he knew exactly how to do that.

That evening there was a grand soiree at Señora Ortega's fine house, organising it had been the first act of the Señora on the French returning. Renard had been surprised to receive an invitation. It saved him acquiring one, and if he was correct in his assessment of Ortega, it would make his work easier.

Renard arrived at Ortega's when the soiree had been going on for half an hour or so. The house windows were all ablaze with light, carriages were coming and going. Renard mounted the steps to the door and handed his invitation to a footman. He handed his hat and cane to another footman in the hall and made his way towards the sounds of chatter and laughter. He found the Señora in the main drawing room, surrounded by French officers. He caught her eye and saw a flicker of something, followed by a small smile. She laughed at those around her, playfully batted them away with her fan, and then she and Renard walked slowly towards each other.

Renard bowed as they came close. "Señora Ortega, it is a pleasure to see you again. I must thank you for the invitation, it is an honour to be at this soiree."

Ortega dropped a small curtsey. "Thank you, Monsieur, it is an honour to have such a senior member of the King's court here. I fear I have neglected you in the past." She gave him a smile that could only be described coquettish. "But let us put all that behind us and let me make it up to you." A wave of her fan summoned a footman with a tray of drinks. They both took one and Ortega sipped it, all the while giving him an appraising look. Renard realised that she was trying to flirt with him. He suppressed a smile.

"Monsieur, I must sit for a while, will you keep me company?"

He nodded his agreement and followed her to a long, low chaise longue. Ortega sank gracefully onto it at the end with the back and patted the seat next to her. He sat, flicking his coat tails clear and over the back of the seat as he did so. They talked, about this and that and the quality of the wine and the welcome cool of the winter and nothing of any consequence. Servants came and went, hovering around her, attentively. After ten minutes or so had passed, she excused herself, saying that she had to attend to her other guests and check the arrangements for supper, she expressed the hope that he would stay for that. Renard expressed his delight and said he would. He stood, gave her his hand as she rose, and then sat again, flicking his tails aside. He smiled to himself, the draft letter that had been in the pocket of his coat had gone. Now that, he thought, was very well done.

The evening went on pleasantly enough. Marshal Jourdan appeared briefly, raising his eyebrows at the sight of Renard, but otherwise ignoring him. At supper Señora Ortega insisted that he sit next to her and she flirted almost shamelessly with him. He wondered what might happen if he reciprocated, but resisted the temptation. He didn't want to antagonise Jourdan or the King. Joseph might not be there, but he was sure he would hear about the way they had kept company with each other. He wasn't going to give any ammunition to those hostile towards him. Servants circulated around the table, removing empty plates, refilling empty glasses. It was excellently done. Eventually Señora Ortega rose and Renard did likewise. As he did, Ortega dropped her fan. Automatically he stooped to pick it up and felt a servant brush past him as he did. He handed her the fan and was rewarded with a slight bob of her head and another coquettish smile. He stepped back to allow her to pass and realised the letter was back in his coat pocket. He had to admire the manner in which it had all been done. Clearly Madrid had pickpockets the equal of any. He wondered how long the contents would take to reach Lisbon.

It was early in the morning when the last of Señora Ortega's guests had departed. She took a last glass of wine and collapsed into a comfortable chair in her private drawing room, kicking off her shoes and wiggling her toes in relief. She was, if nothing else, relieved that Renard had not returned her shameless flirting. She blushed to think of it, but it had served its purpose, it had distracted him. She hoped it had been worth while. There was a soft tap at the door, which opened to admit her butler. He held a piece of paper.

"Señora, I think you should see this."

She held out her hand. "What is it?"

"A copy of what appears to be a draft letter, we got it from Renard's coat tail pocket. It has been returned."

She cocked an eye at him. "Are you sure he didn't realise."

"Quite sure, Señora. Luis did it."

"Good, he is the best,"

Señora Ortega read the letter with increasing surprise. She looked up at her butler. "This must be sent immediately, to Sir Charles Stuart in Lisbon. Send two copies, two messengers, no, send three, to be sure."

"Yes, Señora. I fear the messengers will not be able to leave until tomorrow night, it is too near dawn now, and we will need to make another two copies. Shall I keep a copy for us?"

Señora Ortega thought for a moment. "No. In fact, destroy everything we have that might be compromising. I want to take no risks where that Renard is concerned. If he was to think that we had lifted that letter..." She left the rest unsaid. "Do it tonight. Copy the letter and get the copies out of the house, even if they can't be sent immediately."

"Yes, Señora."

Two days later, Renard called Faucher and Lucroy into his office. "I trust that you are both ready to leave?"

Lucroy answered eagerly. "Yes, Monsieur, I have engaged a smuggler who makes regular trips to Lisbon." He hesitated. "He wants fifty dollars, Monsieur."

Renard surprised him. "Very good, I shall give you both a draft on the paymaster to cover all your expenses. It should be enough for six months and to pay something to Vargas, if you can find him. You should have completed your task and, hopefully established a new network of agents in that time. I look forward to hearing of your success. Faucher, have you made your arrangements?"

"Yes, Monsieur, similar to Lucroy's."

"Then you should meet in Lisbon. Have you arranged that?" Both men nodded. "And when do you leave?"

"In two days, Monsieur," was Lucroy's response.

"Tomorrow," answered Faucher, and he was pleased to see a flash of pique on Lucroy's face.

"Excellent, Faucher. You had better see the paymaster now, here is the order for the money. Lucroy, get yours tomorrow. I don't want you going together and attracting attention." Renard waved his hand dismissively.

As they left the office, Faucher could not help but feel resentment at Renard's behaviour, he hadn't even wished them good luck, as if they didn't matter. Without a word to Lucroy or the other clerks he left for the paymaster's at the military headquarters.

It was short walk across to the headquarters and Faucher was soon in the paymaster's office. He handed the order from Renard to a clerk, who looked at it, saw the amount, gave Faucher a surprised look and disappeared through a door on the far side of the office. Faucher was puzzled, it was, to be sure, not a trifling sum, but nor was it huge. A minute later the door reopened and the clerk waved him over.

"I beg your pardon, Monsieur, but the paymaster would like a word."

Faucher followed the clerk in and walked across to where the paymaster sat behind his desk, holding the order for Faucher's money.

"Ah, Monsieur Faucher, please, forgive me, but I just want to check with you that there has not been some mistake."

"What is the difficulty?"

"Well, you see, it is just that we paid out another large sum yesterday on an order from Monsieur Renard, for three hundred and fifty Portuguese dollars." He gave a little, embarrassed shrug. "I just need to reassure myself that there has not been some unfortunate duplication?"

Faucher was nonplussed. "Monsieur, I can assure you that Monsieur Renard himself gave me that order not half an hour ago, you will understand, of course, that I cannot disclose its purpose? You can, of course, always ask Monsieur Renard yourself."

"No, no, no need for that, your reassurance is enough for me."

Faucher gave him an appreciative nod. He was very tempted to ask who had collected the money, but he did not want to admit to any ignorance. Still he was puzzled. So far as he knew only he and Lucroy were being given funds, and Lucroy not until tomorrow. He said nothing to the paymaster about Lucroy coming tomorrow. If it got difficult for him, that would be just too bad. And he didn't want to do anything that would jeopardise his departure in the morning. The sooner he got away from Madrid and Renard the happier he would be. He'd had enough of Renard and his paranoia about Roberts and his constant demands that they do something. He was also sick of Lucroy's toadying manner.

As Faucher walked back to his office a thought of Lisbon brought to mind the Spaniard who had visited Renard with Lucroy a few days previously. What was his name? Diego, that was it. Renard had asked him about Lisbon. Surely he hadn't paid money to send him there as well, after Roberts? No, no, he knew Roberts wasn't in Lisbon, there would be no point at all in sending Diego after him. He shook his head. It was probably Renard appropriating funds for some mistress or other. He sniggered and walked on.

The day Lucroy left, Renard sat in his office, slumped in his chair, head back, staring at the ceiling. He had done all he could. Diego was on his way, he had left first, and Faucher and Lucroy were on their separate ways. He wasn't sure about Faucher, he had detected a little lack of enthusiasm for their work of late. If he failed it would not be a great loss. Lucroy, he had no doubt, would act energetically in the Emperor's cause and would happily be martyred. If either or both succeeded then it would be to the credit of Renard. He imagined, for one happy moment, the Emperor describing him as the man who won the war in Spain and Portugal. But more than that, much more, he hoped his ploy would place Roberts within Diego's reach. Now, he just had to decide what to do about Señora Ortega, if anything. He would need some very convincing evidence to demonstrate to King Joseph and Marshal Jourdan that their favourite Madrid socialite was in league with the British. He might just let her alone, he thought, and perhaps use her again.

.    .    .

Michael had been in Freineda for a week when Wellington departed for Cadiz. He had been invited by the Spanish to take command of their army, giving him overall control of the British, Portuguese and Spanish armies. Having received the permission of the Prince Regent to accept the offer, he decided that he needed to go to Cadiz, where the Spanish Government had taken refuge, and begin the work of reorganising the Spanish Army. He intended to cover the three hundred miles in six days and, on his return, to go via Lisbon. From his staff he took only Colonel Lord Somerset with him. With Wellington gone, life continued quietly at Freineda, for three days.

It was late afternoon and the light was beginning to fade, Michael and several of the staff were strolling around the square outside headquarters after dinner. They were exchanging gossip and rumours about Napoleon's Grande Armée in Russia. It was being put about that they had been beaten and were in full retreat out of Russia. There was a clatter of hooves on the cobbles and the Spanish guerilla Saornil rode into the square with a small escort. The horses were sweated up and had clearly been ridden hard, the small party became the centre of attention. They were ill dressed and ill equipped, very different, thought Michael, from Sanchez and his lancers.

Saornil leapt from his horse and strode to the headquarters building where he was met by Colonel Campbell.

"Señor Saornil, how might I be of service to you?"

"I must see General Wellington at once!"

"I am afraid that he is not here, may I enquire what it is you want him for? Perhaps another on the staff can help you?"

"No, Colonel, I have important dispatches, I must give them to Wellington himself! I shall wait for him." Watching from across the square, Michael thought the Spaniard was rather excited, he was surprised he did not stamp his foot.

"But, Señor, that is not possible, he has gone to Cadiz."

That rather took the wind out of Saornil's sails, but he persisted. "I have letters from Joseph to Napoleon, they must be handed to a senior officer, Colonel. They may contain information of the utmost importance."

Colonel Campbell hesitated for a moment. "Perhaps, Señor, you would care to come in and have some refreshment and we can discuss the matter further, I am sure we can find a suitable recipient?"

Michael subsequently learnt that Campbell had employed the Prince of Orange in persuading Saornil to give up his captured letters, and had also promised him a dinner with Wellington when he returned. It took some hours and much flattery and wine, but Scovell got the letters and set to work to decipher them. He worked through the night, sending each one to Campbell as he finished his work. They were undoubtedly important, all containing much useful, strategic intelligence, but nothing that couldn't wait for Wellington's return. All, that is, save for one. Michael was at breakfast when an orderly sought him out and told him that Colonel Campbell wanted him at once.

Campbell was in the small room he used as an office and bedroom. With him was Scovell. He wasted no time. "Roberts, read this." He handed Michael a sheet of paper with Scovell's familiar handwriting on it. "It's one of the letters Saornil intercepted. It seems to be your sort of thing. What do you think?"

Michael read Renard's letter to Savary. He read Renard's bold statement that he was organising an attack on the British army's flour supply in Lisbon by two of his staff, an attack that would seriously hamper them and possibly even cause them to leave and return to England. Michael was stunned by the implications. He saw the name at the end, Renard. He looked from Campbell to Scovell and back again.

"Is this genuine?" Michael asked.

"Yes, unless Saornil can forge the main French cipher and knows who Renard and Savary are, which I somehow doubt." It was Scovell who answered.

"But how can you affect the flour supply? I mean, I understand how important it is, but how do you attack it?"

"I don't know," Campbell replied, "but if they can destroy the flour supply the implications would be disastrous. Can you imagine the army with out bread or biscuits? The thing is, Roberts, I believe you know something of this man, Renard?"

"Yes, sir, I do," Michael replied.

"Well then, is this something we need to take seriously?"

"I... I don't know, Colonel." Michael looked at Scovell's writing again. He looked up at Scovell "I suppose your deciphering is correct?"

"What! Yes, it is! Do you think I haven't double checked it?" Scovell was outraged.

"I beg your pardon, sir, please, it's just rather a lot to take in."

Scovell took a deep breath. "Yes, I suppose it is, rather took me aback, I must admit."

Michael considered it again. "If nothing else, I suppose we must take seriously the fact of two of Renard's men going to Lisbon. Renard wouldn't put that in if it wasn't true. I assume they must be French, as he says they are from his staff. That's significant. He's never done that before, he has always used renegade Portuguese or Spanish. That would suggest that whatever he is planning it is something very serious. Something he could only entrust to his own people."

"Ah, yes, I see what you mean," said Campbell.

There was a moment's silence, then Scovell voiced the question they were all thinking. "What are we going to do about it?"

Michael and Scovell both looked at Campbell, who turned to stare out of the window. For a minute no one spoke. Then Campbell turned back and looked at Michael.

"I think, from what little I know, that this might be something for you, Roberts?"

Scovell chimed in. "I think you are quite right, sir, and, forgive me, but I know a little more about Roberts' past activities in this field."

"Well, Roberts, what do you say?" asked Campbell.

Michael gave a wry smile. "I suppose it is, sir. And I do know the relevant authorities in Lisbon." He thought of de Silva. "I shall need orders, sir." He paused to think. "A letter of explanation for Sir Charles Stuart would be useful, I shall need some funds and I would like to take Lloyd and Hall with me."

Campbell looked relieved. "Yes, of course, I'll get De Lancey to write your orders, he's acting QMG until Murray gets back, and I'll write to the Ambassador myself. Can you leave today?"

"Yes, sir, I need an hour or so."

"Very well, I shall have your orders, a letter and funds for you by then."

"Thank you, sir."

"Best get on, then, and good luck."

Scovell also wished Michael good luck as he walked briskly out. In the stables he found, as he had hoped, Lloyd, Hall and Rafael.

"Lloyd, good news for you, we are going to Lisbon!"

Lloyds face lit up. "Duw, there's lovely, sir. When?"

"As soon as we are ready, an hour or so, get the horses ready, all of them. You're coming as well, Rafael. Hall get everything packed. Rafael, you help him." Michael removed his forage cap, and gave it to Rafael. "Pack that, I'll be wearing my shako. Lloyd,

I'll help with the horses." He started to remove his coat. "Come on, the sooner we are away the sooner Lloyd can see his daughter."

# Chapter 8

Late on the third day of their journey, they rode into Mealhada. Michael was on Johnny, Lloyd, as ever, was on Rodrigo, Hall on Castanha and leading Robbie, while Rafael was on Jasper and leading the baggage pony. For Michael and Lloyd the sight of Mealhada brought back memories of the retreat to the fortified lines outside Lisbon, of the long fighting retreat from Buçaco. At the municipal buildings Michael acquired a billet for his party, in a small tavern across the main square. He also made enquiries about the location of the Quinta dos Cavalos Pretos, the Black Horse Quinta that was his. He was taken aback to learn that it lay no more than three miles to the north west. He decided that he could afford to take a small detour in the morning to visit it.

He said nothing until they were ready to leave, just as the dawn was breaking, cold and grey.

"Lloyd."

"Yes, sir?"

"We are going to take a short detour." He paused. "It seems my quinta is only three miles away or so. I think we can afford the time to take a look."

"Ah, right you are, sir."

Michael smiled. "After all, I have waited long enough and I want to see if there's any clue as to why my father bought it. I can have a look at the work that's been done on it at the same time. See if Furtado has spent my money wisely."

The quinta was where Michael had been told it was. It lay at the foot of a low hill, a small stream running in front of it. A high wall surrounded it and Michael led his party through an open gateway. Inside was a large courtyard, a handsome looking two floored house to one side and low buildings all around, some clearly stables. As they clattered in over the cobbles an elderly Portuguese peasant appeared at the door of one of the low buildings. At the sight of Michael in his uniform and the rest of his party he doffed his low, wide brimmed hat. He looked surprised when Michael addressed him in fluent Portuguese.

"Senhor, are you the man looking after this quinta?"

The man bobbed his head, "Yes, Senhor."

"Do you know who owns it?"

The man suddenly looked worried. "No, Senhor, I get my instructions from a lawyer in Lisbon, I get the priest to read them to me. But the Senhorita Cardoso is renting all the land, Senhor."

"Yes, I know. Senhor Furtado asked me to look in and see how things are."

The man looked even more worried.

"Senhor, I have done my best, but workmen and materials are hard to find and very expensive. It is difficult."

Michael turned Johnny and walked him across to the door to the house, closely followed by the peasant. It looked new.

"This door, Senhor, it is new?"

"Yes, Senhor, the French burnt all the wood that they could find. All the doors and windows are new, everywhere, Senhor."

Michael had seen at first hand what the French could do. All in all, he thought, things could be a lot worse. "You have done well, Senhor." The man looked relieved. "Now, show me around."

The house was at least weather proof, glass in all the windows, even if it was completely devoid of furnishings. The outhouses had similarly been restored, but all were standing empty. Michael insisted on seeing everywhere, but got no idea of why his father had purchased it. The tour over, Michael was standing in the main courtyard, taking one last good look around. Everyone was off their horses, who had drunk their fill at a trough, and Lloyd was sitting on the edge of it, talking to Hall. A few more minutes and they would be on their way, and he could decide what to do during the long ride to Lisbon. He could see no reason to keep the quinta, but still he hesitated. He faced the man looking after the quinta and started to speak, but at a clatter of hooves from the gateway everyone turned to look.

Michael cursed under his breath, it was Catarina, with a young gentleman and a couple of servants. She caught sight of Michael and reined in her horse. For a moment they just looked at each other. Michael recovered first and threw her a salute.

"Senhorita Cardoso, it is a pleasure to see you again." Michael saw a puzzled expression on the face of the young man who was accompanying her.

"Lieutenant Roberts! What are you doing here?"

"It's Captain Roberts now." He smiled. "I am just casting an eye over my property."

"What? Your property?" She flushed with anger. The thought struck Michael that it was quite becoming, that she was, as he remembered, quite becoming all round. "What do you mean? Has that, that lawyer, Furtado sold it to you? I told him I would buy it, he told me the owner was in the Brazils. How did you get it."

Michael could not help but smile at her confusion and no little anger. "No, Senhorita, no, he did not sell it to me. I inherited it from my father, it has been mine for some years."

"But, but..." She was speechless.

Her companion pushed his horse forward. "Catarina," he spoke softly, soothingly, "perhaps you could introduce me?"

She looked at him, uncomprehendingly for a moment. "Yes, of course, Filipe. This is, err, Captain Miguel Roberts. Captain, my fiancé, Filipe Carvalho."

Now it was Michael's turn to be surprised. He bowed slightly and said "My congratulations to you both."

An awkward silence fell.

Carvalho broke it. "So, Senhor, you are the mystery owner of this quinta. I think," he said with a disarming smile, "that Senhor Furtado has been a little disingenuous." He waved a hand around. "Senhorita Cardoso has been desirous of buying it for some time. She would rather buy than rent." He gave Michael a penetrating look. "Forgive me, Senhor, but you are an English Captain, not a farmer. Is there any reason why you should not sell?”

Michael looked from one to the other. Then he heaved a sigh and said, “No, none at all.” He took a long look round. “I have no idea why my father bought this. I don’t even know if he ever came here.”

“My quinta is only a league away, towards Coimbra,” the Senhorita informed him. “I am sure that if he had, I would know. I don’t believe he did, but Mateo here,” she pointed to the peasant, “has worked here all his life. Mateo, has there ever been an English gentleman who visited here?”

He shook his head. “No, Senhorita, never.”

“There you are, Captain. I would suggest that it was purchased purely as an investment. Not such a good one since the French visited. I imagine all the rent I pay has gone in repairs?”

Michael gave a non-committal shrug.

“I will give you a fair price for it.”

Michael took another look around. If his father had never visited, then it held no attachment for him. He made up his mind. “Very well, Senhorita. I have no idea of the value of land, I am on my way to Lisbon, I shall instruct Senhor Furtado to agree a price with you and you can have it.”

Senhorita Cardoso visibly relaxed. “Thank you, Captain Roberts.”

Michael nodded to her. “Lloyd, Hall, let’s go.” Hall brought Johnny to him and moments later all his party were mounted. He looked at Catrina and her fiancé, “Senhorita, Senhor, I wish you joy.” Then he put his leg on Johnny and by the time he reached the gate he was in a fast canter. He rode back the way he had come and did not look back.

It took a further four days to reach Lisbon. Faucher arrived while Michael was still two days away. He slipped into the city early in the morning, and made his way to where he believed he would find Vargas. The coffee shop had barely opened when Faucher walked in carrying a valise, which was all the baggage he had. He ordered coffee and bread rolls in his best Portuguese, which seemed to pass. Then he settled down to wait. Workmen came and went, calling in for a quick coffee before going on their way.

Faucher was beginning to get odd looks from the shops owner and his waiter. No one stayed that long in the rather scruffy establishment and no one else had looked in the least like a traveller in search of refreshment. He was just thinking that he might have to leave and try again tomorrow when Vargas walked in. He caught sight of Faucher and for a moment he looked as if he was going to bolt. A relieved Faucher smiled, waved and called out for two coffees. Reluctantly, Vargas came over to sit opposite him.

"Hello, Vargas."

"What are you doing here. Are you..."

"Hush, now. Wait until we have our coffee."

They sat in silence as the waiter came and went.

"Now," Faucher began, "Is all well with you? We have heard nothing from you in Madrid?"

"With the English there..." Vargas shrugged.

"They have not been there all the time." Vargas squirmed uncomfortably. "I sent three men to find you, agents, where are they now?"

"Three? No one came, I thought you had abandoned me." There was a hint of petulance in his voice.

"I am here now."

"Yes, and what do you want?"

"Not much, don't worry." Vargas grunted cynically and Faucher went on. "I need somewhere to stay, somewhere safe. For two. There's a colleague who should also be arriving in the next day or two. Can you find a friend to put us up?"

"Is that all?" Vargas' relief was palpable.

"For the moment, there may be a few things we will need, but you will not be asked to do anything, shall we say, dangerous?"

Vargas looked far from convinced. "Who else is coming?"

"Just a colleague, Lucroy. Did you meet him in Madrid?"

Vargas grunted again. "Just once, that was enough. A bit too Vive L'Empereur for my liking."

Faucher suppressed a grin. "Perhaps, but can you find us somewhere to stay, out of the way, a sympathetic friend?"

"I think so." Vargas looked quickly round the coffee shop. "Lets go somewhere else. We've sat talking for too long, people don't come here to talk." He stood up. "Come on, there's a little taverna I know where people do sit and talk all day."

Faucher followed him out and they set off, away from the river, into the maze of streets just north of the old castle. Across the road, Diego pushed himself away from the wall where he had been standing in the shadows and followed them at a distance. So far the information Renard had given him was correct. He watched them sit in a taverna for half an hour, drinking wine, their heads close together.

When they left, they only went a short distance, their destination a thin, but tall house that stood at the end of a short cul-de-sac. Vargas hammered on the door. After what seemed like an age to Faucher it swung open and he followed Vargas inside.

Inside the entrance hall was gloomy and Faucher could barely make out the man who was introduced by Vargas as Paulo Tavares. Vargas explained to Tavares.

"Paulo, my friend, this is a very important visitor, you should be honoured to give him shelter. You do not need to know his name, just that he is a loyal servant of the Emperor. He should be joined by another friend in a day or two. They need somewhere to stay where no one asks questions and where they will be safe until they leave."

Tavares looked overwhelmed. "Welcome, welcome, Senhor, it is a great honour. Please, come this way, I have two rooms that you can have. And I can promise you, no one pays any attention to comings and goings around here, eh, Senhor Vargas?"

Vargas simply nodded, then asked Faucher, "Do you expect your colleague to come to the same coffee shop to meet you?"

"No. We have arranged to meet on the steps of the Cathedral at midday. We will go there every day until we meet."

"It is past midday, Senhor."

"I know, tomorrow will do, I left Madrid first, I don't expect my friend until tomorrow at the earliest. Perhaps Senhor Tavares can show me the rooms and I can get some rest, it has been a long journey."

The two rooms were on the first floor, one at the front with a window that gave a view  looking down the cul-de-sac to the street beyond. The other was at the back, with the low roof of an outhouse a few feet below the window. There was a small courtyard and an alleyway beyond. Faucher appreciated the alternative exit. He arranged to meet Vargas later that evening back in the nearby taverna, where, Vargas assured him, a reasonable meal could be purchased.

Faucher had two days to wait before Lucroy put in an appearance at the Cathedral. Their greetings were cool. Faucher took Lucroy to their rooms, introduced him to Vargas and Tavares, but, to his relief, Lucroy just wanted a day's rest after his journey. Faucher left him to it. He walked down to the waterfront. There he found a taverna that simply accepted him as Spanish and he was able to get a decent dinner. He spent his time thinking over his situation. He didn't like or trust Lucroy, he wasn't sure about Vargas, who hadn't seemed too pleased to see him, and as for Tavares, he didn't know him, didn't trust him and he wanted out of that house. As for Renard's scheme to blow up the British army's flour supply, he had seen the demonstration, but was sceptical about the whole idea. A spoonful of flour sprinkled into a candle flame was one thing, but a whole warehouse? He shook his head in doubt. He felt that Renard's hatred, there was no other word for it, of Captain Roberts had completely clouded his judgement. But those were thoughts he kept to himself.

As Faucher took his time over his dinner, Michael and his party rode through the gloom of the early evening to the back entrance of his house and the stables. They dismounted wearily and opened up the doors to the stables. As they unloaded the horses, the back door of the house opened and Bernardo and White appeared with lanterns and cudgels. Then they realised who it was and Bernardo called out.

"Hello, Senhor Roberts!"

"Hello, Bernardo, is there hay in the loft?"

"Yes, Senhor!"

"White, get some water on for tea, I've had enough coffee for a while. And we shall need feeding as well."

"Yes, sir, Captain!"

An hour later and everyone was gathered in the large kitchen. The tea had been drunk and Lloyd, with a huge grin on his face, was holding his daughter in his arms, his wife by his side, her arm around his waist. Julietta was staring at Lloyd and clutching at his stubbled chin. The young girl hired to help Mrs Lloyd, Rosa, was serving out stew to Bernardo, White, Hall and Rafael at the kitchen table. Michael had already asked for his to be taken up to the dining room. He wanted to leave everyone to catch up and get acquainted without his inhibiting presence.

In the dining room a cheerful fire was burning and a single candelabra with four candles stood on the table with a single setting. Michael warmed himself in front of the fire and White came in a few minutes later with a dish of stew and a bottle of good wine.

"Thank you, White. How have things been?" As he asked he took his seat at the table.

White was pouring a glass of deep red wine for Michael. "Oh, well enough, sir. Rosa has been a great help, sir. Senhor Furtado has kept an eye on everything, and Bernardo and I have been doing some work inside, what with there not being much to do in the garden in the winter." He paused as he put the bottle down. "And I must thank you, sir, for sending me here instead of keeping me in the field with you, sir. I hope that you will be happy with me and everything and that you'll keep me on here, sir. I like it, I like it very much."

Michael thought he detected a note of concern in White's thanks. "That's good to know."  He took a sip of the wine. "Hmm, this is good, who chose it?"

"I did, sir. Thank you."

"Now, tell me, is there any particular reason why you are so keen to stay? I would have thought you might like to be back in London?"

White hesitated. "Well, yes, sir, there is."

"I see." Michael took a stab in the dark. "What's her name?"

"Oh! Err, ah..., Iolanda, sir."

"Her parents?"

"Very respectable, sir, her father is a baker, sir, got his own little business. Iolanda helps out in the shop, sir."

"Good. Be careful, though, Portuguese fathers are very protective of their daughter's honour."

"Yes, sir, they are." There was a hint of ruefulness.

Michael laughed. "Don't say you haven't been warned. Now, go and join the others."

Michael finished his stew, poured another glass, and turned his chair to face the fire. He stared, thoughtfully into the flames. He was happy to be home, but it was different from the home he had known for so long. The absence of the Santiagos made as much difference as that of his parents. It left him feeling alone, something he had never felt before in his home. The single place setting at the table took on a symbolism of his situation. He thought of Lloyd with his family and Whitmore with his new bride. He thought of White, hopeful over his Iolanda. He'd have to keep an eye on Hall, he was a good looking young man with a pleasant manner, although Lloyd seemed to have taken him under his wing.

He poured another glass. He remembered sitting at this very table with Roberta, now married. Inevitably memories of Elaine came to his mind, bitter sweet as ever. Then Catarina with her fiancé. He must go and instruct Furtado to sell the quinta to her. He felt a slight pang at a vague possibility that something had passed him by. Selling the quinta would bring a close to that particular episode. Then there was Victoria with her farm and her ties to the land. She knew where she belonged. As for himself, he felt detached from his Regiment. A part of it, yet apart from it, a

Captain without a troop, it was a contradiction. His role in the war against Buonaparte was unusual for a soldier. Damn Renard. The man wanted him dead, he was sure one of them would end up that way. It was the only way to end things. He had no doubt the attempts would keep coming. God, even in England. The thought brought the recollection of Elizabeth Trelawney. He smiled ruefully. That had ended badly, thanks to Renard's killer. He finished the glass and took both glass and bottle and the candelabra up to his room.

In his room he rummaged around and pulled out the oilskin package with Elaine's portrait and her letter to him. He read her words, 'do not make my mistake of thinking love comes only once'. He hoped that she was right, but, so far, a second chance continued to elude him. He poured another glass and stood, unseeing, staring out into the black night.

The following morning he shaved carefully, like many light cavalry officers he had started to wear a moustache, he thought it suited him, but he knew it would probably have to go when he returned to England. After a moments indecision he dressed in his uniform. His civilian clothes would not be appropriate today. He instructed Hall to have Johnny and Castanha ready in two hours, Hall in his full uniform, and then he set out on foot for the British Embassy.

Michael was not kept waiting. Sir Charles Stuart, the British ambassador to Portugal, rose from behind his desk and stretched out his arm to shake Michael's hand. "Captain Roberts, a pleasure to see you, sir."

"And to see you, sir, and may I congratulate you on your knighthood?"

"Thank you, thank you. Now, let us make ourselves comfortable." He pointed to two winged arm chairs on either side of pleasant fire. "The coffee will be here shortly." The two men settled themselves and, while a servant entered and served the coffee, Stuart asked, "This is the new uniform, eh? What do you make of it?"

Michael smiled. "It has been described as a little French, sir."

Stuart laughed. "Yes, yes, I see what you mean. Let us hope it does not lead to any unfortunate accidents." The servant left the room, closing the door behind him. "Now," Stuart went on, "tell me why you are here, it's no social call, I'll wager. I thought you were up at Freineda with the staff? And I know Wellington is in Cadiz."

"Yes, sir, that's correct, but information came into our possession and it was thought that I should come to Lisbon and look into the matter."

Michael told Stuart the tale of Saornil and the letter, then handed to him a copy of Scovell's deciphered letter and Campbell's covering letter. Stuart scanned the latter quickly, but carefully read the deciphered letter, twice.

"This, Captain, is quite remarkable."

"Yes, sir, I find it hard to believe myself."

"What? Yes, no, I mean to say, I was considering asking Wellington for your help, he's due to call here on his way back north. Campbell has saved me the trouble, and quite rightly so. You see I have received a rather disturbing letter from Madrid, from Señora Ortega. Well, two copies of the same letter, in fact. Do you know her?"

"Yes, sir, I advised her to send any intelligence to you."

"Ah. That explains that, I know she usually corresponds with Father Curtis who then forwards anything interesting to me. It's a rather roundabout process, but it has worked." He went to his desk, unlocked a drawer and took out a sheet of paper. "This is it, or it's one of the copies. One arrived two days ago and one but yesterday, so your appearance today is more than a little timely."

He passed it to Michael who read it with a growing sense of surprise, then puzzlement. "This looks like a draft, sir, of the intercepted letter?"

"Yes, that's what I thought."

"Did she say how she got hold of it?"

"Apparently Renard attended a soiree of hers, with it in the tail pocket of his coat. It was, err, borrowed, copied and returned without his knowledge."

"That sounds very risky, sir?"

"Yes, but it was successful. I have to admit that I also harboured some doubts about it, until you brought that intercepted letter. A letter to Savary in Paris is something to be taken seriously. However, there are differences from that intercepted letter. The letter you have brought specifies the flour supplies. This one, however, only speaks of a threat to our supplies. It doesn't mention the flour supply. I needn't tell you how important that is? There was a lot of concern when the Americans declared war on us, but it has had no effect on their exports of flour to us. Mind, we are steadily securing alternative sources of supply. Your intercepted letter also mentions that Renard has sent two agents, French, it would seem, but the letter from Madrid speaks of renegade Portuguese. It might be a draft, but it doesn't seem like a draft of the intercepted letter."

"I see what you mean, sir. But does it matter? Whatever is behind the differences in the letters, one thing is clear. Renard has sent two agents here to attack the flour supply."

"Quite correct, but how on earth would you attack the flour supply? There are thousands of barrels of it in the warehouses. I just don't see how it might be attacked, or damaged, let alone destroyed, which is what the letter to Paris would seem to suggest. It would take that to have the effect on the course of the war that is described, but how?"

"I'm afraid that I have no idea, sir, but we do know there are two French agents to track down. Catch them and whatever the plan is, it can't go ahead."

"Yes, yes, of course. I suppose you had better go and see de Silva? I'll have a copy made of the letter from Madrid for you. I think I had better keep both copies from Ortega."

"Yes, sir, I shall, thank you."

"And I shall write to Mister Musgrave, make him aware of the problem and ask if he can shed any light."

De Silva was both surprised and delighted to see Michael and welcomed him warmly into his office. Coffee was again ordered, Michael didn't like to refuse and merely sipped at his. Once they were alone, Michael explained why he was in Lisbon and showed him the copies of the intercepted letter and the apparent draft letter. De Silva read both, carefully. Surprise and apprehension showed on his face.

"Captain, this is rather disturbing intelligence." He read the letters again. "But the differences?" He was as puzzled as Stuart had been. "It makes no sense, I don't understand it. I do understand French agents, however, as do you. That is something definite to work on." He sighed. "Although, you know as well as I do how difficult it will be to find two men in a city of this size. Still, we will do what we can."

"Thank you, General."

"By the way, you should know the da Rochas are in town."

"Who? Oh, ah, yes."

"My wife and I are having dinner with them tonight, I shall mention that you are also in town. Roberta has, of course, given up her work for me, although she still takes an interest and sometimes shares useful gossip."

"Thank you. I can't imagine Roberta, Senhora da Rocha not being interested in, err, our sort of work."

"Indeed, da Rocha is a very patient man." He chuckled and then added, "I can also say that they are very happy." He looked hard at Michael who responded with a rueful smile.

"Rest assured, General, no one is happier for her than I am."

"Good, but I shall not tell her why you are here." De Silva chuckled. "She can discover that for herself. I have little doubt that she will."

Michael returned to his house where Hall was ready at the stables with the two horses. They mounted and set out for Michael's third call, to General Peacock at the British Army's depot at Belem. He wished he could avoid it, Peacock was a paper and pen pusher, a stickler for procedure. He also didn't like Michael, he was outside his knowledge and he knew that Michael only reported to him as a matter of form.

Michael left Hall with the horses in the stables and walked around to the main entrance. As he walked in he was amused to see that Mercurio was still at his post at the entrance, ready to carry out any errand for an officer. The General was both surprised and concerned to see Michael. Surprised because he believed Michael to be at Freineda, concerned because Michael always had that effect on him. There was, he felt, something rather dangerous about him, unpredictable, to say nothing of his activities in Lisbon being shrouded in mystery. He read Michael's orders carefully.

"These are signed by Colonel De Lancey?"

"Yes, sir."

"Isn't that a little unusual? Staff orders are usually signed by the Quartermaster General, or Colonel Lord Somerset."

Michael suppressed a sigh. "Yes, sir, but at the moment there is no Quartermaster General, Colonel

De Lancey is acting QMG until Murray arrives, and Colonel Lord Somerset is in Cadiz with Wellington, sir."

"Humph. And there is no reason given for your coming here?"

"No, sir."

"No, sir! Is that all you have to say?" Peacock blustered.

"Yes, sir, but I am sure Sir Charles Stuart would be happy to vouch for my presence, sir. I have been with him this morning."

Peacock handed the orders back to Michael. "I don't like it Captain, I don't like it at all, it ain't proper. Damn it, I suppose I must be content. Good day to you, Captain."

That could have been worse, thought Michael as he left.

Michael rode back to his stables where he found Lloyd and Rafael tending to the horses. He and Hall dropped down off their horses and Michael handed his reins to Hall. He saw Lloyd nudge Rafael.

"What is it?" Michael asked.

"Senhor," Rafael began, nervously, "I have been to see Pedro."

"And how is he, and his father?"

"Oh, very well, Senhor, he is happy to be back at home, Senhor, and getting on very well with his father, I think they missed each other." Rafael paused.

"Yes?" Michael asked. "What is it?"

"Senhor, Senhor Moreno has offered me a job, Senhor." Rafael looked miserable.

"Ah, I see, with your friend, in Lisbon, and reasonable money, I trust?"

"Yes, Senhor."

"You've had enough of short rations and sleeping in barns and fields?"

"Yes, Senhor, sorry Senhor."

Michael laughed at Rafael's crestfallen face. "Then you had better take the offer. I understand."

Rafael's face lit up with relief. "Thank you, Senhor, thank you."

"Very well, can you help Mister Hall for a day or two to get everything cleaned and sorted out before you leave us?"

"Yes, Senhor, of course."

"Good then I shall settle your wages with you the day after tomorrow. Hall, it means more work for you for the moment, but I expect we will be in Lisbon for a while, which will make things easier."

"Right you are, sir."

As Michael walked up to the house, he saw Bernardo pottering in the garden. "Bernardo! Can you find Carlos and Jorge and I will buy you all a drink tonight, the usual place."

"Yes, Senhor, and Marco is home on leave, Senhor."

"Is he, by God, splendid, I haven't seen him in years."

The five friends met in the tavern on Black Horse Square and with Michael in his civilian clothes it looked exactly like what it was, old friends catching up.

Marco had changed, and Michael told him so. "You are far more serious than you used to be."

"Miguel, my friend, we were just boys, of course we have changed. You and I have seen things no one should see."

"True, and lost friends."

"Ah, yes, Antonio."

The group fell silent. Then Carlos spoke. "I probably saw more of Antonio in recent years than any of you." He paused to look around the table as everyone nodded. "Let me tell you that he was never the same after his father died, and when his mother died he was like a lost soul. Yes, I know you lost your parents, Miguel, for which we are all sorry, but somehow, for some reason, it hit Antonio hard. The laughing joker was only happy when he was living dangerously, by his own rules. He would have had it no other way. Do not regret his death, celebrate having known him, having been able to call him friend." He raised his glass. "Antonio!"

Around the table they all followed suit and drank deeply. Then Carlos raised his glass again. "And here's to the most beautiful woman in Lisbon."

They all smiled and laughed at that and drank deeply again.

Michael and Marco exchanged a few stories. Marco had been on the ridge at Buçaco and teased Michael about the absence of the cavalry. They kept it light, but each could see in the other's eyes that their experiences had been similar and did not need to be discussed. Michael, in his civilian clothes, told his friends about the new uniforms. He had, he said, slimmed down a bit since his tailor had last measured him in London. Jorge offered to fit it for him, and, at Michael's request, agreed that he would also make him a new dress uniform in the old style. He said he would call at Michael's for the old uniform to use as a pattern and to reuse the silver plated buttons. They agreed that he would call at the house the following day. Once he had seen Michael in it, he would refit the new uniform in a couple of days and return it to him. The new uniform would take a little longer and he would let Michael know when it was ready for a fitting.

There was no news of their other friend, Ricardo, who had last been heard of as a sergeant in an infantry regiment somewhere. When Michael was asked how long he was going to be in Lisbon, he said he didn't know, a few weeks he thought. For one thing, he said, he needed to find a new groom and a servant to say nothing of another baggage animal. He asked Carlos if he might be able to help, to recommend someone. Carlos said he would give it some thought. It was a good evening.

# Chapter 9

Michael woke with a sore head. He groaned into his pillow. His bed was warm and comfortable. He opened his eyes briefly, then screwed them tight against the morning light. He heard the door open and heard Hall's cheerful voice.

"Good morning, sir, coffee here for you. I'll have some hot water for you in five minutes, sir."

"What time is it?"

"Nearly eight o'clock, sir."

"Hall."

"Yes, sir?"

"Why are you so damned cheerful?"

"It's a glorious day, sir, not a cloud in the sky, and I had a really good night's sleep, sir, in a bed. There's hot rolls and butter and cold meat for you, sir, in the dining room."

Michael groaned again. "Thank you Hall."

The coffee helped, the bread and meat more and a second large coffee finally got him awake. He had dressed in his civilian clothes again and now went in search of Lloyd and Hall to tell them to do the same. White, Lloyd and Mrs Lloyd were in the kitchen, enjoying the warmth from the range where Rosa was stirring something, Lloyd was bouncing his daughter on his knee.

As he entered White and Lloyd started to rise.

"Sit down, all of you, before you drop Miss Julietta, Lloyd." He smiled and looked around. "Where's Hall?"

Lloyd answered, "He's down at the stables, sir, with Rafael. I think Bernardo is with them, sir."

"White, go down and fetch Hall."

"Yes, sir." White disappeared on his errand.

"Begging your pardon, sir," said Lloyd, " but it's a shame about Rafael, he had a way with the ponies."

"Yes, he did, but I hope we will find replacements for him and Bradley as well as another baggage animal before we leave again. I mentioned it last night and I'm rather hoping Carlos might know someone." He paused to smile at the baby. "When Hall comes in, I want both of you to come up to the study, then I'll tell you what's going on."

"Right you are, sir."

Michael made his way upstairs to the main hallway of the house and the study off it. The shelves that lined the walls where his father's books had been were still empty, as was the large safe, it's door standing ajar. He wondered about doing something to replace the books. Perhaps it would benefit from repainting and new curtains on the window might be a good idea. The portrait of his parents was still in place, over the empty fireplace. As always, he stood and looked at it for a moment and wondered what his mother would say. He smiled as he remembered that she always said his father's study was entirely his affair. Then, as he lowered himself into his father's chair, the door opened and Lloyd and Hall came in.

"Close the door, Hall." Michael waited until the door was shut and then went on. "You both need to know why we had to come to Lisbon so suddenly. You remember that guerilla leader, Saornil, who brought in captured dispatches?" They nodded. "Amongst them there was a letter from Renard." Lloyd's eyebrows shot up in surprise. "Major Scovell deciphered it and its contents reveal that the French are sending two agents here from Madrid, they may well be here already." He paused before saying, "Their purpose would seem to be to destroy the supply of flour for the army."

Lloyd muttered something under his breath while Hall said "Bloody Hell, beg pardon, sir."

"Yes, quite." He took a breath. "The difficulty is that we have no idea how they intend to attack the flour supply. The suggestion is that they are planning to destroy it, but how you would destroy thousands of barrels of flour..." He shrugged. "However, to start, we will go and have a look at the warehouses for ourselves, see if anything occurs to us. You will need your civilian clothes, no obvious weapons, and no firearms at all, for the moment. I want to leave in half an hour. White and Bernardo can stay at the house. Unfortunately we lose Rafael tomorrow, so White and Bernardo will have to do their best with the horses while we are about our business, Lloyd, you can keep an eye on that."

"Yes, sir."

"I hope it won't be too long before I can get more help, Hall, as I just told Lloyd, I asked my friend Carlos last night to see if he knows anyone who might do."

"That would be good, sir," Hall replied.

"It would. Right then, half an hour back here, and we shall see what we can discover."

There were three warehouses, large warehouses, standing side by side. Michael had not realised the scale of the operation to keep the army supplied with flour for bread and hard tack biscuits. There was a constant stream of mule trains leaving for various destinations, laden with barrels. The warehouses were on a dockside, and tied up next to one was a large, American merchant vessel in the course of being unloaded. Michael could not begin to imagine how many barrels it carried. There was little in the way of security, it seemed unnecessary for barrels of flour. There were a few clerks checking what the mule trains took, a few labourers helping with the loading, a couple of officers from the commissary and that was it. For the life of him, Michael could not even begin to envisage how an attack might be staged. He could see that it might not be difficult to gain entry to one or even all of the warehouses at night, but then what?

Michael and his men quickly fell into a routine of keeping an eye on activity around the warehouses during the day, and paying a few randomly timed visits during the night. That is, he and White did. He had the impression that White rather enjoyed sneaking about with his cudgel, ready for anything. He left Lloyd with his wife and daughter at night, he and Hall checking on the horses. Hall he sent to sleep in the room off the stables. Rafael was paid off and departed for his new job. He would be missed, but Michael understood entirely why he had left.

Jorge came and went with Michael's uniforms, the new style and the old. Two days later and Michael was summoned for a fitting. The new uniform fitted perfectly, the replacement for the old uniform required a little more work, and Jorge said it should be ready in two days.

Michael also managed to go and see Furtado. Together they went over Michael's financial situation and then Michael told him about his visit to the quinta, meeting Senhorita Cardoso and agreeing to sell the quinta to her. He was more than happy to leave the negotiations in Furtado's hands and instructed him to get a reasonable price without haggling overmuch.

Michael and his men were not the only ones interested in the warehouses. Separately, so as not to attract attention, Faucher and Lucroy strolled past the warehouses, once a day for almost a week, at different times and wearing different coloured coats and hats. Just as Michael had, they noted the lack of any serious security around the warehouses. Lucroy was enthused, Faucher not so much, he just found the whole scheme difficult to take seriously. Then the news of Napoleon's disaster in Russia started to reach Lisbon. At first both Faucher and Lucroy were inclined to dismiss the reports as mere rumours. Lucroy was sceptical and bullish.

Faucher was more concerned and fretted about his younger brother and two cousins in the Emperor's Grande Armée. He was worried and distracted, constantly on the look out for more news. The attitudes of Lucroy and Renard, who he had begun to suspect was becoming mentally unstable, were causing questions to arise in his mind. Three years in Spain, surrounded by a hostile population who did not welcome their liberation from their King and the imposition of a Buonaparte as their new King, had also had an effect on him, making him increasingly uncertain about what he was doing. He began to have an idea, which became a plan. He could, he realised simply disappear into Lisbon. He had some money from Renard to pay for the setting up of a new network. Instead he could use it for himself. Perhaps, he thought, he might even get a job, posing as a displaced Spaniard. The more he thought about it, the more attractive the idea became. He wondered what he might do about Lucroy.

At the British army depot at Belem, the news from Russia was talked about by all. There was much speculation about what it might mean for the war in the Peninsular. Michael, on a quick visit, listened and made the point that it might not affect them at all, or not for a long time. It was, as he pointed out, a long way from Moscow to Lisbon. Of more immediate interest to Michael was a letter that was waiting for him. It had come in on the latest packet ship from Falmouth and was only three weeks old. It was from his grandfather. He saved it until he got home and was settled in his drawing room with a steaming pot of coffee.

Usually his grandfather's letters were full of parish gossip and, at this time of year, reports from the hunting field. This one was different. The Reverend Isles wrote that he had been finding the winter very hard. Travelling around his parish had got difficult, he was feeling the cold more than ever, he had been ill with several bad colds, he admitted that Mrs

Menwynick had despaired of him. She had, on one occasion, even persuaded Scobell to tell him that his horse was lame. Michael smiled at the thought of the battle of wills. His grandfather did further admit that the weather had been very wet and the roads almost impassable at the time. To his shame he had begun to feel that he was neglecting his parish. He had, he wrote, after much soul searching, decided that the time had come to retire. He had written to the Bishop and got his agreement. He was going to move to Falmouth and live with Michael's uncle Jocelyn, in the house that one day would be Michael's. He assured Michael that he had enough money to live comfortably and not be a burden on Jocelyn. Moreover he had made an offer to help the incumbent of the church in Falmouth, which had been accepted, so he would not be giving up on the ministry entirely.

At that point Michael stopped reading and put the letter down. He was more than a little taken aback. The idea of the Reverend Isles retiring was one that had never crossed his mind. On reflection, however, he was also more than a little relieved that his grandfather had taken the decision. He would undoubtedly find life in Falmouth much easier, and he thought that it would be good for his grandfather and uncle to provide company for each other. A lawyer and a priest. He smiled. Now that could be interesting.

He took up the letter again and discovered that Mrs Menwynick and the Scobell's were to stay on for the new incumbent. That news was followed by a little parish gossip, and then the letter turned to recent news from the hunting field. In the middle of that came an item of news that Michael found particularly of interest. So much so that he read it over several times as if hoping to extract more from the words on the paper.

It had happened, his grandfather wrote, that Miss Trelawney had come down to Cornwall for the hunting and had been good enough to call upon him. She had, he said, asked to be remembered to Michael. The letter went on that she had asked about Michael and seemed, as the Reverend put it, to be more than politely interested in his well being.

"Good God!" Michael exclaimed, once again putting down the letter. Miss Trelawney, Elizabeth, taking the trouble to visit his grandfather, enquiring after him and then asking to be remembered. That, he thought, was no chance visit and comment. No, he knew Elizabeth had a house in Truro, knew she hunted around there, but that was a fair way from his grandfather's in the middle of winter. He sat thinking, his mind running on at speed. A tiny flicker of hope was kindled. Perhaps, he thought, she hadn't been as repelled from him by events in Truro, in her house, and by what he had told her, as he had thought. Then reality set in. She is in England, he thought, I am in the Peninsular with the army and unlikely to return to England any time soon, possibly not for years. He sighed, and read the rest of the letter.

Another communication arrived at the house. It was from Roberta, Senhora da Rocha. It invited him to join her for coffee the following morning at the coffee house below the cathedral. Michael smiled at that and wondered if the location was significant. Roberta had uncovered a French spy network on a visit there. That, he reminded himself, was back when she was one of de Silva's best agents in Lisbon. It seemed a long time ago, but it would be good to see her again.

In the morning he sent Lloyd and Hall off to wander around the warehouses again and set off for his rendezvous with Roberta. It was cold, with the promise of rain later. The coffee shop windows were steamed up and Michael pushed his way through the door into the welcome warmth, looking around for his friend as he did. Roberta was sitting with her maid Constanca, at a table that gave her a view of the window, and both doors, one from the street, one behind the counter. It was arguably the smartest coffee house in Lisbon, its customers representing the best of Lisbon society, but her careful habits had not left her. The interior was richly decorated, white cloths on the tables, red velvet covered chairs, and heavy curtains at the window.

When Michael walked in, Roberta gave a little wave to him, a look of surprise on her face. He crossed the room to their table and gave Roberta a small bow.

"Senhora da Rocha, how good to see you."

"Captain Roberts, what a pleasant surprise, will you join us?" She spoke loudly and clearly, plainly for the benefit of two well dressed ladies at a nearby table.

"With pleasure, Senhora, thank you." Michael took a seat opposite the two ladies and ordered coffee from a waiter who appeared. Until he had returned with it and then departed they sat in silence.

"You will understand, of course," Roberta spoke quietly, "that I have certain proprieties to maintain?" Michael smiled and nodded. "Constanca here knows everything of course and, as you know, can be relied on completely. Moreover, I can tell you that Senhor da Rocha knows I am meeting you." She smiled at Michael clear surprise. "Of course he does, my husband knows everything, Miguel, even about my work for de Silva, both in the past and now. I still pass on bits of gossip from time to time. Now, I want to know why are you here, in Lisbon? But first, how are things with you?" She smiled mischievously.

Michael knew exactly what she meant, and he told her about his grandfather's letter and  Elizabeth. He also told her that he did not hold any great hopes, given his circumstances.

"But you like her?" Roberta asked.

"Yes, yes, I do."

"How much?"

Michael smiled at her, "A lot, but just how much it is too soon to tell."

Roberta looked at him thoughtfully for a moment. "Then you must hold on to that and hope. It will be good for you and might just be the saving of you, Miguel. I know what you have done, what you have seen, I probably know as well as anyone and better than most. I know it was all necessary, but you must not let it become who you are. I know how much difference da Rocha has made for me, being able to talk to him, to trust him completely. It has been good to talk to someone not involved, to hear what they think. You need the same, Miguel. I would not say this if I did not care very much for you."

Michael noticed the slightest of blushes. Constanca looked pointedly out of the window.

"Thank you, Roberta, I shall think about that." They both sipped their coffee. "By the way," Michael went on, "I saw Senhorita Cardoso a few days ago."

"What? Now, Michael, I think that ship has sailed, a long time ago."

Michael laughed. "I know, Roberta, all too well." He gave her a rueful grin and told her all about the meeting at the quinta and his decision to sell it to her.

"I think that is a very good idea, you treated her badly, it is the least you can do."

"Roberta! Please, but you are right, and I have instructed Furtado to see to it."

"I'm pleased to hear that. Now, tell me, why are you in Lisbon? I know you paid my uncle de Silva a more than social call."

"Nothing gets past you does it?"

"Of course not, you should know that by now, so either tell me and make me pleased with you, or..."

Michael laughed, but grew serious as he told her, explaining about the two letters, about the puzzling differences between them.

Roberta nodded thoughtfully. "That is odd, of course, it might not mean anything, but the general threat seems real enough."

"It does, and it's enough for me to be here."

"And you have no idea about the two French agents?"

"None at all. I hardly know how to start looking for them."

"And what did my uncle say?"

"The General said he will do what he can, but we have nothing to help us even begin to look. So far we are just keeping a watch on the warehouses." He shrugged. "Any ideas would be very welcome."

"I shall give it some thought, and keep my eyes and ears open as well."

"Thank you, but be careful, Renard is an evil man."

Roberta laughed. "Don't worry, Miguel, nowadays, as a respectable lady I go nowhere without my maid, do I Constanca?"

"No, Senhora, and it is all terribly boring, not like the old days."

They all laughed and the conversation moved on to other things, such as Michael's need for a new groom and servant.

# Chapter 10

There had been the rumours, but in early January came confirmation. Copies of The Times newspaper for the 17th of December arrived from London and carried the news of the disaster that had befallen Napoleon's Grande Armée in Russia. The massive army that had marched into Russia and had taken Moscow had been driven back, through the cruel Russian winter with devastating losses. Napoleon was reported to have abandoned his army and to be back in Paris. The news was the talk of Lisbon with wild speculation as to what it would mean for the war in the Peninsular.

Michael sent Lloyd and Hall to watch over the warehouses and rode out to Belem to see if there was any more news to be had there. At the entrance he saw Mercurio, waiting patiently as ever for errands to run. He saw nothing to lose and spoke to him

"Mercurio, how are you?"

Mercurio squinted up at him from where he squatted against the wall. "Ah, I know you. What do you want with me?"

Michael put his hand in his pocket and flipped a dollar to Mercurio who snatched at it eagerly. "Not an errand, that's far too much."

"No, not an errand, information."

"What about?"

"I want to know if you hear anything, anything at all about strangers in Lisbon."

"There are always strangers, Senhor."

"Yes, but I think you know the sort of strangers I mean. Strangers who aren't what they seem, who might even be French. There will be another dollar if you do."

Mercurio scratched himself. "Of course, Senhor."

"Do you know how to find me?"

Mercurio laughed. "Of course I do. I know your house, Senhor."

"Good, see that you don't let me down."

Inside the headquarters the rumour was that the French retreat hadn't just been a disaster, it was worse, most of the Grande Armée was said to have been destroyed. A quarter of a million men lost, some said, some said half a million. It was difficult to give any credence to the idea. The numbers were beyond grasping. After chatting to various officers and clerks for an hour about it, Michael rode slowly back home, deep in thought. Perhaps, just perhaps, this was the beginning of the end for Buonaparte. To Michael, who seemed to have lived most of his life with Britain at war with France, that was a difficult idea to contemplate. Buonaparte and the war was just a fact of life. That all that could change was difficult to grasp. Perhaps he would get home and, well, he left that thought alone.

When he got home and rode into the stables he was surprised to find Carlos there, talking to Bernardo. He was accompanied by a young lad of fifteen or sixteen years. Michael dismounted from Johnny and greeted Carlos.

"Hello, Carlos, what brings you here?"

"Hello, Miguel. It's what you said the other night about needing a groom and a servant and a baggage animal." He pointed to the boy, "This is Jacinto, Jacinto Pires, he is a second cousin or something to me, not sure exactly what." Jacinto rolled his eyes. "His mother and mine are great friends. Anyway, he would like to be your servant." He grinned at Michael. "And my mother says I have to go along as your new groom to keep an eye on him!"

"What!" Michael was surprised.

"Well, maybe it wasn't all her idea." He shrugged his shoulders, "I am selling my mules, Miguel. It has become too difficult, irregular pay, competition from the big mules trains. It's no longer worth it, or any fun."

"Oh, I see." He paused. "Horses are not mules, Carlos."

"I know that, Miguel, but they are half horse!" He chuckled, "The more intelligent half as well."

Michael laughed. "But are you sure? It's a hard life, probably harder than being a muleteer."

"Humph, I doubt that."

"I don't know, Carlos, you are a friend, and..."

"So is Bernardo!" Carlos broke in. "And who is looking after your horse now, eh?"

"What? Well, this is different..."

"Is it? Bernardo tells me you and your two dragoons are off everyday, not in uniform either," Michael frowned at Bernardo who merely grinned and shrugged, "and he and your house servant are doing their best with a little help from your dragoons. I think you need someone, Miguel, and where will you find better? Tell me that?"

Michael thought about it. He did need a groom and another servant. There was no real doubt that Carlos could look after horses, and he knew he could trust him entirely. If the lad was a relation of Carlos, however vague, that was itself a recommendation. But he still hesitated. He knew why.

"I'm sorry, Carlos, but I'm not sure I can do it."

"Why not, Miguel? Tell me, please?"

Michael hesitated. "Look, Carlos, this war has already cost me too many friends, I don't want to lose anymore."

"Oh, you mean like Antonio, don't you?" There was suddenly a hard edge to Carlos' voice.

"Well, yes."

"Miguel, tell me this, was Antonio doing anything you had asked him to do and that he didn't want to do? Did you ask him to go to Madrid? Did you force him to help you? No, he was doing what he wanted to do, like he always did. He was his own man and so am I!" Carlos paused, took a breath. "Miguel, if I didn't want to do this, if Jacinto didn't want to, we wouldn't be here."

Michael had to recognise the truth of what Carlos said. The two men stood staring at each other for a moment. Bernardo broke the silence.

"Senhor Miguel, Carlos, my friends, please, Antonio would not like this, I don't like this. I do know that I would like it more if you were together, looking out for each other."

Michael slowly nodded. "You're right, Bernardo. I'm sorry, Carlos. Of course you are your own man and I will be glad to have you with me." He held out his hand.

Carlos laughed. "No, Senhor Miguel, we agree terms first, and then we shake!"

"Very well, muleteer pay for you, half that for Jacinto, and if you still have your mules, I'll buy two as baggage animals. I have a horse you can ride, and a pony for Jacinto."

"Now that is very fair," said Carlos, and the two friends shook hands on it.

Michael turned to Jacinto and offered him his hand. "Is that acceptable to you, Jacinto?"

"Yes, Senhor," and Jacinto shook hands with him, beaming all over his face.

"Good, now that is settled. When can you start? I suppose you will need to collect your things?"

"Err, no, Miguel, sorry, Senhor Miguel. Mine are in the room here," he pointed at the stables, "and Senhora Lloyd has given Jacinto a room in the house."

The expression on Michael's face was astonishment, that rapidly changed as he began to laugh, and he roared with laughter and called Carlos a rogue.

·       ·       ·

The news of the Russian disaster arrived in Madrid a few days after it had reached Lisbon. It left Joseph's court and army reeling from shock. Renard was stunned. He sat in his office staring into space for some time. Then he began to think. With the Emperor back in Paris communications would improve. He might even give more attention to Spain and the plight of his brother, Joseph. He would need, more than ever, some devastating blow to be struck against the English. He smiled. The destruction of the English flour supply would be perfect. He began to imagine himself recalled to Paris, welcomed as a hero, feted by all, rewarded by the Emperor. The possibility that the plan would not work no longer featured in his thinking. The death of Roberts, which he now considered as good as achieved, would be the crowning glory of his work.

·     ·     ·

The effect of the news from Russia on Faucher was rather different. He was shocked and horrified. As more news arrived it became clear that the Grande Armée hadn't just suffered bad losses, it had been almost wiped out. He thought of his young brother, of his cousins and in the privacy of his room he wept for them. He thought of everything that had happened in the last few years, looking back as far as he could. He didn't remember the Revolution, for as long as he had been aware of such things, France had been ruled by Napoleon, initially as First Consul, then as Emperor. As such, in Faucher's mind, he was responsible for all the ills that had befallen France. He saw no benefits for France. Any enthusiasm he had for Imperial France, for the Emperor, for his own role, for his current mission, slowly ebbed away and vanished.

Lucroy, in contrast, seemed to be even more animated than ever by the news. When Faucher emerged from his room Lucroy was at him immediately.

"Faucher, this news from Russia, it means our mission is more important then ever. If we can destroy the flour and force the English to leave, it would be of great service to the Emperor, to France! We must get on with it, we must strike a blow that will leave the Emperor's enemies reeling."

"Really?" Faucher replied, his voice dripping with sarcasm. "Do you think it will make the slightest difference? Do you even think this scheme will work? You've seen the warehouses. Do you really think we can destroy them, make all that flour blow itself up?"

"Yes, of course I do, Monsieur Renard believes it, so do I!"

Faucher, in his despondency, spoke rashly. "Don't be a fool Lucroy. It won't work, it's a stupid idea, we will just end up dead and forgotten."

"You damned traitor," yelled Lucroy, who hurled himself at Faucher.

They grappled, fell to the floor, ineffectually flailing at each other. Faucher managed to push Lucroy off and got to his feet. Lucroy got up as well and they stood, panting and staring at each other, neither willing to renew the struggle. Lucroy straightened up and brushed himself down with his hands.

"I'm going out, but I shall report this to Monsieur Renard when we get back to Madrid!" He turned and stormed out.

"If we get back to Madrid," shouted Faucher at his retreating figure.

Faucher stood in the middle of the room for a few minutes. Then he made his mind up, walked into his room and started to pack his few belongings. He took all the money he had. He reckoned he had a good hour before Lucroy returned, and he was out of the house in fifteen minutes. Diego had seen Lucroy storm out and chosen to follow him. Faucher's exit was unobserved by anyone. Swiftly he walked away and into the maze of streets that was Lisbon's old quarter.

He walked west, passed through the new streets built after the earthquake and went on into older streets. Eventually he settled on a taverna he found on a narrow street winding its way up hill. Inside it was gloomy and quiet. A bored looking innkeeper sat behind a counter of planks. He was in luck. He asked about a room and was offered one at the back of the building, on the first floor. His said he was a Spaniard and apologised for his bad Portuguese. The innkeeper seemed to accept that. Faucher paid for two weeks and said he hoped to find work. The innkeeper wished him luck, said he might be in luck with so many men away in the army.

After two days, Lucroy decided that Faucher wasn't coming back. He had, he decided, either been caught, somehow, or simply run away like the coward he appeared to be. In case it was the first possibility he found Vargas and told him he had to move. Vargas grumbled, but found another house, this one owned by a widow. She was deaf and knew little about what was going on, but she liked the money Lucroy offered. Lucroy's relocation was observed by Diego. He too had concluded that Faucher had lost his nerve and run. He had already followed Vargas once and knew where he lived. Confident that he could find Lucroy should he move again, he set about finding out if Captain Roberts had arrived in Lisbon. He started to make enquiries about his friend who was an officer in the English army, if anyone asked how he knew him, he tapped the side of his nose and, with a wink and a grin said he had supplied the good Captain with, err, certain commodities. It always worked.

Meanwhile, Lucroy told Vargas that he needed gunpowder. He wanted enough to make half a dozen small charges, two for each warehouse, but he didn't tell Vargas that. Vargas was taken aback, he tried to prevaricate, but Lucroy said there was a lot of money available, if he could get the powder, Vargas asked for a week, Lucroy gave him five days.

Faucher lay low for a couple of days and then put the next part of his plan into operation. His landlord had suggested that he try down around the docks, to see if he could get work as a clerk or similar, as it was obvious he was an educated man not used to working with his hands. Faucher had no intention of going anywhere near the docks, there was always the chance he might run into Lucroy. Instead he looked for areas where there were lots of businesses. He decided the best thing to do was keep an eye open for anyone who looked like a clerk, particularly around midday when they might be out at a taverna or coffee house to eat. He could engage them in conversation and see if they had any ideas where work might be available.

His story of being a Spaniard looking for work held up, no one challenged him, but after two days he hadn't found a job either. He got a little braver and tried his luck in a taverna on the Praca do Carmo. It was closer to the centre of the city than he had tried before. His gamble paid off. The innkeeper told him about a mercantile house that always seemed to need clerks. He said they seemed to have a reasonable reputation as an employer and it was only a short walk away.

Faucher said "That sounds like just what I am looking for. Where is it?"

"Walk west, take the first left, then the first right, left again at the church and it is on your left."

"What name is it?"

"What? Oh, yes, of course!" The man laughed, "Palacio Quintela, big place, you can't miss it."

Faucher found it easily. It was indeed big, not as big as some buildings in Paris, but big enough to give him pause. Then he took a deep breath and walked up the steps and through the double doors that stood open. Inside was a large, vaulted entrance hall, with chairs around the walls. As his eyes adjusted to the gloom, a porter appeared and asked him, politely, his business. Faucher explained to him that he was from Madrid, had fled the French and was now looking for a job, perhaps as a clerk. The porter told him to take a seat and he would go and see Senhor Rodrigues, the head clerk, and ask if he would see him.

Faucher took a chair in the corner near the door and settled down to wait. Time passed. The porter returned and told him that Senhor Rodrigues might be able to see him in an hour or so, if he would care to wait. Faucher said he would. More time passed. Faucher tried to be calm, he wondered what was going on, perhaps he should just get up and leave? He tried to avoid looking at his watch. Gradually he relaxed and the tension of the last few days ebbed away enough that he began to doze.

He was vaguely aware of a Portuguese gentleman walking in. When the porter saw him he smiled at the newcomer.

"Senhor Roberts! A pleasure to see you, Senhor, I shall tell Senhor Rodrigues you are here, please, take a seat for a moment."

Faucher's head had jerked up at the name. He had been half asleep, had he heard correctly? It couldn't be? The man's right profile was towards Faucher. Then at the porters bidding he took a chair to Faucher's right, some five yards or so away. As he turned and sat down Faucher could see his left profile clearly, could see the vivid white scar that ran down his cheek from cheekbone to jawbone. He froze in fear. It was, it had to be, it was Captain Roberts! He sat, rigid, his mind blank, he couldn't think. Then the porter returned.

"Senhor, Senhor Rodrigues will see you now, please?" He gestured to a door way, Michael rose and followed him along the familiar corridor to Rodrigues' office.

Rodrigues rose from behind his desk. "Senhor Roberts! What a delight, I had no idea you were in Lisbon." He came around the desk, hand outstretched.

Michael shook the offered hand. "Senhor Rodrigues, I have only been back a few days, but I came to see you as soon as I could." The two smiled at each other.

"Tomas, coffee for us!" Rodrigues instructed the porter. Then to Michael, "Please, please, sit down, sit down."

He returned to his own chair, "Now, what can I do for you? Not more spies, I trust?"

Michael laughed. "Not in your service, but possibly in Lisbon." He smiled disingenuously. "But then, that is nothing new, is it? No, Senhor, I have merely come to pay my respects to an old family friend."

The porter entered with coffee, placed it on Rodrigues' desk and left.

"I am very glad to hear that, and it is always a pleasure to see you." Rodrigues served the coffee and they chatted about things and relaxed in each other's company.

Michael left the Palacio an hour or so later, strolling out through the entrance hall, empty save for the porter. Standing on the steps he pulled his watch out and opened it. Time to get something to eat, he thought. He snapped his watch shut and as he put his watch back he looked to see if old Priscilla was in her usual spot. She wasn't. Of course she wasn't, it was January, no time of year for a flower seller. He chuckled at himself. Then he caught sight of a man looking in his direction, who turned away as soon as Michael looked his way.

Michael turned up the hill from the Palacio, strolling slowly, heading for a small taverna that served good food a few minutes walk away. Something about that man tugged at his memory. He strolled on. Eventually it came to him. He had been sitting in the entrance hall of the Palacio. And now he was hanging around outside and avoiding Michael's eye. He continued to stroll on, thoughtfully.

In the taverna he took a table towards the back, with a view of the door. He exchanged pleasantries with the owner and ordered fish stew and a jug of red wine. The owner brought the wine over and Michael chatted with him a little more. Out of the corner of his eye he saw the door open, saw the same man come in and take a table towards the front of the low ceilinged room. He ordered a single glass of wine. Michael was puzzled, both by the man and by what to do. He was clearly following Michael, now, but how, why had he been at the Palacio? He slowly finished his stew and poured another glass. As he did so, the man stood, slowly, and hesitantly walked towards Michael. Michael's cane with its hidden blade was propped in a corner, to reach for it would be too obvious. His hand slipped inside his coat and he readied his knife under the table. He left it lying on his lap and placed both hands in clear view, one lifting his glass to his lips. The man stopped by his table.

"Senhor Roberts?

Michael looked up and smiled. "Yes?"

"Captain Roberts?"

"Yes, can I help you?"

"May I speak with you, please?"

Michael gestured to the seat opposite.

"Thank you, Captain."

There was something about the man's accent...

"Now, how may I help you?"

"I'm not sure, Senhor. I have.., I have heard much about you, I thought it would be helpful to talk to you."

Michael laughed. "I can't imagine what you have heard, I'm just one cavalry officer amongst many, and only a Captain."

"I have heard that you are a decent man, Captain."

Michael raised his eyebrows at that. "I would like to think I am. Who told you that."

The man was silent for a moment. "Another cavalry officer."

"Very good. Now, tell me what were you doing at Quintela's?" The man looked surprised. "And why did you follow me here?"

"I was hoping to get a job, then I wondered if you might help me."

"What? Get a job?"

"No, no."

"Then what?"

Faucher hesitated. Then he decided to take a chance, a great chance, and all because of a conversation with a French cavalry officer.

"The cavalry officer, Senhor, the one who told me about you, it was Lieutenant Lapointe."

The name took a moment to register, Michael had not expected to hear it again, and certainly not in a taverna in Lisbon. He was shocked into silence for a moment. "Lapointe? Really? Can you prove that?"

Faucher's hand went to his coat. "May I, Senhor?"

"Slowly." Michael dropped his hand on to his knife.

Faucher pulled a folded document from his coat, opened it out and laid it on the table in front of Michael. Michael glanced at it and realised with shock that it was Lapointe's safe conduct, signed by Wellington.

"If you have that, then you are..?"

"French, Senhor." Faucher paused, took a deep breath and said, "I surrender to you, Captain, and if Lapointe is correct, I will be safe as your prisoner."

The innkeeper appeared at the side of the table to take away Michael's dish. "Was the stew to your liking, Senhor?"

Without taking his eyes off the man in front of him, Michael replied, "Yes, yes, it was. And I would like another jug of wine and another glass for this gentleman."

"Yes, Senhor, of course."

Michael and Faucher sat in silence, looking at each other as the innkeeper brought the wine and poured two glasses before going away.

"So, Monsieur, just who and what are you?"

"My name is Faucher, Gaston Faucher. I am, or was, a senior clerk to Monsieur Renard, he is the..."

Michael cut in, his voice carrying a hard edge. "I know who Renard is."

"Of course, Senhor, my apologies."

"Are you one of the two agents sent to Lisbon to attack the flour supply?"

It was Faucher's turn to be shocked. "How did you know that?"

"That is no concern of yours, Monsieur"

Faucher nodded wearily. "So you know everything?"

Michael lied. "Yes, everything."

Faucher sighed. "To tell you the truth, I am not sure that it would work."

"Why not?"

"Well, the idea that you can get flour to blow up, I know that I've seen the theory demonstrated, but a small quantity of flour is very different from a warehouse full of barrels of the stuff."

"Good God!" Michael could not restrain his exclamation. Faucher looked at him, sharply.

"You didn't know that?"

"No, about the attack, yes, but not how."

Faucher gave a wry smile. "You do now."

Michael took a mouthful of much needed wine. "I think you should tell me everything, and why you decided to surrender?"

"The second one is easy. I think Renard is unstable, becoming irrational and this operation was likely to get me killed. I have also been hearing about Russia." Michael saw the sadness come over him. "I have a younger brother and two cousins in the Emperor's

Grande Armée, they are quite probably dead. Coming on top of what I have experienced here over the last few years, put simply, my love for Napoleon has died."

"I'm sorry about your brother and your cousins."

"Thank you."

Faucher took a drink and told Michael everything. He told him about Renard's obsession with Michael, hating him for killing his son, holding him responsible for all his setbacks, for the death of Lopez and Montero, about his reaction to Lapointe's message. He told him about Lucroy and Vargas. He finished his story and fell silent, draining the last of the wine from his glass. Michael followed suit.

"That is quite a story." Faucher merely nodded. "Now," went on Michael, "I think we both need some coffee, but not here. The British ambassador serves very good coffee, I think we should go and see him." He remembered the safe conduct and picked it up from the table. "I think I had better keep this."

Faucher looked drained and shrugged. "If you think that is for the best." He looked hard at Michael, "But, remember, I am your prisoner and under your protection."

"Of course."

"You give me your word?"

"I do."

"Then let us go."

The Ambassador's coffee was good, very good, but, afterwards, Sir Charles Stuart would have been pressed to say what he had drunk. He listened, incredulously, as Michael introduced his companion and related what had happened. His amazement only grew as Faucher told his story.

"Well, I'm damned," was his first comment. "But exploding flour? I beg your pardon, Monsieur, but I find that difficult to believe."

"Perhaps I can demonstrate?"

"Good God, can you? Well, um, yes, I suppose so."

A small amount of flour, a spoon and a lit candle were soon available on Stuart's desk. He cleared off the papers on it.

"There you are, Monsieur, please, show us."

Faucher took a spoonful of flour and sprinkled it so that it fell in the candle flame. The flame went out and the flour dusted the Ambassador's desk. Stuart and Michael shared sceptical glances. Faucher tried again. Instead of sprinkling, he flicked a small amount off the spoon, it formed a little dust cloud, it fell, there was a bright flash as the flour ignited. There was a stunned silence.

"The plan," Faucher explained, "is to have two small charges in each warehouse, the first destroys a number of barrels, creates a cloud of flour dust, the second..." He shrugged. "I have no idea if it will work."

Stuart reached for a small handbell on his desk. In response to the tinkle of the bell his secretary appeared. Stuart looked up from the candle. "Send for General Peacock. I need to see him, urgently."

"Yes, Sir Charles." The secretary disappeared.

"Roberts, do you have any men with you?"

"Two, sir, they're keeping a watch on the flour warehouses."

Stuart rang the bell again. "Are they in uniform?"

"No, sir."

"Their names?"

"Lloyd and Hall, sir"

The secretary came in again. "Send one of the clerks, an intelligent one, down to the warehouses where the flour is kept. He is to find two dragoons, in civilian clothes, their names are Lloyd and Hall. I suggest he walk around shouting their names." The secretary went out again.

"Captain Roberts, when your men arrive you are to take our, err, guest here to your house and keep him safe. I think we must treat him as a friend, after all, he came to us, to you, of his own free will. Did you not Monsieur?" Faucher nodded and Stuart continued his instructions to Michael. "Then go and tell all to de Silva. I shall write you a note for him as well. I shall inform Peacock of the threat and arrange for additional guards on the warehouses. Wellington is due here in a few days. He will want to hear all this from you, Captain."

"Yes, sir."

Stuart looked at Michael and Faucher. "I don't know about you two, gentlemen, but I need a drink."

It took a little time, but eventually Faucher was safely in Michael's house, watched over by Lloyd, Hall and White. The only difficult moment had come when

Lloyd had insisted on searching Faucher to make sure he wasn't armed. Realising it was a reasonable demand, Faucher had simply smiled and complied. Michael walked quickly to police headquarters and brought de Silva up to date. Not surprisingly, de Silva was as sceptical as Michael and Sir Charles Stuart had been. Michael tried a demonstration. To his surprise it worked and de Silva was convinced. He also told Michael the contents of the note from Stuart.

"He has asked me to put a guard on your house, to keep your Monsieur Faucher in and others out. Don't worry, they will be discreet, you won't know they are there. Tell me, do you trust this Frenchman?"

Michael thought for a moment. "Yes, I believe I do. I saw his face when he told me about his brother and cousins in Russia, he was..., I'm not sure, but I believed him." Michael gave a hollow laugh. "Never thought I'd see the day I trusted a Frenchman." But then, he thought, there were two he could think of that he would, Lieutenant Lapointe and Marshal Ney. He left the General to his arrangements and walked home for dinner.

<h1 align="center">Chapter 11</h1>

Sitting down for dinner in his own home with a Frenchman was a novel experience for Michael, that he was also a member of the French secret services made it a little disturbing. His experiences with that organisation had, until now, always involved violence and death. White served them, he knew that Lloyd and Hall were just outside the room and he knew Faucher was unarmed. It was still difficult to relax and make conversation. Over their dinner he asked Faucher about his background. He was from central France, he had, he told Michael, never seen the sea until he was on his way to Spain and saw it as he passed Bayonne. When Michael asked after his family, Faucher's face darkened.

"I don't know, Captain. I have heard nothing for over a year. I don't know if my parents are still alive, I do know that the units my brother and cousins were in went to Russia." He stared at his wine glass, absently turning it round on the table. "I hate this war, I wish it were over, France would be a better place without Napoleon."

Michael watched him carefully for a moment before speaking. "You could help to bring that about."

Faucher looked up and Michael could see tears on his cheeks. "Could I? How? I have no wish to be a traitor to my country."

Michael realised that he needed to proceed cautiously. "No, no, of course not, and I wouldn't ask you to." He gestured to White, "Another bottle," then, quietly, "take your time." White nodded and left the two men alone.

Faucher took up the conversation, "What would you have me do?"

"Nothing that would harm any Frenchman."

Faucher looked at him, his face angry, "Do you expect me to believe that, Monsieur? You are at war with France, if I help you how can I not harm any Frenchman? Do not take me for a fool."

At the raised voice Lloyd and Hall appeared in the doorway, Michael waved them back. He let Faucher calm down for a minute and then spoke to him, keeping his voice soft and unthreatening. "No, Monsieur, I think you are anything but a fool. I think you are an intelligent man who loves his country dearly, but not its present ruler who has, surely, caused the deaths of more Frenchmen than anything you or I could do."

"Thank you, and you are quite right."

"Then will you help me to stop the attack on the flour supply? That will harm no Frenchman."

"It will mean the war goes on, that will result in harm to my countrymen in Spain."

"They are in Spain because Buonaparte sent them. Had he not..." Michael left the sentence unfinished.

"And if I do help you, afterwards, what will become of me?"

"No harm, I give you my word."

Faucher startled Michael by laughing. "You realise, don't you, that there is no guarantee that this plan of

Renard's will work? That little conjuring trick with the flour is one thing, but a warehouse full of barrels?" He shrugged, "Who knows?"

"I agree, but we cannot take the chance that it would not work."

Faucher nodded. "That I understand. Very well, Monsieur, what do you want to know?"

"Tell me about your contact here in Lisbon and tell me about Lucroy, please?"

Faucher told him all he could, told him what sort of a person Lucroy was, about his enthusiasm for the task they had been given and his blind faith that it would work. As he talked Michael realised there was no love lost between the two. He suspected that the wish not to harm any Frenchman might not be rigorously applied in Lucroy's case. He asked Faucher where they had been staying and Faucher told him about Vargas and the rooms he had found for them.

Michael asked him, "Will you show us where the rooms are? Perhaps we can find Lucroy there?"

"Yes, gladly, but I would rather Lucroy didn't see me."

"I think we can manage that."

Faucher also talked about Renard, repeating his belief that Renard was becoming increasingly unbalanced, and that he held Michael entirely responsible for, well, everything that went wrong. Michael detected a note of scorn in Faucher's voice as he spoke about Renard and his attitude toward his staff. There was clearly no love lost there either.

Eventually, Michael could see that Faucher was exhausted. The release of telling all, of being safe and having eaten and drunk well finally told on him. White had eventually brought in a second bottle and it was now empty, most of it in Faucher. White had diplomatically withdrawn, leaving them to talk, but now Michael called him in.

"White, make sure Monsieur Faucher gets to his room and has everything that he needs."

"Yes, sir."

Faucher rose, slightly unsteadily. "Thank you, Captain Roberts, I am grateful to you."

Michael rose with him. "It has been, um, interesting, Monsieur, and now I will bid you goodnight. Sleep well, and there is no need to rush in the morning, someone will doubtless be on hand when you wake."

Michael waited until Faucher had followed White out of the dining room and started up the stairs. He headed downstairs. In the hall he found Lloyd and Hall. "I want one of you outside Faucher's room all night. I don't think he will be any problem, but just in case. Ask White to take over from you before first light."

"Very good, sir," Lloyd answered, "we'll just take a stroll up now and make sure Mister White is managing, sir." He and Hall went quietly upstairs and Michael unbolted the front door and stepped out into the silent street.

"Officer?" Michael called out softly.

A shadow detached itself from a larger shadow and slid up the street to him.

"Good evening, Senhor, is all well?"

"Ah, so you are out here, I wasn't sure."

"Thank you, Senhor."

"Now, I have a message for General de Silva."

He explained about his success with Faucher and the intention to visits the rooms he and Lucroy had occupied. He asked if de Silva would be so good as to let him have the help of a dozen of his officers? The officer smiled and said he was sure there would be no difficulty and would it be acceptable if they waited for Senhor Roberts at his stables? It would be more discreet. Michael agreed whole heartedly and suggested nine o'clock to meet. He wanted Faucher fresh and fed.

Michael was not surprised when de Silva himself appeared in his coach, along with a dozen men who drifted into the stable yard in twos and threes. Carlos leant against a wall and grinned at the police, one or two of whom clearly knew him, but ignored him. Michael greeted de Silva.

"Good morning, General, thank you for this."

"It's a pleasure, Captain." He looked across to where Faucher stood between Lloyd and Hall. "Is that your Frenchman?"

Michael followed his gaze, "Yes, that's him."

"Hmm. Trust him, do you?"

"So far, General, so far."

De Silva broke off his stare. "You know some of my men, Horta there is in charge," Michael caught the man's eye and they nodded to each other, "they know what to do and will take your instructions. I shall await developments at my office. Good luck." He banged on the roof of his carriage with his stick and it moved off.

The raid went well, except Lucroy wasn't there. The afrancesado landlord was arrested and taken away. The rooms were thoroughly searched but nothing was found. Faucher was crestfallen.

"I am sorry, Captain."

"It can't be helped, at least we got the landlord. He won't be giving any more help to Renard."

Faucher suddenly perked up. "No, but there is Vargas. He brought us here. He might know where Lucroy has gone."

"And how do we find him?"

"There's a coffee shop he frequents, that's where we found him."

"Where is it? Just a moment." Michael called the senior policeman, Horta, over. "Now," he asked Faucher, "where is this coffee shop?"

Faucher gave an accurate description. Horta spoke. "I know where that is."

"The French agents' contact uses it, man by the name of Vargas. Do you think we can take him?"

Horta thought about it. "It won't be easy, particularly if we have to wait for him, we could be spotted." He thought some more, then asked Faucher, "This man, Vargas, is he a violent man, is he usually armed?"

"I don't think he is armed, and he likes his food and drink a lot, he is not an energetic man."

"Have you been there with him before?"

"Yes, Senhor."

Horta addressed Michael. "I think our friend here should go in to wait for Vargas. They will know him as a friend of Vargas who is waiting for him. I will send in two men at a time to wait with him. We can change them every now and then." He looked at Michael. "I beg your pardon, Captain, but you are too well dressed, you will stand out too much. Perhaps you should go and wait with the General?"

Faucher looked worried. "I do not wish to be separated from Captain Roberts!"

Horta gave him a look. "There is nothing to worry about, Monsieur. I know that you are helping us, I shall take great care no harm comes to you." He gave a little chuckle. "I would not wish to fall foul of the General or the Captain here."

Michael chimed in. "I have worked with Senhor Horta before, you may rely on him."

Faucher looked from one to the other. He looked resigned. "Very well."

"And my men," asked Michael.

"I think they had better go with you, Captain, even out of uniform they look like soldiers."

"Very well. Hopefully I shall see you soon."

Two hours later Horta bundled Vargas into de Silva's office where he was impatiently waiting with Michael. Behind him came Faucher. Horta was grinning.

"It went perfectly, sir, he strolled in, Monsieur Faucher greeted him, our men took him. No fuss, no shouting or any great disturbance."

De Silva looked very pleased. "Well done, Horta." He walked to the very nervous looking Vargas. "Now, Senhor, tell me, please, where can we find Monsieur Lucroy?"

"Who Senhor?"

De Silva looked disappointed. "The French agent who arrived in Lisbon with this gentleman." He gestured at Faucher.

Varges started to speak. "I don't.."

He got no further. De Silva's hand shot out and delivered a resounding slap to Vargas' face. "I shall ask you one more time, Vargas, and if I am not happy with your answer, I shall hand you over to Captain Roberts here. He has a way of extracting information that leaves me in awe of his skills."

Michael wasn't too sure how to take that, but it had an effect on Vargas who went very pale. He looked at de Silva who looked very grim. He looked at Michael, who smiled at him. He looked at Faucher, who avoided his eye.

It all came out in a rush. "He is staying with an old widow woman up in the old quarter, near the Praca da Figueira. She is old and deaf, she knows only that he is paying good money."

De Silva smiled at him. "And I am sure that you can lead my men there?"

"Yes, Senhor, of course." Vargas glanced across at Michael and unconsciously licked his dry lips.

"Horta, take this man and raid the house. We will wait here."

It was another fruitless wait. Horta returned with Faucher to report that Lucroy was gone, had left the day before. The widow said she didn't know where he'd gone and he believed her.

De Silva glared at Vargas. "You must know something, where has he gone?"

"Please, General, I don't know, I swear, by all the saints, I don't know."

Faucher suddenly leant in close to Michael and whispered something. Michael looked a little surprised and then nodded his understanding.

"Excuse me General. Vargas, one question." Michael paused. "Have you supplied Lucroy with any gunpowder." Sweat broke out on Vargas' forehead and he looked terrified. "I see that you have. When and how much?"

"Err, two days ago, Senhor, it was not much. About six arrátel, Senhor."

That's nearly six pounds, thought Michael, enough for six small bombs, enough, in theory, for three warehouses.

"General, if we might speak together?"

"Horta, have Vargas locked up. Monsieur Faucher, if you would care to go with Horta, no, you will not be locked up, he will look after you while the Captain and I confer."

Once they were alone, de Silva asked, "What is it Captain?"

"I think Vargas has told us all he can, the man is terrified. The main thing is that Lucroy now has the means for an attack on the flour warehouses."

"Yes, but, really, Captain, do you think six arrátel of powder will do any real damage?"

"It's enough for six charges, General, two for each warehouse, it's what Faucher described. As to whether or not that could do any real damage, well, I just don't know. It seems to me that it would either do next to nothing, or destroy the warehouses completely. I don't want to gamble on which it is."

"No, no, of course not. What would you do, Captain?"

Michael thought for a moment. "We could try scouring the streets and lodging houses of Lisbon, but that would take weeks and might not work. It seems to me that Lucroy now has what he needs to make an attack. All we can do, it seems to me, is watch the warehouses and hope to intercept him."

"That would seem the best course, Captain, if not the only course." De Silva consulted his watch. "It will be dark soon, the warehouses will close." He put his watch away. "I understand that General Peacock has put additional guards on the warehouses?" Michael nodded. "That area is usually deserted at night. Lucroy would be seen instantly. I think he will probably come during the day, the warehouses are open and there are many people coming and going. That would be the best time for him to attack. I suggest that from first light you and your two men are down there with Faucher. You can keep a watch for Lucroy. After all, Faucher is the only one we have who knows what Lucroy looks like and is at all trustworthy. God help us, we are relying on a French member of their secret service. Not that we have much choice. I'll have Horta down there, with a couple of dozen men all around to help as necessary. How does that sound?"

"Like the only thing we can do, General."

For two, long, tiring days Michael, Lloyd and Hall accompanied Faucher in a constant patrol around the three warehouses. Faucher had tried to describe Lucroy, but only he could be sure of recognising him. They each, apart from Faucher, carried a pistol concealed under their coats. Michael, as ever, carried his cane with the concealed blade that had been a gift from Lady Travers, Elaine. It seemed a long time ago now. He touched his cheek where the long scar ran. He remembered the touch of Elaine's hand. He smiled at the recollection, sad, but reconciled and glad for what he'd had.

On the second day more news arrived of Napoleon's retreat from Russia. It confirmed the horrendous losses suffered by the French. Napoleon's much vaunted Grande Armée had effectively ceased to exist. The news further depressed Faucher, who became even more outspoken in his criticism of Napoleon. Michael was particularly interested in the news about the role played in the retreat by Marshal Ney. He had commanded the rearguard and fought his way out of Russia in the face of overwhelming numbers. Michael could not help but admire his bravery and determination. He thought back to when Ney had saved his life near Ciudad Rodrigo. He was, without doubt, indebted to the French Marshal, even if the debt was likely to remain unpaid.

He glanced across at Faucher, leaning on a street corner, his eyes constantly sweeping everyone he could see. De Silva's men had recovered what little baggage Faucher had and he had a clean shirt and was freshly shaved.  There was one Frenchman with no love for Buonaparte, Michael thought, and he knew there were others and the French King's court was in England. He thought of Lapointe and wondered what had become of him. Janvier, lying in that damned awful hospital in Oporto came to his mind. He had struck Michael as a decent man. He wondered if he had kept his arm, he hoped so. Michael's hostility towards the French was becoming less generalised and more specific. Most specifically towards Renard, but just at the moment Lucroy would do. He waved to his companions and they moved slowly on to another warehouse.

At nightfall they gave up and returned to Michael's house. The Portuguese police would keep a watch all night, backing up general Peacock's sentries. At home, he found that Jorge had delivered his new old style uniform. He wondered when he might get a chance to wear it. There were also two notes waiting for him. The first was from Stuart who simply informed him that a third copy of the draft letter had arrived from Ortega. The second was from Roberta, asking him to join her and her husband for dinner that evening. He was tired, and had Faucher to consider, but there was something in the note that made him resist the temptation to make his excuses. Some of the phrasing gave a sense of urgency to the invitation. He explained to Faucher that he had received an invitation from a dear friend that he could not refuse, and left him in the care of Lloyd and Hall.

For no good reason that he could think of, almost as an after thought, he took White along with him. The two men left by the front door, Lloyd closing it after them. Diego watched them go. Discovering where Roberts lived hadn't been difficult, although he had been a little surprised to find that the cavalry officer had appeared in Lisbon as Renard had predicted. He had expected to be doing little more than taking a holiday at French expense. What was going to be difficult was getting close enough to kill him and get away. The man was constantly in the company of competent looking men, if not members of the Lisbon police. He had quickly spotted the police watching Roberts' house. It made his watch harder, but he managed. He had watched Roberts and his men as they hung around those three warehouses for two days. He thought he recognised one of the men with Roberts as one of Renard's clerks, although he had no idea what he was doing. Not that Diego cared very much, he only had one thing to do, anything else was Renard's problem.

At Roberta's White was whisked away to the kitchen and Michael was warmly welcomed by her husband, Senhor da Rocha. Michael felt a little awkward, da Rocha knew that he and Roberta had been and still were the very best of friends. He also knew that they had been lovers. He knew they no longer were and had extended the hand of friendship to Michael because of his importance to Roberta. It had been a long time ago, but it still left Michael feeling uncomfortable. Still, there was not the slightest thing in da Rocha's demeanour to suggest he saw Michael as anything other than a good friend of his and his wife.

Da Rocha's house was warm and comfortable, the dinner was pleasant and most enjoyable. It took Michael away from his present troubles as they talked. He told them that he had instructed Furtado to sell the quinta to Catarina Cardoso. Roberta left no doubt about her approval. She, mischievously, then asked if he had heard any more of Senhorita Trelawny. Michael had said he hadn't and she had given a little, sympathetic pout. Dinner finished and the servants left them alone in da Rocha's elegant dining room.

"Miguel," Roberta began, "I have to confess to an ulterior motive in inviting you to dinner."

"Ah, I thought there was a sense of urgency in your note."

Da Rocha laughed. "When Roberta demands, one complies."

"Now, Alexandre, please, this is a serious matter, and it is all your fault."

"Then you had better explain to Captain Roberts..."

Michael interrupted, "Please, Michael, or Miguel, I feel I am amongst old friends."

Da Rocha inclined his head in acknowledgement. "Thank you, Miguel, obviously I know my wife and you are old friends, and I am honoured to be considered the same. And now, Roberta will explain, Miguel."

Roberta paused, gathering her thoughts. "It is the matter of the two letters."

"The ones from Renard?"

"Yes, I have been puzzling over them, and the differences between them. One is a genuine letter, we know, because it was taken from a French courier while on its way to Paris. It is the other one that bothers me."

"The draft?"

"Yes, if that is what it is."

"What do you mean?"

"If it is a draft, it leaves a lot out that is in the letter to Paris. You said it doesn't mention the flour supply and it doesn't mention sending two French agents. Surely, if anything gets left out, it gets left out of the final version, not the draft?"

"I see what you mean."

"And the way it was obtained. Does Renard strike you as the sort of person to go to a social event with the draft of a very important letter in his coat pocket?"

"Err, well, no, although Faucher believes he is becoming unstable."

"Perhaps, but not stupid."

"So, what do you think?"

"It was Alexandre's thought, Miguel. He suggested to me that perhaps the draft was meant to be read and sent to us. Perhaps Renard did it quite deliberately, leaving out the very important details, but making what would appear to be a very real threat to the army's supplies."

"But why, in God's name would he do that?"

"Miguel, you came to Lisbon because of the intercepted letter?" He nodded. "What would have happened if that letter hadn't been intercepted?"

"Sir Charles said he had been going to ask Wellington to send me to Lisbon because of the draft letter."

"And if Renard meant that letter to be copied and to reach us, what does that mean?"

Light dawned on Michael. "Renard wanted me sent here, to Lisbon!"

"Exactly, and why would he want that? To stop his plan to blow up the flour? I think not, and that is not in the draft letter that, let us assume, was intended to get you to Lisbon. Miguel, there is only one explanation."

"What is that?"

"It's a trap, Miguel. It was intended to get you away from the safety of the army and into Lisbon where you would be easier to get to. I think he is planning to have you killed."

Michael sat, stunned, thinking hard. "But.., Faucher has not said anything."

"He might not know."

"Faucher has said that Renard seems obsessed with me, blaming me for all his failings and demanding that someone kill me. Damn it, Roberta, you might be right."

Alexandre spoke. "I must take some responsibility for this idea, Miguel, but I do think it is worth considering. It is too big a risk to ignore as fanciful."

"Like the idea of blowing up the flour. Would it work? No one is sure, but we can't take the chance."

"Quite."

"Roberta, excuse me Alexandre, but would you be so good as to speak to your uncle about this?"

Alexandre chuckled. "Excuse you, Miguel? Do you think I would stand the slightest chance of stopping her? No! And what is more I shall go with her. It was my suggestion, and I find it all rather stimulating." Michael looked a little shocked. "Forgive me," Alexandre went on, "a threat to your life is not a thing to be taken lightly."

"And you, Miguel, what will you do?" Roberta asked.

"I shall have to inform Sir Charles." He looked at the da Rochas. "Thank you, both of you."

It was early the following morning and Sir Charles Stuart listened intently as Michael expounded the da Rochas theory. When Michael had finished he added his own interesting news.

"Senora Ortega has communicated with us again. I was going to speak to you today anyway. According to her, and bear in mind she is only aware of the, shall we call it the draft letter? And that says nothing of the number of agents sent. As I was saying, according to her three agents have been sent to Lisbon, not two."

"What!"

"Yes, quite. And it seems to me that Paris was not to be informed of the third person and that neither Faucher nor the other one knew about them either. She believes she knows the identity of the third man, a Spaniard, in fact, name of Diego, known as a killer for hire. My suggestion to you, Roberts, given the da Rocha theory, is that Renard has deliberately set about contriving to have you sent to Lisbon and has despatched a killer after you. He didn't inform Paris because, for him, this is a personal matter. He wants you dead, Roberts. Your friends the da Rochas are correct, your being here is a trap."

At that moment there was a soft tap on the door, and Sir Charles' secretary looked in. "I beg your pardon, Sir Charles, but the Marquess of Wellington has arrived."

"Ah! Thank you, arrange for some coffee, will you?"

"Yes, Sir Charles." The door closed again.

"Very timely, Roberts, you can tell him what you are doing here."

The door opened again and Wellington strode in, looking rather travel stained. He offered his hand to Stuart and as they shook he said, "Hello, Sir Charles, damn glad to get here, hope you've ordered some coffee. Roberts! What the devil are you doing here?"

"My Lord, Colonel Campbell thought I should come because of intelligence received after you had departed for Cadiz."

"Oh, he did, did he? And just what was that?"

A servant entered with coffee and there was a pause while Wellington was served and the servant left.

"Well, Roberts, explain."

Michael explained about the letter intercepted by Saornil and deciphered by Scovell. Stuart joined in to tell Wellington about the letter obtained by Señora

Ortega. Michael then told Wellington about Faucher and the latest developments and the conclusion they had just arrived at. Wellington sipped his coffee as he listened.

"Is there anything in this idea about blowing up the flour warehouses?" he asked.

Stuart answered him. "Remarkably, yes, it seems that there is. The Frenchman, Faucher, gave us a most, err, interesting demonstration and while it was not entirely convincing, I am convinced that there is a threat and a possibility it might be done."

"I see. And you, Roberts, what do make of this man?"

"So far, my Lord, he has been dependable, he does appear to have become genuinely disenchanted with Buonaparte. He also does not like Renard, of that I am sure."

"Hmm. Are you sure that the warehouses are adequately protected?"

Stuart answered him. "Yes, my Lord, Peacock has put extra guards on and General de Silva has also deployed men around the buildings and adjacent streets. I hope, however, that the French agent will be taken before he can do anything. Roberts and his men have been looking out for him, with Faucher to identify him."

"Good. Roberts, make sure you get him. The third man as well, but then you seem to have a knack of dealing with Monsieur Renard's schemes. Now, you had best get along and do just that." Wellington smiled. "I have to arrange the investing of Sir Charles here with the Order of the Bath.

# Chapter 12

As soon as he had got the gunpowder, Lucroy had decided to put some distance between him and Vargas, he didn't like the man and didn't trust him. He had simply walked out of the widow's house taking everything with him, she had neither seen nor heard him leave. An anonymous taverna in a remote back street suited him better. He had spent some time constructing six charges and fixing the fuses. They had long, slow fuses that he had brought himself from Madrid. He reckoned he would have about ten minutes in each warehouse before having to make a speedy and long escape. The explosions would, he hoped, be massive and he had no intention of being killed by his own hand.

He had deliberately kept away from the warehouses since he had moved his lodgings. He didn't know what had happened to Faucher and if he had been captured and given anything away, he wanted to allow time for things to quieten down. He was determined to destroy the warehouses and his caution was a result of his belief that he would only get one chance. He would move slowly, carefully, checking everything, waiting for his opportunity. Now, as soon as the streets got busy, Lucroy slipped out of the taverna and strolled downhill towards the river, the docks and the warehouses. The six powder charges were hidden away in his room, slipped inside his mattress. His intention was to spend two, perhaps three days watching the warehouses to decide on the best time to gain entry, where to get in and most importantly, how to get away.

When he and Faucher had first visited the docks to look at the flour warehouses they had noted the lack of any serious security. This time, however, he slipped around the last corner from the warehouses and almost walked into an English soldier. A quick apology, in muttered Portuguese, and he walked on. To his horror, he realised things were different. There were small groups of soldiers at each warehouse entrance and at all the street corners. Forcing himself to stroll casually, he took the first turning away from the area and entered the first coffee shop he came to. It was scruffy, small and dark, but, most of all, it was almost empty. He needed to think.

Nursing a large coffee he sat towards the back of the shop, not far from a door that led, he hoped, in case he needed it, to a back entrance. He realised that the sudden appearance of the additional guards suggested that the English were aware of a threat to the flour. With that many soldiers around it would be impossible to get into any of the warehouses with his charges. They were not big, but too big to imagine he could smuggle them in. He decided that he would have to come back after dark and see if the night offered any possibilities. There was nothing he could do until then, so he just sat quietly, considered his bad luck, and speculated about how the English could have got wind of the planned attack. As only he, Renard and Faucher knew about it, he came to the tentative conclusion that Faucher, somehow, had indeed been captured and made to talk. He had little time for his colleague, he doubted his loyalty to the emperor, and he wondered how the fool might have given himself away. He had been right to change his accommodation.

He sat in the coffee house until he started to get filthy looks from the owner, dragging out his single coffee. It wasn't even very good. He got to his feet, smiled at the owner, and made his way slowly towards the door. He was only a few feet away from it, only a few seconds from opening the door, when he saw Faucher walk past. Lucroy almost dashed out, but stopped himself when he realised he was not alone. He was walking and talking with a Portuguese gentleman. As he watched and wondered what on earth Faucher was doing, he saw that Faucher and the gentleman were accompanied by two men in the clothes of the Portuguese lower classes, but he realised immediately, from their manner and bearing that these were two soldiers. He let the little group pass, and then he slipped out and followed at a safe distance, keeping to the wall, watching out for doorways he might disappear into.

They were walking towards the warehouses, back the way Lucroy had come. At the street corner Faucher stopped and seemed to be looking up and down the street that ran past the warehouses. The Portuguese gentleman turned to speak to him, and Faucher saw the scar that ran down his cheek, white against his tanned face. He turned his back and walked slowly away.

He walked back to the taverna where he was staying. First he went to his room and checked that nothing had been disturbed. It was all in order. Then he went down to the public room and ordered a meal and a jug of wine. As he ate and drank, he thought. The man with the scar could only be Roberts, surely? But what was he doing with Faucher? Faucher hadn't looked like a prisoner, he didn't look like a man who had been interrogated, so what did that mean? He thought about Faucher and his opinion of him. Was it possible, he wondered, that Faucher had become a traitor? Was there any other explanation? Not that he could see.

It was clear to him that he was not going to be able to destroy the English flour supply. He might as well go back to Madrid. Renard would be furious, and with him when it was clearly Faucher's fault. Then it occurred to him that he could take back to Renard the victory that Renard clearly wanted above all others, he could kill Roberts, Faucher as well with any luck. He thought long and hard about it. He would have to be careful and very quick, if he wanted to get away, and he certainly did want that. He assumed that Roberts and Faucher were keeping a watch on the warehouse, presumably for him. So they would be there again tomorrow. He would watch the watchers and then take his chance.

He returned to his room, extracted his pair of pistols from their hiding place, and settled down to clean them. He checked them very carefully, he checked the flints and dry fired them to see the sparks fall into the empty priming pan. He would load them in the morning, taking great care, his first shot would have be perfect. He was unlikely to have a chance to reload, but a few spare cartridges would not go amiss and he could easily carry them in his coat pocket. His preparations complete, he went out for a walk for a few hours, just relaxing and enjoying the bustle of the city. He missed Paris. Then he had dinner, a few glasses of wine and went to bed. Perhaps surprisingly, he had no difficulty sleeping.

Just before dawn, Michel, Faucher, Lloyd and Hall set out yet again to walk to the warehouses. Michael was beginning to entertain doubts about the attack on the flour supplies. He had lain awake for an hour or more before Hall had appeared with coffee and hot water for shaving. He didn't doubt Faucher was telling the truth, so far as he knew it, but Michael had woken to an idea that kept him awake and thinking. If there was a trap to attempt to kill him, who was to say, other than Renard, that the attack on the flour was no more than a ploy to get him where Renard wanted him, in Lisbon and vulnerable to attack. No, that wasn't right, he had eventually concluded. The attack on the flour was mentioned in the letter to Paris, which Renard could not have relied on falling into their hands as it had. So it had to be a genuine plan, with a real intent to destroy the flour. So, was there a trap at all? After all, that was purely guess work on the part of the da Rochas. He decided that he would put the idea of a trap to Faucher, see what he made of it.

By mid morning, Michael was desperate for a coffee. He thought it would also be a good opportunity to talk quietly to Faucher. They had been watching the early morning surge as workers arrived in the dock area and went to their jobs. Michael had begun to recognise a few of de Silva's men, looking like dock workers and hanging around street corners and near the entrances to the warehouses. Peacock's sentries were in place and Michael supposed they made a fairly daunting deterrent. He pulled his watch out, made a show of consulting it and spoke to Faucher.

"I think we can afford a break, treat ourselves to coffee." They had become familiar with the area over the last few days. "Let's try the coffee shop around the corner."

Faucher nodded. "Yes, that would be most welcome, Monsieur."

Lloyd and Hall were standing nearby. "Lloyd, Hall, we're going for a coffee. Just round the corner. Follow on."

Side by side Michael and Faucher walked along the street, Lloyd and Hall following a few yards behind. Around the corner it was a little quieter, but there were still warehouses lining the street on both sides, with porters moving about and carts waiting to be loaded or unloaded. A hundred yards or so brought them to the coffee shop. Mchael was thinking about how best to put his questions and not taking much notice of his surroundings. He pushed the shop door open and turned to Faucher.

"After you, Monsieur,"

He saw Faucher start to say something, saw his eyes glance over Michael's shoulder, looking further up the street. He saw a look of horror flash across his face, then Faucher threw himself at Michael, sending them crashing into the street. As he did so there was a loud crack and the window of the coffee shop shattered, shards of glass flying everywhere. Faucher rolled off Michael.

"It's Lucroy!" He yelled.

Michael heard Lloyd shout, "I see him, sir!"

Michael got to his knees, groping for the pistol tucked in the waistband of his pantaloons, but trapped under his waistcoat. All around people were shouting, crouching behind carts, crates, anything. Up the street he could see Lloyd and Hall pistols in hand, running hard, people scattering before them and between them he glimpsed a running figure, a man in a grey coat. He pushed himself upright and ran after them. Suddenly the man in the grey coat dived sideways and disappeared. Alleyway, thought Michael and ran on as hard as he could.

Ahead of him Lloyd got to the alleyway first and swung around the corner and out of sight, Hall only a couple of yards behind him. As Michael ran on there was the sound of a shot. He forced himself to stop and look cautiously around the corner. Lloyd was lying prostrate on the ground, Hall crouched behind a barrel.

"Hall, what happened?"

Hall glanced back over his shoulder. "He took a shot at us, sir, Lloyd ducked, slipped, I think he's knocked himself out against the wall. I don't think he was hit, sir."

Michael became aware of someone standing close by him, it was Faucher. "Look after Lloyd," he snapped. "Come on Hall, he's fired twice, probably got a brace of pistols, can't fire again until he reloads. Did you see where he went?"

"Down to the left, sir."

"Come on, sharp!"

They ran on to another corner and Michael peered around it, carefully. He was just in time to see the man run though a pair of high gates.

"There he is, come on."

The gates opened into a yard, and as they reached them they were met by porters, clerks, labourers, all running out of a warehouse on the far side. Michael grabbed a man who looked like a clerk and stopped him.

"Where did he go?"

The man tugged to free his arm, "Into the warehouse, Senhor, he had pistols!"

"Is there a way out?"

"No, Senhor, that is the only entrance."

Michael released his grip and the man took off a fast run. Got you, you bastard, he thought.

"Did you hear that, Hall?"

"Yes, sir."

"Good, now you go around that side, I'll take this side." He pointed with his pistol.

Cautiously, keeping to the walls, they made their way around the yard. There were carts and barrows, bales and barrels everywhere and they made use of them to keep covered from the dark entrance into the warehouse. They reached the wide entry, its double doors open to the outside. Hall looked at Michael for orders. He held his hand up to tell Hall to stay where he was. He removed his hat, laying it with his cane on the ground behind him, then he took a quick look around the door. He glimpsed a low ceilinged space that seemed to stretch away in all directions, with more crates, bales, barrels, all sorts of goods piled up to head height. He pulled his head back.

"Hall, it's damned dark in there, he could be anywhere. Take a quick look yourself."

Hall stuck his head out for a second and then ducked back. "I see what you mean, sir."

Michael shouted into the dark, "Lucroy, can you hear me? There's no way out. Put down your pistols and surrender."

There was no response.

Michael glanced across at Hall. "It looks like he's not going to come out. We'll just have to go in." He paused to think. "He's probably reloaded by now. We'll go together, just as far as the first cover, it's only a few yards."

"Yes, sir."

"Ready?"

"Yes, sir."

"Then,...go!"

Michael hurled himself around the open door and across the cobbled floor before crashing down behind a large bale of what looked like cloth. He glanced across to see Hall, now also hatless, with his back to a large barrel. He glanced at his pistol, the flint was in place, he checked the priming pan was still full, and then brought it to full cock. He saw Hall do the same. He risked a quick look around the side of the bale. There was a passageway, about ten feet wide running into the warehouse interior between all the crates, barrels and bales. His quick glance revealed nothing beyond some thirty feet as the interior got darker.

He realised there was a similar passage going off to left and right along the front wall. He listened carefully, but heard nothing. He cupped his ear and looked quizzically at Hall. Hall shrugged and shook his head.

A voice called from outside in Portuguese, "Captain Roberts, are you alright?"

A man appeared, one of de Silva's, edging closer towards the door. Michael waved at him, put a finger to his lips, waved him back. He disappeared. Michael realised he could just leave the whole problem to de Silva's men, but they would probably bring Lucroy out dead and Michael wanted to question him.

Michael pulled out his knife, opened it and held it in his left hand. He caught Hall's eye and pointed down the passage that ran away behind Hall. Hall nodded and then surprised Michael by taking off his boots. Michael realised what he was doing and smiled approvingly. Then Hall put down his pistol, took his knife in his right hand, got on his hands and knees and moved cautiously into the passage and away, rising to his feet as he went. Michael wanted to keep Lucroy's attention on him, to the front.

"Lucroy, it's useless," he called out in French, "surrender and you will live. Don't be a fool. You can't escape. There are Portuguese police outside, do you want them to take you? They won't care if you come out alive or dead."

Michael slowly raised himself to his feet and could just see over the top of the bale. His view down the passageway was blocked by other things stacked up.

He wondered how far Hall had got, he had no idea, but the man could move as silently as a cat.

"Come on, Lucroy, be sensible, man, you don't have a chance except to surrender to me."

There was no response.

"Let me come and talk to you, is that alright with you?"

Still no response.

"Lucroy, I'm going to walk slowly towards you."

Silence.

Michael took a step into the passageway, nerves taut and ready to dive to the floor at the slightest hint of danger.

"Lucroy, I just want to talk, don't shoot." He took a step forwards, keeping close to the right side of the passage, edging forwards with his back against the stacked goods, trying to use bits of crates for cover. He held his pistol levelled at waist height, his knife was point down, hidden against his left leg. He listened carefully, nothing. Another step. The only sounds came from outside, it sounded as if the infantry were out there as well.

Confirmation came when an English voice shouted. "Captain Roberts? Officer of the guard here, do you need help?"

Just shut up, thought Michael and he took another cautious step, every sense alert. Then another step.

Then a shot rang out, deafening in the confines of the warehouse. Michael ducked instinctively. The shot went he knew not where, but he had seen the flash and had an idea where Lucroy was, on the other side of the passageway, perhaps thirty feet away.

Suddenly there was a grunt, a thud, French curses, the sound of a scuffle. Michael ran forward, ignoring any danger. There was another passage way, to the left, between all the goods stacked up, and at its mouth Hall and Lucroy were struggling furiously, rolling on the floor. Lucroy had a grip on Hall's knife hand, a pistol in his other hand, which was grasped in turn by Hall, Michael glimpsed another pistol lying on the floor. The pistol in Lucroy's hand went off with a deafening crash and blinding flash, it hit nothing. Then Michael was on them, the point of his knife pricking Lucroy's neck, a small bead of blood appearing. Lucroy froze.

"Just give me one reason, Lucroy, and I'll kill you."

Slowly, Lucroy released his grip on Hall's knife hand and let the empty pistol fall from his other hand. Hall got to his knees.

"Thank you, sir."

"That's quite alright, and thank you, you did well, very well."

In the gloom the two men grinned at each other.

At Michael's shouted summons the police came rushing in, followed by a young English infantry subaltern. Lucroy was secured and dragged away to the Police headquarters. Michael advised the subaltern that everything was under control and he could carry on until further orders. He walked out of the warehouse into the bright daylight, anxious to find out what had happened to Lloyd.

As he retrieved his hat and cane, a pale looking Lloyd came in through the yard gates, Faucher lending him a steadying arm.

"Lloyd, are you hurt?"

Lloyd gave him a wry smile. "Only me pride, sir. Slipped on a damned turd and knocked myself out against a wall."

"Thank God for that."

**Chapter 13**

By mid-afternoon, Lucroy was safely under lock and key at de Silva's headquarters. Michael was back at his house with Faucher, Lloyd and Hall, Mrs Lloyd fussing over Lloyd and trying to suppress a grin at how he had knocked himself out. Outside, all the security precautions were still in place. Michael had still not spoken to Faucher about the idea of a trap and now he was determined to do so. It was the last loose end. They were sitting in Michael's drawing room, White served coffee and withdrew.

"Thank you for what you did this morning. You probably saved my life."

Faucher looked startled at Michael's words. "Oh, um, well, you have been good to me, and you believed me." He smiled. "And what would happen to me if anything happened to you?"

Michael chuckled. "Oh, I am sure you would be well looked after."

"Yes, perhaps, but what is going to happen to me?"

"To be perfectly honest with you, I don't know. I hope to talk to the ambassador about it, hopefully Wellington as well. He's in Lisbon for a few days, so I don't have long."

Faucher was impressed, but asked, "Don't have long for what?"

"To work out what exactly is going on."

"But you know, Lucroy and I were sent to destroy your flour supply. Or at least to try, I don't know if it would have worked."

"No, no one does, and there's no way to find out." Michael paused to take a sip of his coffee. "But there's another problem." He hesitated.

"Another problem, Monsieur?"

"Yes, we don't know if blowing up the flour was Renard's plan."

"Oh, it was, I was with him when he thought it up, it was all his idea, Captain, I assure you."

"My apologies, I wasn't clear. We don't know if the destruction of the flour was what Renard was, is trying to achieve. There is a suspicion that there may be another objective, more important in his eyes."

"I don't understand."

"No, and I don't think you were supposed to." Michael wanted to lead Faucher gently, to see if he came to the same conclusion that he had. "You see there was a letter, or what appeared to be a draft of a letter, a copy was obtained. It was written by Renard, addressed to Savary, it spoke of an attack on our supplies, that's how we knew something was going on, but it didn't mention the flour supply."

Michael watched Faucher's face closely as he absorbed what he was being told.

"Obtained? How?"

"I can't say exactly, but it was direct from Renard."

"No, no, Renard is too careful with all documents. Nothing is allowed out of the offices, everything is stored in massive locked chests. It's impossible"

"Faucher, I can assure you it was obtained from Renard, copied, and returned to him, never mind how. Now, just accept that for a moment, please?"

"Very well."

"Now, there was also a letter we intercepted on its way to Paris."

"Oh!"

"Would you agree that Renard would expect that to reach Paris and for its contents to remain confidential? For us to remain unaware of the plan outlined in it?"

"Yes, of course he would. In any case, it would be in cipher and meaningless. Oh," realisation struck him, "you deciphered it?"

Michael suppressed a smile at that. "Yes, we did. So why would he deliberately allow a similar letter to be communicated to us?"

"Who says it was deliberate?"

"Why else would Renard break all his own rules for the security of confidential documents? From what you say it couldn't have been an accident, so..."

"But why?"

"I'll come back to that. The point is that the intercepted letter resulted in my coming to Lisbon, to investigate."

"Yes?"

"But if it hadn't been intercepted the copy of the draft letter would have had the same result."

Realisation crept into Faucher's expression. "You mean the draft letter was intended to bring you to Lisbon?"

"Yes, now, why would Renard want to get me away from the army and to Lisbon? Given what Renard thinks of me."

Faucher was silent for a moment. Michael could almost see the thoughts settling. "Because it would be easier to have you killed?"

"Exactly. I fear that you and your operation were just the bait to get me here, and the thing is, Faucher, we have received information that another man has been sent to Lisbon by Renard, a known killer."

Michael sat back as Faucher worked it all out.

"The bastard! He didn't care about me, or Lucroy, it was just a scheme to get at you!"

"I'm afraid so. At least we have some idea about the man sent. He's Spaniard called Diego. Do you know him?"

"No, I don't. No, wait a moment." Faucher frowned. "There was a Spaniard, visited Renard a few days before Lucroy and I left Madrid. He was alone with Renard for some time. I remember, as he left, Renard asked him how well he knew Lisbon. He said almost as well as he knew Madrid." He thought for another moment. "And when I went to the paymaster to collect my funds for this operation, the paymaster was surprised. He had paid a similar amount out the day before on an order from Renard, but I know it wasn't for Lucroy, he was due to go the next day."

"What do you know about this man, Diego?"

"Nothing, I don't think I would even know him again. It was Lucroy who brought him to Renard."

"Then I think we need to speak to Monsieur Lucroy."

Accompanied by Hall, Michael and Faucher walked over to the police headquarters. DeSilva had them shown into his office where he looked at Faucher for a long moment before speaking.

"I understand, Monsieur, that you saved the life of my friend here." He gestured at Michael. "I never thought I'd ever say this to a Frenchman, but thank you."

Michael added, "He could have slipped away in all the confusion as well, but he stayed to help my man, Lloyd."

Faucher looked surprised. "I didn't think of that."

"And how is your man?" de Silva asked.

"He has a sore head and a bruised dignity, but he will recover."

"I'm pleased to hear it," de Silva said, "now, what can I do for you? And, please, do take a seat."

Michael explained the situation to de Silva who sent to have Lucroy brought up from the cell he was in. While they waited he asked, "How do you wish to proceed, Captain? I would like to know before we begin."

Michael smiled at the recollection of their interrogation of the killer Janardo. "I was thinking of letting Faucher here do all the talking."

"What?" Faucher sat bolt upright.

"I thought he might be more likely to believe you than me."

"Oh, well, I can try."

"One word of advice," offered Michael, "talk as if we know everything, make it clear that we know all about Diego being sent here, that all we want is a description. You might make sure he understands that Renard was willing to sacrifice the pair of you to get at me."

Faucher nodded his understanding and sat, collecting his thoughts.

Lucroy was brought in by two guards, his wrists manacled, looking dirty and unshaven. When he saw Faucher he snarled and swore. "What are you doing here, you damned traitor, if I was free I would kill you with my bare hands!"

Michael stood up and walked close to Lucroy. He spoke quietly, but the tone of menace in his voice was clear to all. "Shut up, sit down and listen to what Faucher has to tell you. It might save your scrawny neck."

Step by step, Faucher took Lucroy through the story, the two letters, the differences, how they brought Captain Roberts to Lisbon, how they knew all about Diego, how Faucher knew about him, about the money he had been given by Renard. He explained carefully that it meant that Renard was prepared to sacrifice them in order to get at the Captain. He laid it all out, quietly, logically, calmly. Michael watched Lucroy carefully, saw his expression change slightly as he went from disbelief to belief. He finished and silence fell.

Michael let Lucroy stew for a moment then spoke. "You see, Lucroy, Renard didn't care what happened to you, didn't care at all. We know everything."

"Then what do you want from me?" Lucroy snapped.

"What we want is a description of Diego and any idea you have of where he might be found in Lisbon."

"And if I do that?"

Michael sighed, it always seemed to come down to bargaining. "It's more a matter of what happens if you don't. If you don't you will hang. If you do, well, I am sure the Lisbon courts can be persuaded to show mercy. What do you say, General?"

"Oh, I think that can be arranged." He paused, looking thoughtfully at Lucroy. "And, of course, if someone was to prove particularly helpful, there's always exile to the Brazils."

"Is that what you offered him?" He gestured at Faucher with a thrust of his chin.

Before anyone else could respond Michael spoke up. "What happens with Monsieur Faucher need not concern you."

Lucroy looked at all of them in turn. "It would seem that I have no choice, and if you know everything else a description seems a small price. As for how you might find him, I didn't even know he was being sent.

All I do know is that Renard wanted him to kill the Captain here."

De Silva rang a small bell on his desk. The summons was answered a moment later by his secretary. "Take this man somewhere. He has a description to give to you. Once you have it, see it is circulated to everyone. The man is a Spanish killer. Oh, and before you circulate it, bring it here, I want to see if Monsieur Faucher here recognises it as the man he saw in Madrid."

Faucher did recognise it and de Silva smiled with grim satisfaction.

Still accompanied by Hall, Michael and Faucher's next call was at the British Embassy. They had to wait for almost half an hour, but Michael was then shown into Stuart's office, leaving Faucher in the ante room with Hall. Stuart and Wellington were the only people in the room. Quickly and succinctly Michael brought them up to date with events.

Wellington listened carefully to everything, then said, "Excellent work, Captain Roberts, excellent." Stuart nodded his agreement. "it was also good work to persuade Monsieur Faucher where his best interests lie. Would you say his change of heart to oppose Buonaparte is permanent?"

"Yes, my Lord, he had a younger brother and two cousins in the Grande Armée, he fears they are lost in Russia."

"From what I hear they most likely are." Wellington looked grim. "It was a huge army and now it no longer exists. What that will mean for us here I do not know. Time will tell. However, Sir Charles and I have been discussing your Monsieur Faucher and what to do with him. Sir Charles has suggested that as a senior clerk for Renard, and given Renard's seniority in the secret police, Faucher probably knows a lot about how they operate, might even know something about agents around Europe, even if he has been cut off out here for some years. We have agreed that it would be for the best if Monsieur Faucher was sent to London and handed over to Mister Musgrave, in the friendliest way, of course. We are sure Musgrave will find him a source of much useful intelligence. A dispatch has already gone to Musgrave on the packet telling him he will be receiving Faucher as soon as we can get him there. We have also concluded that you should escort him to London. That will get you away from this man Diego as well. Hopefully he will give up and return to Renard."

Michael was stunned.

Wellington chuckled. "There is no one better, Captain. He knows you, trusts you. Sir Charles has been in contact with Admiral Martin and there is a sloop leaving on the late tide tomorrow, sailing to Falmouth, from there you can coach it to London. I have also written to Earl Harcourt warning him of your arrival and asking for billets for you. Lord Somerset has your orders, you may take one of your men with you." Wellington looked across to Stuart. "I believe that covers everything?"

"Indeed it does, My Lord."

"Good. Forgive me, but I would like a private word with the Captain."

Stuart nodded, rose silently and left the room. Wellington turned to Michael who was wondering what on earth this was about. "While you are in London there is something that you can do for me."

"Of course, My Lord."

"There will be no orders for this, nothing written at all." He paused, hesitating for a moment. "It may come as no surprise to you that I am already contemplating this year's campaign." There was another thoughtful pause. "The outcome of the Russian campaign will undoubtedly have an effect on Buonaparte's plans. He will be desperate for a new army. He will look carefully to see what is happening in Spain. It would suit me if he saw what I want him to. While you are in London I want you put it about that the army is in no condition to take the offensive this year. Exaggerate the losses from Burgos. Suggest that if there is an offensive, which you think is unlikely, it will be directed at Burgos as I am most vexed at having been thwarted there. It would be helpful if that view became known in Paris. As an officer on my staff you may be considered to be well informed on these matters. Speak to Musgrave, I warned him in my letter that you would be seeking help from him with something for me. He may be able find you some French agent to give this intelligence to. Perhaps something might appear in that damned rag, The Morning Chronicle. Do what you can, but do it quickly. D'ye understand?"

"Yes, My Lord," was all a stunned Michael could manage.

"Off you go then, Roberts, good luck. Oh, and be back by the end of April, I may have more work for you."

Michael rushed home, explaining as he went to a confused Faucher that they were sailing for England the next day. At the house he set Hall and White and young Jacinto to packing everything he would need. He told Hall he was taking him, told Lloyd he was leaving him to look after the horses with Carlos. Lloyd looked pleased. Then he rushed Faucher to the tailor's where Jorge worked and got Faucher some more clothes. They didn't quite fit, but Michael refused to let Jorge alter them, there was no time.

Finally, lying in bed, he had time to think about the task given to him by Wellington. He didn't quite understand The Peer's thinking, but, if that was what he wanted, he would do it. How he would do it was another matter, but he had the voyage to England to think about it.

Diego had watched Lucroy's attempt to kill Michael, he had sneered at the amateurish effort. He had hung around to see the fracas when Lucroy had been captured. To his surprise he recognised one of the men with Roberts as the other of Renard's clerks who had come to Lisbon. That puzzled him. He kept a discreet watch on Michael and realised the clerk was staying there. He did no more than watch, it had very quickly become clear that he was not going to get close enough to Roberts to kill him and get away. He saw baggage loaded on a cart, followed it to the docks, saw Michael along with Faucher and a dragoon rowed out to a Royal Navy sloop. Another dragoon, a corporal, had seen them off, along with some servant or other. He picked up among the dockside gossip that the ship was bound for Falmouth. He watched it sail and then set about returning to Madrid.

.        .        .

It took Diego the best part of three weeks to get to Madrid. His reception by Renard was not warm, but no more than he expected, he was ready for it. He told Renard what he had seen, what he believed had happened. That Lucroy was a prisoner, that Faucher was a traitor, the flour was undamaged and Roberts, who he couldn't get close to, had left for England on a Royal Navy ship. Along with Faucher.

For a moment Diego thought Renard was going to explode with fury. But, somehow, he calmed himself and maintained his equilibrium. Diego was impressed. Then Renard spoke.

"What you are telling me is that you have failed? Did I not get Roberts to Lisbon, where you said you would be able to kill him? I did my part, but you, Señor, you failed. Get out and never bother me again. Get out, before I have you arrested."

"No." Diego said, quite calmly.

That triggered the explosion of anger Diego had been expecting.

"No? No? What the devil do you mean, no?" Renard screamed at him, spittle flying from his lips. "How dare you defy me? What do you mean by it? Are you a fool, do you want me to have you executed, because I will!"

"You will not."

"And why not?"

"Because you do not want to die."

The door opened and a clerk looked in. "Is everything alright, Monsieur?"

"Get out," Renard screamed at him and the door quickly closed. He took a deep breath. "Explain yourself, Señor, quickly."

"Roberts has said he is going to kill you. Who is going to keep you alive? Who can stop him? I can. Monsieur, I can."

"But you saw him leave for England!"

"Indeed, Monsieur, but before he left, who has he sent to Madrid to act on his behalf? Just as you sent me to Lisbon."

Renard went quiet, he seemed to shrink as the implications of Diego's words hit him.

Diego went on. "There is a solution, Monsieur."

Diego saw a flicker of hope in Renard's eyes. "There is?"

"Oh, yes."

"What?"

"Let me keep you safe, let me look after your security." Diego shrugged as if he didn't care. "Or just wait to die."

Renard looked beaten. "Very well, Señor Diego." A slight smile flickered on his face. "As I no longer have to pay either Faucher or Lucroy, I shall pay you what they received."

Diego smiled. "Then we have an arrangement, Monsieur."

.        .        .

Michael discovered that Faucher was not a good sailor. For the first three days of the voyage he was constantly sick. The ship's doctor was unsympathetic, pointing out to Faucher that Lord Nelson had suffered in the same way and reassuring him that in a few days he would recover and regain his appetite. The captain of the ship, a Lieutenant, didn't really help when he told his passengers that the Bay of Biscay was unseasonally quiet. But, on the fourth day, Faucher took a little soup, and kept it. On the fifth day he was able to join Michael in the Captain's cabin for dinner. With three of them it was cramped, the food was basic and the wine copious.

The voyage gave Michael time to think about Wellington's task. He was far from sure how to go about it, a few vague ideas occurred to him, but he decided he would definitely need Musgrave's help. The voyage also gave Michael a lot of time to get to know Faucher, and through him he learnt more about Renard. He heard many tales of Renards unreasonable demands on his staff. Faucher explained that Marshal Jourdan, acting, he claimed, for King Joseph, piled pressure on Renard, demanding information, demanding results when his own cavalry patrols were daily threatened by Spanish guerillas, rendering the army almost blind and in ignorance of affairs any distance from them.

It seemed as if Renard had transferred his own failings to meet the demands onto Michael, blaming him for everything, even when it was obvious that

Michael could not have been involved. Above all Renard hated Michael for killing his son. It drove him, had become an obsession. It was, Michael had to admit to himself, nothing new, but it was confirmation and reinforced the idea that only one of them, either him or Renard, would see the end of the war. He was determined it would be him.

As for Faucher himself, Michael learnt a little of his childhood, he was clearly very fond of his brother and the very thought of him and what might have befallen him in Russia was enough to bring angry tears to his eyes. He harboured feelings of guilt that he had a civilian job while his young relations fought with the Grande Armée. Michael could not help but sympathise with him.

It was early morning when the sloop sailed into the Carrick roads, exchanging salutes with Pendennis Castle. Faucher stood next to Michael who was watching Falmouth come into view.

"Your home, I think, Captain?"

"One of them, here and in Lisbon."

"I wonder if I will ever see my home again."

Michael tore his eyes away from Falmouth to glance at Faucher. He could not help but think of Strenuwitz. "I am sure you will, the war cannot go on for ever, Buonaparte will be defeated."

"Yes, perhaps, but if he is, will I be able to go home? I served in his secret police, that would not be popular with many."

Michael had no answer.

As soon as the ship had anchored, Michael, his travelling companions and all their baggage had been rowed ashore and he had used his orders from Wellington to get through customs quickly, but it was still after midday before all the formalities were completed.

"Hall, can you remember where my Uncle's house is?"

"Yes, sir."

"Then find a porter and get the baggage taken there. I will go with Monsieur Faucher to Wynn's and see about coach tickets. If you get to my uncle's first, explain, but perhaps don't mention our friend is French."

"Very good, sir."

At Wynn's Michael had a long argument about tickets for the coach. It was full. He would have to wait a day. Michael produced his orders from Wellington, threatened to have the coach stopped by the local garrison, accused the ticket agent of treason, of being a Francophile. Faucher stood by, uncomprehending as the Cornish accents defeated his limited grasp of English. Eventually, money changed hands and Michael obtained two inside seats and one outside seat, on the understanding that Michael would pay for any subsequent additional accommodation at Wynn's for the displaced passengers. He was advised to be there an hour early if he wanted to get all his baggage aboard.

With that settled, Michael led Faucher through Falmouth's narrow streets to his uncle's house. Before he could bang on the door it opened to reveal both his uncle and his grandfather.

"Michael, my boy, this is a surprise, your man got here no more than five minutes ago. Come in, come in, and your friend. Come in." Uncle Jocelyn practically hauled him by his arm.

The Reverand Isles was just as effusive. "Michael, how simply splendid." He grasped Michael's hand and squeezed it. "This is such a surprise, a wonderful surprise. Did you get my letter? I am living here now, Jocelyn and I are getting on like an old married couple."

Michael and a bemused Faucher were shepherded into the drawing room and Jocelyn called out for tea at once. In the drawing room a roaring fire was a welcome sight.

"Uncle, Grandfather, may I introduce Monsieur Faucher. Monsieur, my uncle Mister Roberts and my grandfather, the Reverend Isles."

"Good God," spluttered Jocelyn, "a Frenchman?"

"Yes, uncle, a Frenchman, but here, I can assure you, as a friend."

"A friend, you say?" the Reverend asked Michael.

"Indeed."

The Reverend held his hand out to Faucher. "Then you are most welcome, Monsieur."

Faucher shook the offered hand and then that offered by Jocelyn. Then the tea arrived, brought in by Mrs Trevellick, who gave Michael a broad smile, said she was glad to see him and that nice Mister Hall was in the kitchen talking to Mister Trevellick and Mister Choak.

Michael explained to his uncle that they were leaving on the London coach, which departed from Wynn's at a quarter to three in the morning.

"Then we will give you a splendid dinner and provide you with provisions for the journey," Jocelyn responded.

Over dinner the Reverend explained that he had only been in Falmouth for a week, but that he had already been made to feel very welcome. He had also arranged to help the Reverend Hitchins at Falmouth's church. Much to Michael's relief, his grandfather made no mention of the visit to him by Elizabeth Trelawney. In turn, Michael was able to tell of Lloyd's marriage and becoming a father, with Mrs Lloyd currently acting as Michael's housekeeper in Lisbon. Conversation with Faucher was limited to explanations and descriptions concerning Falmouth, and the local hunting.

It was well after midnight that the evening broke up. Michael had to insist that his uncle and grandfather said goodbye in the warmth of the house and did not come to Wynn's. Hall had been well looked after, and Choak had found an old, but serviceable coachman's coat for him. It was big enough to go on over his cloak. Michael had his cloak and Jocelyn found a heavy coat for Faucher. As Hall and Choak wheeled away a handcart with their baggage on, Michael said goodbye and promised that he would call again before returning to the Peninsular.

The next two days were uncomfortable. With the exception of brief stops at inns to change horses and allow the passengers some relief, they were squashed in the coach as it rattled its way towards London. Michael's uniform and the presence of a Frenchman caused some staring, but no awkward questions. Sleep came intermittently. Occasionally there was a hot drink to be had as horses were changed.

In the early hours of the morning the coach rolled into the yard of the Swan with Two Necks off Cheapside. Tired and aching they gathered all the baggage together and Michael set about hiring a Hackney carriage to take them to Earl Harcourt's house. Faucher was tired and clearly nervous. As they travelled through the dark streets he was constantly looking around, his face expressing amazement and apprehension together. At Earl Harcourt's house the gates to the yard were closed and Michael sent Hall to hammer on them. He was a little surprised at the speed with which they were opened.

The man behind them asked "Captain Roberts?"

"Yes, he's in the carriage."

"You are expected." He opened the gates wide as Hall climbed back into their carriage and then called to the driver, "Straight to the front door, I'll keep the gate open for you."

As the carriage came to halt again, the front door opened and a footman appeared. "Good morning, Captain Roberts, a pleasure to see you again, sir. If you and your guest would care to go to the drawing room, I'll see to your baggage with your man. Mister Markham will be with you presently."

Michael remembered the way and led Faucher through the large hall, looking larger with a single candle lighting it. In the drawing room another servant was just lighting a fire and more candles were already alight. Both men welcomed the warmth that followed. The door opened and Markham, Harcourt's butler came in.

"Good morning, gentlemen, I have ordered coffee for you, I trust that will be satisfactory, Captain?"

"Very much, Markham, thank you."

"His Lordship's valet knows you are here, sir, he is informing his Lordship who will join you as soon as he is dressed. Breakfast is being served in the dining room shortly, sir. Your man, Hall, is being fed in the kitchen and your baggage is in your usual room, sir. I have been given no instructions as to Monsieur Faucher's baggage, sir, I understand he is to be accommodated elsewhere."

"Thank you, Markham."

"Err, forgive me, sir, I wonder if I might enquire after young James, sir?"

"What, oh, yes, of course. He is at my house in Lisbon, helping to look after it. That has suited him better than serving me in the field and it has been no bad thing for the house either."

"Thank you, sir, his mother will be gratified to know that, sir."

"He's also walking out with a local girl."

"Oh. Perhaps that is something I won't share with my sister, sir."

"I don't see why not, very respectable family, her father has his own bakery."

"Ah, thank you, sir."

The door opened and a footman entered with coffee. Markham served and Michael and Faucher were beginning to get warm when the door opened again to admit Earl Harcourt.

"Mornin', Roberts, good to see you, this our guest?"

"Yes, my Lord, may I present Monsieur Faucher? Faucher, this is General Earl Harcourt."

Faucher bowed low, and Harcourt smiled at him. "Welcome to England, Monsieur. Now, I expect you are both hungry? Come along, breakfast should ready."

Harcourt led the way into the dining room where bread rolls, cold meat and cheese awaited them. "Sit down, gentlemen, don't stand on ceremony, it's too damned early."

"This is quite a welcome, My Lord." Michael said.

"Yes, well, Wellington commands and we all obey. Got his letter a few days ago, been expecting you ever since." He coughed. "Err, I've sent to Musgrave, let him know you've arrived."

Faucher looked up from his breakfast. "I am to meet him?"

"So I believe, Monsieur."

"But he is the head of your Alien's Office! Surely he is too important to meet a simple clerk like me?"

"Ah, you know about the Alien's Office? But then I suppose you would. No, Monsieur, he is very keen to talk to you."

Faucher looked worried, but Harcourt reassured him. "Do not be concerned, Monsieur, let me assure you that you will be well looked after, you have my word on that!"

Once again the door opened and John, the footman came in. "A note for you, My Lord."

Harcourt took and read it. "Here we are, Mister Musgrave says he will be pleased to meet Monsieur Faucher at ten o'clock at his office." He looked up. "You know where that is, Roberts?"

"Yes, My Lord."

"Excellent. You can deliver our friend into Musgrave's care and then your task will be completed. It is not yet seven o'clock, so might I suggest that you finish here and then get a little sleep? I am sure you must be tired after two days in a coach at this time of year." He gestured at Michael's uniform. "While you're escorting our friend here, you'd best stay in uniform, just in case of any difficulties, might help, eh?"

At a few minutes before ten, Harcourt's carriage drew up at the entrance to the narrow alleyway off Crown Street where Musgrave's office was located. The imposing black door opened at Michael's knock and he and Faucher were ushered upstairs and into Musgrave's office.

Musgrave rose from behind his desk and strode forward, smiling, his hand outstretched to Faucher. "Monsieur Faucher, a pleasure to meet you sir, a pleasure." They shook hands and Musgrave offered his hand to Michael. "And a pleasure to see you again, Captain." He waved at three armchairs arranged before a healthy fire. "Please, gentlemen, take a seat, coffee or tea?" Michael requested tea, and Faucher followed his lead.

Under the window of the office was a small square table, two chairs drawn up to it, and a chess board laid out on it. Musgrave noticed Faucher give it a long look.

"Do you play, Monsieur?"

"Yes, yes I do."

"Splendid, I have difficulties finding opponents. We shall have a few games, eh? But I warn you, I am ruthless!"

The tea came and a few minutes were spent in inconsequential chatter. Musgrave enquired after their journey from Lisbon and was endeavouring to put his guest at his ease. Eventually, Musgrave addressed Michael.

"Captain, Monsieur Faucher and I have much to talk about and I fear that much of it will be of no interest to you. I believe that Wellington has granted you some leave?" Michael nodded. "Then let me detain you no longer, you may leave Monsieur Faucher safely in my care."

"Thank you, but I do need a few words with you on another matter."

"Ah, yes, of course." Musgrave consulted his watch. "Perhaps in an hour? I am sure you will be able to find some entertainment until then." Musgrave reached for a small bell and rang it. In response one of his men appeared at the door, Michael recognised Mason. "Mason, the Captain needs to speak to me, I have asked him to return in an hour." Mason gave a little bow.

Michael rose and offered Faucher his hand. "It seems I am dismissed, Monsieur," he said with a smile. "However, I hope we meet again, and may I wish you good luck."

Faucher stood and took Michael's hand, squeezing it and shaking it. "Thank you, Captain. Thank you for everything."

Michael left the room, pulling the door shut behind him and started to walk towards the stairs down to the front door, his sabre tucked under one arm, his shako under the other. There was a decent looking coffee house nearby where he could catch up with the newspapers and pass a quiet hour.

Mason coughed, "I beg your pardon, Captain, but there is someone Mister Musgrave would like you to meet, but doesn't want Monsieur Faucher to see here."

"I don't understand?"

"Well, sir, we will be easing the Monsieur into French loyalist society, sir, and we will have people keeping an eye on him, sir, for his own good, sir, and its best he doesn't know who they are. After all, he is not a prisoner."

"Ah, I was wondering what would be done with him."

"Oh, he will be well cared for, sir, I expect he is a veritable well of information for us. Pays to look after him. Anyway, sir, there's someone who might become involved with that who you need to meet, sir, help avoid any difficulties in the future. If you'd just step this way."

Mason led Michael down the corridor, opened a door, ushered Michael in and closed the door behind him. The room was a sparsely furnished drawing room, a few armchairs, a low table, a single window. A woman, her back to him, was looking out of the window. She turned.

Elizabeth smiled at him. "Hello Michael."

# Chapter 14

"Elizabeth?" Michael almost shouted in his surprise.

"Yes, Michael, it is me." She smiled at him.

"But.., but what are you doing here?"

"Working for the Alien's Office, for Mister Musgrave."

"What! What do you mean?"

"I mean that I am helping to keep a watch on the French émigrés here in London. To make sure that they are what they say and not agents of Buonaparte." She smiled again. "And since you might come across me in Monsieur Faucher's company, Mister Musgrave suggested we meet now to avoid any future difficulties." She glanced up and down. "Is that the new uniform? I have to say, I'm not sure about it, or the moustache."

Michael ignored the light hearted jest, his mind was flooded with memories of Elaine, from their first meeting at Carlton House to holding her in his arms as she died, of his love for her. The thought of Elizabeth putting herself in the way of such danger, of history repeating itself, was too much.

"But you can't, you mustn't," he blurted out.

The smile vanished from Elizabeth's face. "And just why can't I, Captain Roberts?" Anger flickered in her eyes, but Michael was too overwhelmed to notice.

"Because it's damned dangerous, that's why. It's no work for a woman!"

"Did you try to stop Lady Travers?"

"What? Elizabeth..,"

"Miss Trelawney, if you don't mind, Captain!"

"But, Eliza.., Miss Trelawney, please..."

"No, Captain. I am well aware of Lady Travers and her sad death. You will recall that you told me your story in Truro, after I had shot and killed Rochambeau in the hall of my house, so do not presume to lecture me on danger, sir! I am my own woman and I will do as I please, including working for Musgrave and I will beg you to remember that I am not Lady Travers!"

Michael was speechless and stared at Elizabeth as she stared right back at him, her anger clear to see. Then she turned to a bell pull and tugged on it. Almost at once the door opened and Mason came in.

"Yes, Miss Trelawney?"

Her voice cold and clipped she answered him. "Captain Roberts is leaving."

Mason stood to one side, holding the door open. Michael stared at her for a moment, then swivelled on his heel and marched quickly out, followed by Mason. As soon as Mason had close the door, Michael turned to face him.

"Mason, I must see Mister Musgrave at once."

"I beg your pardon, sir, but he is still with Monsieur Faucher, he said they were not to be disturbed." Michael swore and Mason, ignoring the curse, went on. "There's a very pleasant little coffee house just around the corner, sir..."

"Yes, I know, damn it. Oh, damn, my apologies, Mason."

"Yes, sir. Then perhaps you might retire to it for a short while, sir? I shall send for you the moment Mister Musgrave is free to see you."

Michael sat, staring without seeing at some newspaper or other, his coffee going cold. He had been caught completely off balance by meeting Elizabeth like that. He had also been knocked further off balance by his reaction to her working for Musgrave. That memories of Elaine had washed over him was, on reflection, no real surprise. What had surprised him was the immediate strength of his concern for Elizabeth's safety. He had, he realised, suddenly found that he genuinely cared about her. It had been a year since they had parted. He had convinced himself that his revelations about his role in the intelligence war would make him less than attractive in Elizabeth's eyes. He had put thoughts of her behind him, or so he had believed. He was angry and disappointed with himself for the way he had reacted, overreacted, and had angered Elizabeth, but he could not deny the power of the emotions he had felt. Before he could reach any conclusions about what to do, one of Musgrave's men came for him.

Musgrave was alone in his office and greeted Michael warmly. "Come in, come in, take a seat, please. Your Monsieur Faucher is safely in the care of Mason, you need have no concerns. A splendid young man, I think he is going to prove most helpful. I am grateful to you Captain, for his, err, shall we say acquisition? It was well done. Now, I expect this concerns the matter the Marquess of Wellington warned me about? I must admit I am intrigued to know how I might be of service, so far away from Spain." As Musgrave spoke they both took their seats either side of the fire.

"Yes, sir, it is, but I must speak to you about Miss Trelawney."

"Ah, yes, yes, of course. I, ah, gather the reunion was not as cordial as I might have hoped."

"No, sir, it was not, and I am sure you can understand why."

"No, I don't, not at all. Miss Trelawney gave me to understand that you think the Aliens Office should not employ women? Now why do you think that? After all, Lady Travers was a most valuable agent. I don't recall you raising objections about her work? Indeed, you worked with her."

"That is the very problem, sir, I did work with her and..." Michael hesitated, then blurted out, "and I loved her!"

"Ah, yes, of course." Musgrave steepled his fingers on his chest and looked thoughtfully at Michael. "And, consequently, you fear the same fate befalling Miss Trelawney?" Musgrave smiled. "I refer, of course, to her being killed, rather than loved by you." Michael glowered at him and Musgrave hurried on. "Forgive my flippancy, it is an unfortunate characteristic of mine in serious situations." He paused again. "I think your concerns are ungrounded, Captain. Miss Trelawney is not Lady Travers. For one thing, Lady Travers was motivated by a desire for revenge on the French who she held responsible for the disappearance of her husband. Much, I believe, as you are for the loss of your parents. She sometimes took unnecessary risks, driven by her thirst for revenge. Miss Trelawney, however is motivated by a sense of duty. She sees others taking their share of the fight against Buonaparte, and I believe that includes you, and she wishes to take her share."

"But I would never expect anyone to..."

"Perhaps not, but she came to me of her own volition and offered her help. She speaks excellent French, is a very sociable, intelligent and well educated young woman. She is able to move easily in society, including amongst the French émigrés as occasion demands. Unlike Lady Travers, she takes no apparent active role in their affairs. She simply watches and listens to the gossip. She is young, and that helps, she is not taken very seriously, but that's the French for you. Now, I hope that I have put your mind at rest? For my part, I have no wish for a repeat of that dreadful night, you must believe that."

Michael nodded, slowly, reluctantly, he could not deny the truth of what Musgrave had said.

"Now, please, tell me what it is Wellington wants me to help you with?"

Michael carefully repeated to Musgrave what Wellington wanted him to achieve. Musgrave listened intently and when Michael had finished he sat in silence for a few minutes, staring into space before he responded.

"That is no small task you have been given. I spend most of my time trying to stop the French getting any intelligence, so this is quite a novelty." He fell silent again. "It seems to me that, put simply, we need to find a French agent, let them hear this intelligence from a reliable source and then allow them to communicate it to Paris. It is, of course, far easier said than done. Particularly as we have been quite effective at, err, eliminating French agents. One possibility, however, does come to mind, but it is a challenging one."

"I beg your pardon, sir, but if there is a possibility I think it must be attempted regardless of the challenge."

"Well, yes, but let me explain. I know from my agents in Paris that there is one French agent in London who is considered to be particularly reliable. He doesn't send a lot to them, but what he does is always high quality material. I would very much like to catch him, but, so far, he has eluded us, partly because he does limit his activity. I believe he is a member of the French émigré community here and in Paris he is only known as L'Ange Bleu, The Blue Angel, a little melodramatic, but he has successfully concealed his identity for some time, possibly years. Anything coming from him would carry weight."

"But if you don't know who he is, what can we do?"

"Look harder, but gently, we do not want to frighten him off. I shall give it some thought and set Mason to work, as you know, he has a skill where these things are concerned. I shall also think about the best way to pass on the required intelligence when we find him, and find him we will."

"Thank you, sir. There is one other thing, Lord Wellington's suggestion that something in the newspaper could be helpful. He suggested the

Morning Chronicle, which is no friend to the Government."

"That is certainly true, far too much useful intelligence has appeared there, from letters home by officers in the army."

"Yes, and I have one officer in particular in mind."

"Ah, who would that be, I don't see how an officer in Spain can help?"

"This officer is recently returned, Colonel Gordon, our late Quartermaster General."

"Good Lord, are you serious?"

"Completely. It is already known that intelligence he sent to England, intelligence known only to three men, Gordon, Lord Somerset and the Marquess, appeared in the Morning Chronicle."

"Yes, I heard about it from Bathurst, who read it in the Chronicle before he received Wellington's dispatch. He was singularly unamused. But what do you propose?"

"If you approve, I will ask Earl Harcourt to help, to invite Gordon to dinner, then I shall, over dinner, let it be known that the army is in a parlous condition and incapable of taking the offensive and it is Wellington who has brought the army so low. Gordon will like that and, I trust, pass it to his newspaper friends."

"But why should he believe you? He must have some knowledge of you from his time in Spain?"

"He does. And he was given the idea that I am an incompetent officer only on the staff because I can't be trusted with a troop and as a favour to the Earl. If I suggest that Wellington sent me home, supported in that by the Earl, he will believe I am no friend of Wellington. That will give veracity to anything critical that I say."

Musgrave was quiet for a moment, then spoke. "May I say, Captain, that is a very, very devious plan, and it might well work. By all means see if you can enlist the Earl. And if he needs an excuse, I believe that the Colonel is soon to be a Major General. A congratulatory dinner would be in order."

When Michael left Musgrave's office he had much to think about. He decided that a straightforward approach to Earl Harcourt would be best. That left him thinking about Elizabeth. He had, for a fleeting moment, thought that Musgrave was going to ask him if his concerns over Elizabeth were due to his loving her. He realised that while he didn't love her as he had Elaine, he could very easily come to love her and that was why he was scared for her. He had lost Elaine in the intelligence war, he didn't want the same to happen to Elizabeth. He would have to take Musgrave's assurances at face value and trust her to be as careful as Musgrave had suggested she was. After all, he reminded himself, Roberta had been a very successful agent without problems, much in the same manner as Elizabeth was, according to Musgrave. And now Roberta was married and no longer an agent, at least not to the extent she had been. Marriage. It changed things. Then he thought about the row with Elizabeth and wondered if he had ruined things so far as she was concerned. He was now unlikely to find out whether or not she had been repelled by his part in the dirty war, if there was anything in her visit to his grandfather. He walked on slowly towards Harcourt House. It had been a very long day coming after two days in a stagecoach. He was tired. He knew the Earl and his wife were out that evening and he was glad of the chance to go quietly to bed and get some much needed sleep.

Elizabeth was still angry. Her aunt, suffering from an attack of gout and housebound, listened to her furious description of her argument with Michael. Gradually, she ran out of words and energy.

"How dare he, just how dare he take that attitude with me?" She glanced at her aunt and detected a small smile. "What? What are you laughing at? Aunt Mary?"

"Oh dear, Elizabeth. Have you no idea why he objects to you working for Musgrave?"

"Of course I do. He is an unreasonable man who thinks a woman should take no part in the defence of her country,"

"But you said yourself he took no objection to Lady Travers."

"Yes, he didn't, which makes his objection to me all the more infuriating and inexplicable."

"My dear, have you considered that he feels so strongly because he feels strongly about you?"

"What? Oh!" Elizabeth was taken all aback.

"Oh, indeed. And, may I ask, why do you care so much about the views of a man you haven't seen in a year? Hmm?"

"Aunt Mary, I do not care, he will be back to Spain soon enough and may never return, or marry some

Senorita." But aunt Mary saw the slight blush that appeared at her neck.

Later, she lay in her bed and remembered that fateful night in Truro. It wasn't the fact that she had shot and killed a man that was at the forefront of her recollection. What she thought most about was why she had opened the door of her house and called out to Michael. How she had given in to desire and how she had wanted him. In the dark she blushed again.

In the morning, Michael found Earl Harcourt already at breakfast, Markham in attendance.

"Mornin' Roberts. I trust you are recovered?"

"Yes, My Lord, thank you."

"And our French friend safely delivered?"

"Yes, My Lord."

"Good, good, now, what are you doing with yourself?"

"If I may, My Lord, I would like to speak to you about that."

"Hmm, no time like the present, eh? Markham, see we are not disturbed."

With a "Yes, My Lord", Markham left them alone in the dining room.

"Speak away, Roberts."

"It's something Lord Wellington has asked me to do for him. It's a sensitive and difficult matter and I hope that you might be willing to help."

Harcourt looked at him under a lowered brow. "Sensitive and difficult, you say? Tell me more, Roberts, and let me decide."

"I am afraid that it would mean deliberately misleading a senior officer."

"I am intrigued, tell me, who is this officer."

"Colonel Gordon, sir, our late Quartermaster General."

"Him? Man's a rank incompetent!"

"My Lord!"

"Roberts, I am a General and the Colonel of your Regiment, I do hear things, ye know."

"Yes, My Lord. Are you aware that he sent confidential information, from a dispatch from Wellington to Lord Bathurst, to a correspondent in England, which then appeared in The Morning Chronicle, before Bathurst had received the dispatch?"

"Good God, no!"

"My Lord, there is certain information that Lord Wellington would like the French to know. It occurs to me that if Colonel Gordon were to learn it, as it is not favourable to Wellington, there is every chance of it appearing in The Chronicle and thus coming to the attention of the French. I might add, sir, that Mister Musgrave approves of this idea and that he and I are working on another plan to get this information to the French."

"And just what is this information?"

"That the army is in a parlous condition and unlikely to be able take the offensive this coming campaign season, and if it does, it is thought that Lord Wellington will want to advance through Salamanca to try to take Burgos again, he being somewhat vexed at having been thwarted in that."

Harcourt sat silent for a moment, absorbing what Michael had said. "I assume this information is false?"

"To tell you the truth, My Lord, I don't know, Lord Wellington was not forthcoming on that point."

"Hmm, I don't suppose he was, but I know that he is being substantially reinforced this winter."

"My Lord."

"How would you propose to reveal this information to Gordon?"

"That, My Lord, is where I hope you might help."

"Go on."

"Mister Musgrave informed me that Gordon is to be promoted Major General. Given that, you might wish to invite him to dine, to congratulate him. I shall be present. He thinks, thanks to Sir Stapleton Cotton, that I am an incompetent who only has his position thanks to your wish to gratify an old friend, my grandfather. I shall let him think that Lord Wellington finally lost patience with me and sent me home. Consequently, I am no supporter of his and will complain bitterly over dinner that Wellington's incompetence in the Burgos campaign has put everything at risk, ruined the army and so on. I believe he will take that up eagerly."

Harcourt looked thoughtful and then smiled. "I like it, Roberts, I believe we might arrange something suitable. Now," his smile broadened, "tell me just what Sir Stapleton told him about you?"

Michael did, and Harcourt roared with laughter.

Michael spent the next few days kicking his heels. No word came from Musgrave and until that happened the dinner could not be arranged. Michael borrowed a horse from Harcourt and took to riding in Hyde Park in the mornings. Hall had little to do, looking after Michael, so he sent him to help Jackson, Harcourt's groom, and to learn from him. Michael had a lot of time on his hands to think. He thought a lot about Elizabeth and how he might undo the damage done by their argument. He began to hope that he might, and to hope that she thought better of him than he had suspected, at least, that was, until they had argued. He wanted to repair things between them and then see where things led. His evenings were spent dining with Earl and Lady Harcourt. It was pleasant, but Lady Harcourt's presence limited the conversation between the two soldiers.

One evening, Harcourt mentioned that he had heard that the 10th Hussars, preparing to go out to the Peninsular, were being issued with a number of rifled versions of the carbine, produced by Ezekial Baker in Whitechapel, the same Baker who produced the rifles weapons that were so effective. The following day, with nothing else to do, Michael paid a visit to Whitechapel to see for himself. Baker's premises included a small range and Michael was able to test one of the guns for himself. He was impressed, the weapon was far more accurate than the ordinary carbine. He ordered two with all their appurtenances to be delivered to Earl Harcourt's.

Musgrave and Faucher were sitting in Musgrave's office, the chess board between them. Musgrave had quickly discovered that Faucher was an excellent player and a daily game or two had become routine. Musgrave also found that it made Faucher more communicative, it was less intimidating than a formal questioning. Musgrave had already learnt a lot about how the French Secret Service was organised and operated. Faucher's willingness to help had been reinforced by the emerging news of Buonaparte's debacle in Russia. He had become increasingly opposed to the Emperor, holding him responsible for France's sufferings and the loss of his brother and cousins, for whom he held little hope.

Today, however, Musgrave was a little distracted. Despite applying the full resources of the Aliens Office nothing had come to light about L'Ange Bleu. He remained as elusive as ever. He had sent an urgent request for information, any information, to his agents in Paris, but he did not expect much if anything, and it would take time even to learn nothing from Paris. He was deep in thought when Faucher moved a piece and declared 'Checkmate!"

Musgrave started in his chair. "What? Oh! Oh dear!"

"Pardon, Monsieur, but that was too easy. I think your mind is elsewhere?"

"Yes, yes, I fear it is." Musgrave looked thoughtfully at Faucher who had started to rearrange the pieces for another game He decided to ask the question. Faucher was waiting for him to make a move.

"Monsieur, let the game wait for a moment, there is something I would ask you."

"Of course, Monsieur."

"As I am sure you realise, I have hesitated to ask you anything that might directly result in harm to any of your countrymen."

Faucher bowed his head in acknowledgement. "Indeed, and I thank you for your consideration. But, perhaps, the time has come for me to choose sides? And I choose France, not the Emperor. So, please, ask."

It was Musgrave's turn to bow his head in acknowledgement. "Thank you, Monsieur. There is an agent we are looking for, and have been for some time. It is preying on my mind, I fear. I wonder if you might be able to help us find him?"

Faucher smiled in return. "A reasonable request, but I have never dealt with our agents in England, I do not see how I might help?"

"Perhaps you can't, but I shall ask anyway. We are looking for an agent who we know is in London and has the nomme de guerre of L'Ange Bleu. So far we have failed completely. I hope you might give us some small lead that will help."

"L'Ange Bleu?" Faucher beamed, "In London? The last time I heard anything of her she was in Vienna."

"Her!" Musgrave exploded. "She's a woman?"

Faucher's smile widened. "Ah, you thought L'Ange Bleu was a man! Oh dear!"

"Yes, well, ah, thank you for clarifying that matter for me, Monsieur. Is there anything you can tell me? Anything that might help us to identify her?"

"I am afraid I never met her, but I understand she always circulated in the higher levels of society, went about as a lady, a gentlewoman, which helped to keep her safe. She was not someone who you would ever imagine was a spy."

"Thank you. Now, I must ask you to forgo another game, I fear, I am sure you understand that there are things I must do."

"Yes, of course. I wonder if I might beg a favour?"

"Of course."

Faucher fingered his coat. "I could do with some new clothes, these are more than a little tired and not a good fit. Captain Roberts got them for me in Lisbon, in rather a hurry."

"But of course, forgive me, I should have taken steps already. I shall have Mason take you to a good tailor. The Aliens Office will settle the bill."

As soon as Faucher had departed with Mason, Musgrave summoned a messenger. "Go and find Miss Trelawney, try her home first. If she isn't there, her aunt may know where you can find. Tell her I need to see her, urgently."

The man left and Musgrave sat down to think. His guess was that L'Ange Bleu was hiding in plain sight amongst the women of the French émigrés in London. If that was the case, no one knew them better than Elizabeth Trelawney. He was going to need her help. He would also need to inform Captain Roberts. He sincerely hoped that there would be no trouble between the two of them. He smiled at the recollection of almost suggesting that Roberts was in love with her. It seemed perfectly obvious to him that there was an attraction between the two young people. He was confident they would work it out, they were not unintelligent.

# Chapter 15

Michael was relieved when a messenger arrived during breakfast, asking him to be at Musgrave's for ten o'clock. Harcourt looked askance at him across the table.

"Good news, I hope?"

"I think so, My Lord. Musgrave asks to see me at ten o'clock."

"Excellent. Perhaps we can organise that dinner we have discussed. Do you want to take my carriage?" The Earl gestured to the window, outside rain was falling heavily.

"Thank you, My Lord, but I think I will take a hackney, I have no idea how long I shall be gone."

A little before ten o'clock Michael paid off his cab a short distance from Crown Street. The rain had eased to a light drizzle and he wanted a short stroll and some fresh air to ready himself. The doorkeeper recognised him and sent Michael up the stairs to Musgrave's office.

He knocked, heard a muffled "Come!" and walked in. Musgrave was there with Mason and, to his surprise, Elizabeth.

"Captain Roberts, please, take a chair, there is tea on the table if you would care for some." Michael poured himself a cup, mostly to give himself time to wonder what Elizabeth was there for. From what Musgrave had said the hunt for a French agent was hardly something she might take part in. He took a seat and Musgrave addressed them.

"The reason I have gathered us together is that I have some new information, but first, Miss Trelawney, you need to know that we are actively seeking a French agent known as L'Ange Bleu, not the sort of activity that you are usually involved with," Elizabeth acknowledged this with a nod, "but new information about L'Ange Bleu, courtesy of Monsieur Faucher, suggests to me that in this case you will be able to help. It seems this agent is a woman!" A ripple of surprise ran through his listeners. "More than that, she moves in the higher levels of society and as a lady is above suspicion. She has previously been active in Vienna, but whether that will help us, I do not know. We do know she is now operating in French émigré society here, but we were, unfortunately, looking for a man. You," he spoke directly to Elizabeth, "know the ladies of this society as well as anyone, hence your involvement." He glanced at Michael. "I see no reason why this should be any more risky than anything else you have done, but we will take steps to ensure you have a high level of protection. That is, if you become more actively involved rather than in your usual role as an observer."

Musgrave glanced at Michael again, who gave a slight nod of acknowledgement of his words. Elizabeth did not notice, she was staring thoughtfully at her tea cup. She looked up and spoke.

"Gentlemen, Mister Musgrave, I appreciate your concern, but I believe I can look after myself." She shot a cold look at Michael. "There is, however, something I should like to know. Why do you want to find this woman? I suspect there is more to this than just shutting down a French agent. If it were just that, there would be no need for the Captain to be present."

Michael was impressed by her perception. Musgrave smiled broadly.

"Miss Trelawney, you are quite right. Your analysis does you credit. Yes, there is more to it. Captain, would you care to explain?"

Elizabeth turned her gaze on Michael and he felt the piercing inquisitiveness of those striking blue eyes. Briefly, stammering occasionally, he explained to her what Lord Wellington wanted him to do. He finished and she nodded, slowly.

"I see. That is clever." She turned to Musgrave. "It occurs to me that, at the moment, you have no plan for how to discover the identity of this woman?"

"None at all." Musgrave looked forlorn.

"Then, perhaps, I may make a suggestion?"

"Please, do." Musgrave gestured, giving Elizabeth the floor.

Elizabeth began, a little hesitantly, as if still working things out. "If this woman is part of French émigré society, then I have probably met her. I have met, I think, all the French ladies of any standing, they do say the most indiscreet things about their husbands." She smiled. "They also like nothing better than to gossip at a grand soirée. If there was to be a grand enough soirée, particularly one where there might be people of importance and things to be learnt, then this L'Ange Bleu would no doubt be there. Perhaps the information Wellington wants made known to the French could be put about there? That way it doesn't matter if you have identified her or not."

"Very good, Miss Trelawney, very good indeed, but how to put the information about?" Musgrave asked.

Elizabeth smiled, disingenuously. "I think the Captain here could do that. He is recently returned from the army, his position on the staff would mean he is well informed. A little careless talk and there you have it."

Musgrave rubbed his chin contemplatively. "Yes, yes, but if she reports her source to Paris, Captain Roberts is a known person, known for his counter intelligence successes. He is not the sort of person who would broadcast anything that might be considered confidential. They would be suspicious in Paris."

Silence fell. Then Elizabeth chimed in again. "But what if it were someone else, someone well informed, someone who the Captain tried to stop saying what they were saying, tried to contradict them, but unconvincingly? Would that not give weight to the information?"

"Good Lord, yes, that might work, but who? It has be someone who we can rely on. Someone willing to play the part."

"Might I make a suggestion?" All eyes turned to Michael. "I have a friend who recently left the army, but who could claim to be in correspondence with a great number of former comrades. If he claimed they were all saying the same thing, that would be very difficult to counter. I am sure such a scheme would appeal to him."

"Who do you have in mind?" Musgrave enquired.

Michael smiled, "Henry van Hagen. He left the army only last year, he has inherited an estate in Buckinghamshire and he has recently married. He was a good friend, and just the sort who might correspond with former comrades. I rather think something like this would appeal to him."

"In that case," said Musgrave, "can you arrange for him to come up to town?"

"I am sure I can. I shall write to him today, but when?"

"Quite," mused Musgrave. "We need to organise a grand soirée, Miss Trelawney, do you have any suggestions? We need a suitable host and venue."

"Well, it needs to be some prominent personage, someone who will attract the best. I wonder, perhaps Viscount Petersham? He has a grand house in St James' and as a half pay colonel I am sure he would be eager to help. He is also a friend of both the Prince Regent and the Duc d'Angoulême, if there were any possibility of them attending, any rumour..."

"Ah, yes," Musgrave broke in, "but, of course, they mustn't, it could all be rather embarrassing. They must not be associated with anything like this."

"No," Elizabth countered, "but rumours do get around, I could see to that."

"Very well." Musgrave spoke decisively. "We have a plan. I shall speak to Petersham. Do you think we can manage it all in a week?"

Elizabeth said, "Once we have Petersham involved it should be perfectly possible.".

"Splendid," Musgrave responded.

"In that case," put in Michael, "I think the Earl Harcourt's dinner should be arranged for the following evening." Elizabeth looked at him quizzically. "It's another scheme for disseminating this intelligence."

Her response was limited to "Ah!"

"More tea anyone?" Musgrave interrupted. "Ah, this is cold, I shall ring for more. Mason, while we wait we can think about how to manage this little affair."

The following week was a busy one, there were many more meetings and Michael saw at first hand exactly how competent Elizabeth was. She was plainly in her element amongst the French émigré society. She also had the ability to charm Petersham, which helped more than once. Michael's admiration and respect grew, but there were no opportunities for socialising. He promised himself that he would correct that once the current situation was resolved. He did, however, manage to make a start in putting things right between them. They were in Musgrave's office, Musgrave had left them for a moment to speak to Mason about some detail of the forthcoming event.

Michael took the opportunity to speak to Elizabeth. "Miss Trelawney?"

"Yes?"

"Miss Trelawney, I owe you an apology. These last few days I have come to see that you are more than capable of working for The Alien's Office. Please, forgive me for doubting it."

"Thank you, Captain. And perhaps you will forgive me for getting so angry with you?"

"But of course." They smiled at each other.

Harcourt had also set to work, organising the dinner for Gordon. Lady Harcourt was in London, but Gordon's wife, it transpired, was at their estate on the Isle of Wight and thus not available. Harcourt set about inviting people who could be relied on and making the dinner party large enough to be a convincing celebration. He had the advantage that as Gordon's promotion was not yet official, a smaller, discreet party would not seem strange. He decided ten should be about right and issued invitations.

The soirée at Petersham's was going well. The Viscount was enjoying himself hugely, surrounded by the best of London's French society. Elizabeth was drifting from group to group, her senses keenly tuned for anything that might indicate L'Ange Bleu. The reception rooms of Petersham's home were ablaze with candles, footmen circulated with trays of drinks, some of them Musgrave's men. Petersham himself had entered wholeheartedly into their enterprise and could not have been more cooperative once Elizabeth had charmed him. She glanced at a clock on a mantelpiece. Another ten minutes and things were going to get interesting. She scanned the assembled guests, but no one stood out for any reason. She caught Petersham's eye and nodded to him, they both began to move.

In a corner of the room, Henry van Hagen was speaking apologetically to a small group of émigrés. "I am very sorry," he was saying, "but the army in Spain, or rather back in Portugal with its tail between its legs, is not about to liberate France, nor Spain for that matter. Wellington overreached himself with his move against Burgos, the army is in no state to do anything except lick its wounds."

Elizabeth saw Petersham move to listen. Henry was going on. "I have no idea what Wellington is thinking of, but I do know the army is weak, ravaged with disease, short of horses and will be going nowhere this year." There were some long faces amongst his listeners, who were slowly increasing in number as Henry warmed to his theme.

Then there was a slight stir at the door and Michael appeared, in his new full dress uniform, the old style, not the new. The silver braid and buttons shone on his chest with reflected candle light. He had his pelisse slung carelessly over his shoulder and his sabre hung low by his side, the red leather of his sword belt and the blue and silver of his sabretache contrasting with his highly polished hessian boots. As intended, he drew the attention of the whole room. He looked, Elizabeth admitted to herself, very handsome and dashing.

He stood in the door for a moment before Petersham caught sight of him and hailed him across the room. "I say, Captain Roberts, a moment, please." His raised voice caught the ear of all. "I believe you are just returned from the army?"

Michael strode over to him, "Indeed I am, My Lord."

"And you were on Wellington's staff?"

"Yes, My Lord."

"Then tell me, what is your opinion of Mister van Hagen's assertion that the army is in no fit state to take the field this year?"

Michael looked shocked, "My Lord?"

Petersham turned to Henry. "Mister van Hagen, would you be so kind as to repeat your view of the condition of Wellington's army for Captain Roberts here?"

"Of course, My Lord, although I must say it is not my view, but that of the many correspondents, former comrades, that I know with the army. They all inform me, quite independently, that the campaign against Burgos was an unmitigated disaster, the regiments are decimated and will take months to recover. They say there is no possibility of them taking the offensive this year."

Petersham turned to Michael. "What do you say, Captain?"

Michael looked horrified. "My Lord, it simply isn't true. Yes, the army suffered greatly on the retreat from Burgos," here Henry gave out a great guffaw, earning a glare from Michael, "but I am confident that his Lordship will soon put matters right."

"So the army will take the offensive?" Petersham asked. "After all, you are a staff officer, you should know."

"I... I cannot say, My Lord," Michael was looking very uncomfortable, "I am not privy to Lord Wellington's plans."

"But do you deny Mister van Hagen's description of the state of the army?"

Michael looked miserable. "No, My Lord."

A loud chattering broke out in the room. Elizabeth looked around, listening to, but not watching the performance. Then Henry's voice cut through.

"Even if he does manage to put some sort of force in the field, I have it on good authority that he will make another attempt on Burgos. He is, by all accounts," Henry put a lot of stress on his words, and then repeated them, "by all accounts, rather vexed at his failure and wants nothing more than a second bite at the cherry."

Petersham turned to Michael. "What do you say to that, Captain?"

Michael looked crestfallen. "Nothing, My Lord."

The chattering broke out again.

L'Ange Bleu was intrigued, excited at this exchange. She observed Michael closely. She noted the scar. It had to be the Captain Roberts that Renard and gone on about before he was sent to Spain. A dangerous man, apparently, although at the moment he looked anything but dangerous, handsome, yes, but very crestfallen. She was tempted to speak to him, who knew what she might learn, but she would wait until things settled down a little.

Elizabeth noticed a woman standing slightly apart, not joining in all the excited chatter produced by Henry and Michael. She knew her by sight, she wasn't a frequent presence in French society, except for the finest events. She turned to one lady she knew quite well.

"Madame, forgive me, but can you tell me who the lady is over there, in the rather striking red dress?"

"Who? Oh, her, that's Mademoiselle Celeste Gabrielle. She would be here. Keeps herself to herself unless there's a few Lords about."

"Thank you, Madame." She looked at the woman again. Celeste Gabrielle, she thought. Something stirred in the back of her mind, what was it? She saw Michael slope miserably away towards the refreshment room. Watched Gabrielle watch him. Henry was once again holding forth, and Gabrielle moved closer to listen, but kept glancing in Michael's direction.

Suddenly, Michael returned and placed himself squarely in front of Henry. "Mister van Hagen, I think you should stop, you should be more careful about what you say."

Henry glared. "Stop? Who the devil are you to say I should stop?"

Michael's arm shot out and he slapped Henry in the face with a glove. "I shall be happy to meet you at a time of your choosing, sir!"

Then Petersham was between them, two of Musgraves burly footmen joining him.

"Gentlemen, that is quite enough. I must insist that you both leave, now."

Michael spun on his heel and strode out of the room. In the hall he picked up his shako, stuck it on his head and left the house, with a small grin of pleasure on his face. Back in the reception room, Henry tried to bluster, but Petersham gestured and the two footmen closed on Henry, who turned and walked away with as much pride as he could muster.

Elizabeth realised that Mademoiselle Gabrielle looked a little cross. Clearly she had wanted to speak to Michael. She was an attractive woman and Elizabeth realised she was glad that she had been thwarted. Then it came to her. Celeste Gabrielle. Celeste meant heavenly. Gabrielle was the feminine version of Gabriel, the Archangel Gabriel, whose colour was said to be blue. She was the Blue Angel, L'Ange Bleu, she had to be. Heart pounding with the excitement of her realisation, she walked quickly across to one of Musgrave's men and whispered quietly to him. He nodded and left the room.

Outside Petersham's Michael had waited in the shadows until Henry came out. He called softly, "Here, Henry."

Henry joined him. "That was rather fun, Michael, but did you have to slap me quite so hard?"

Michael chuckled, "I'm sorry, Henry, but it had to look good. Come on, there's a carriage waiting up here to take us back to Harcourt House."

At Harcourt House, the Earl was in his drawing room, waiting for them. As Markam showed them in he leapt to his feet.

"Come in, come in, how did it go? Well, I hope? Tell me!"

Both men laughed and Michael replied. "Well enough, My Lord, I hope. Our little play was well received."

"Good, good, a glass of port for you both?"

"Thank you, My Lord, it was rather fun." Henry was grinning.

"I am sure it was, but has it worked, eh? That's the thing."

"Time will tell, My Lord," Michael said, "Musgrave has promised to let us know as soon as anything develops."

"And Miss Trelawney, she is safe?"

"Yes, My Lord."

"Splendid, her father would never forgive me if anything happened to her." The Earl looked at Michael. "You must take care of her, Roberts, great care."

Somewhat confused, Michael could only respond with "Yes, My Lord"

Markham handed glasses to Michael and Henry and then withdrew. They described to the Earl the scene at Petersham's, Henry rubbed his cheek ruefully and said he received less harm when he had been serving. He asked Michael if the retreat from Burgos had been as bad as he had heard. They discussed the loss of Pelly, Harcourt informed them Hay was getting the Lieutenant Colonelcy and command of the Regiment. It would all be confirmed before Michael returned. Harcourt also said he had heard that Michael had done well during his brief time in command of B Troop. Michael expressed the hope that one day he might have his own troop. The need for more horses was discussed and Harcourt said he had arranged to send out all he could and had contacted Guthrie, the horse dealer, for more horses.

They had been talking for an hour or more when there was the rattle of a carriage outside followed by knocking at the front door. A Minute or two later and Markham opened the door to announce "Mister Musgrave, My Lord."

A worn and tired looking Musgrave came in and Harcourt quickly poured him a port.

"Thank you, My Lord." He took a deep draught and looked at the three men anxiously watching him. "My Lord, Gentlemen, I think I can say, in all honesty, that tonight went better than I could possibly have imagined."

There was relief all round and Harcourt ushered Musgrave to a chair, saying, "Now, tell us all, please."

"I am very happy to be able to tell you that we have identified L'Ange Bleu. Or, rather, Miss Trelawney did, worked it out in a moment, remarkable, quite remarkable. We have her and her house under surveillance and should be able, in a few days, to identify anyone who works for her intelligence organisation."

"Are you quite sure you have the right woman?" Harcourt asked.

"I believe so, but now we have, let us say, a suspect we are looking into this woman's history most carefully. I expect confirmation of Miss Trelawney's identification within a few days." He addressed himself to Michael and Henry. "I am told your performance was most convincing, and our woman was a keen observer of it. I would expect, given the importance of what Mister van Hagen said, that she will send a messenger off to Paris as soon as possible."

"Is that easily done?" It was Harcourt who asked.

"Unfortunately, it is. The smugglers on the south coast frequently carry messages and people across the channel as well as fine French wines. In this case, it is rather to our advantage." He rose to his feet, putting down his empty glass. "And now I must return to my office, the next few days will be busy. Mister van Hagen, thank you for your help in this matter. I know, of course, that you will say nothing of it to anyone."

Henry bowed to Musgrave. "You may be quite sure, sir."

"Captain Roberts, perhaps you might come to my office tomorrow, say at eleven o'clock? We should know more by then." Michael nodded. "Then I shall bid you all goodnight."

The three men talked for little longer, Harcourt extolled Elizabeth's intelligence in identifying L'Ange Bleu and Henry declared that he should like to meet her one day, but that he must return to his estate in the morning. Then they all retired for the night. Later it occurred to Michael that he had no idea who was coming to the dinner tomorrow, he had been too engrossed in the arrangements for the soirée.

Michael had his chance to ask Harcourt who might be at the dinner when they met for breakfast. As usual, Lady Harcourt was taking her breakfast in her room.

"Ah, yes, I have been meaning to speak to you about that. I have put together a small party, after all, Gordon's promotion is not yet official, it must be a discreet gathering. Now, his wife is unavailable, and with you that made two single men. So, I have, err, invited the two Trelawney ladies. I understand that the elder has sufficiently recovered from her attack of gout. In addition Colonel Archer and his wife and Collyer, my agent, and his wife. Archer and Collyer both know that they may hear some odd things that must be kept confidential. Archer understands, Collyer will do as I say. I think that should give you a suitable audience. Oh, and I have also taken the liberty of informing the Trelawney ladies about what is going on. Had to really, Elizabeth can manage her aunt, I think we may rely on their discretion. What do you think?"

"I think that will do very well, My Lord," answered Michael, thinking he was very glad that he had at least begun to make his peace with Elizabeth, and wondering why she hadn't thought to tell him that she would be coming.

As had become a habit, Michael rode across to Hyde Park after breakfast. Harcourt had made available a fine chestnut hunter and he thoroughly enjoyed its forward going nature combined with admirable manners. He was riding quietly along, there were not many out in the cold weather, but at least it was not raining, when he became aware of someone riding up alongside him. He twisted in the saddle to see who it was.

"Lord Petersham! Good morning My Lord!"

"Mornin' Roberts. Glad to have met you."

"My Lord?"

"Yes. I take it that from your point of view that all went well last night?"

"Yes, My Lord, it was all very satisfactory."

"Good, glad to help. Enjoyed that little performance that you and your friend put on, most convincing.

And I understand it was, ah, err, heard  in the right quarters?"

"It was, My Lord."

"Hmm, yes, Miss Trelawney seemed very pleased, very pleased indeed. I gather from Musgrave that she pulled off a bit of a coup. Remarkable young woman, that."

"Yes, indeed, My Lord."

"Thinks a lot of you, ye know."

"My Lord?" Michael was astounded, both at what Petersham said and his frankness.

"Well, so her aunt tells me, she should know, practically raised her as her own."

Michael rode on in silence.

Petersham went on. "Now, there's a gentleman over there I must speak to. Think on what I say, Roberts, and take good care of her. Good morning to you."

"Good morning, My Lord," Michael managed as Petersham rode away. He rode on, thoughtful. If Elizabeth's aunt thought that, it must be true. Perhaps there was a possibility for him. Perhaps she did consider he might be more than a friend. Unbidden, a memory of that fateful night in Truro came to mind. Why had she opened her door and called out to him? He decided there could be many reasons, none important.

That evening, Colonel Archer and his wife were the first to arrive. Michael immediately thought that he looked far better than when he had last seen him in Spain. He greeted Michael warmly. "Hello, Roberts, glad to see you. I gather we are not to be surprised by anything you say tonight? Don't entirely understand it, but the Earl says and the Earl must be obeyed, eh?" He smiled broadly as they shook hands.

Michael just managed to say, "I hope I shall be able to explain in time, sir," when Markham announced "Miss Trelawney and Miss Elizabeth Trelawney."

Lady Harcourt swooped on her friend and Elizabeth approached Michael. "Good evening, Captain, not in uniform this evening?"

"No, the Earl thought not, not for a discreet little dinner. May I say that you look very fine this evening."

"Why, thank you. For myself, I am rather looking forward to your, err, forthcoming performance. Two in two nights. Shall we see you on the stage Captain?"

Michael caught the twinkle in her eye. "No, you may rest easy, this is for one, or rather two nights only."

Collyer and his wife were the next to arrive, followed closely by the guest of honour, Colonel Gordon. Gordon seemed surprised to see Michael, but there was no opportunity for the two to speak until they were seated for dinner. Michael was seated not quite opposite Gordon, with Mrs Archer to his left and Elizabeth on his right. It was well into the dinner that a slight lull in conversation gave Gordon a chance.

"I see you are returned from Spain, Captain, on leave or more permanently."

Michael looked petulant. "Permanently, I am sorry to say, Colonel." He made as if to say more, but stopped. Gordon rose to the bait.

"I do hope there is nothing wrong? I thought you were comfortably established on the staff?"

"I thought too, Colonel, but apparently the Marquess thought otherwise, sir. He decided he could dispense with my services. I think he did not like my stating the obvious."

"And what was that?" Gordon asked as the conversation around the table died away.

"To be perfectly frank, sir, I told him that Burgos had been a damned bad scrape, begging your pardons ladies, and that the army was so knocked about as a result that I didn't see how it could possibly take the field this year. I fear Lord Wellington don't like criticism, even when intended to be helpful."

"Helpful, you say. How so?"

"I picked up a hint that he wanted another crack at Burgos, he was certainly very out of sorts at being baulked of his prize there. I was merely trying to suggest that another such attempt, with the army in its present condition, would be inviting another disaster."

"Hmm. The army was certainly in a bad condition when I, unfortunately, was forced to leave for health reasons." He turned to Harcourt. "My Lord, what is your opinion?"

"Truly, I cannot say. Unlike Captain Roberts, I am not recently returned from the army, I have not seen it with my own eyes. I think we must take his observations at face value."

Archer joined in the conversation. "I understand our Regiment suffered badly, particularly in losses of horses. May I ask, My Lord, if you are able to put this right?"

Thanks to Archer's careful intervention, the conversation moved on and became general again. Elizabeth leant towards Michael and spoke softly. "Very well, done, Captain, another fine performance."

Two days later the Morning Chronicle carried a piece that could not have met Wellington's wishes more if he had written it himself. In a coruscating editorial it accused Wellington of the destruction of the army's offensive capabilities as a result of his disastrous attempt to take Burgos, a mistake that he seemed to be set on repeating. It suggested that the French in Spain could rest easy for the next year.

Michael read it with a considerable sense of satisfaction.

A summons to Musgrave's office came a few days later. He found him and Mason looking very pleased with themselves.

"Captain Roberts! I am delighted to be tell you that, no small thanks to Mason here and his men, that we have identified Mademoiselle Gabrielle's network. We watched as one of her servants, a Frenchman, departed her house the morning after the soirée, he took the Folkestone road, completely unaware that he was followed all the way. He contacted known smugglers on the Kent coast and was taken across two days later. I think we can safely assume that your false intelligence is now in the hands of Buonaparte. And may I congratulate you on the piece in the

Morning Chronicle, which, no doubt, has also reached Paris. Now, I am just waiting for Miss Trelawney and then we can discuss what is to be done with our L'Ange Bleu and her minions."

There was a tap at the door and Elizabeth came in. Musgrave welcomed her. "Miss Trelawney, thank you for coming. I was just telling the Captain that we have successfully identified Mademoiselle Gabrielle's people and can now set about arresting them all."

"Ah, yes. I have been thinking about that. I have a proposal to make concerning the Mademoiselle." Musgrave raised his eyebrows. "I think we should allow her to escape, to return to France."

There was a chorus of "What!" from the three men.

Musgrave objected. "But Miss Trelawney, why on earth should we do that? She is a foreign agent working against this country."

"Of course she is," Elizabeth began to explain, "but let me ask you, what would she be able to do if she escapes to France? She would never be able to return here now we know her. As an agent she will have been rendered useless. All she would be able to do is report to her masters in Paris. They would, undoubtedly, ask her about the surprising intelligence she had sent, and that they have read in the Chronicle. She would tell them how she witnessed the, err, debate between Captain Roberts, known to the French, and Mister van Hagen. She will describe how the Captain endeavoured to contradict Mister van Hagen and failed, failed entirely. It would add a huge degree of veracity to the intelligence."

There was a stunned silence, then Musgrave spoke. "Good God, Miss Trelawney, that is a brilliant stroke. Now, how do we do it?"

# Chapter 16

The people L'Ange Bleu, or Mademoiselle Gabrielle as they now referred to her, had working for her on intelligence matters were few in number. After watching them all carefully for a few days, they began to make arrests, slowly, starting with the least important. They had one stroke of luck when an arrest was observed by another of Gabrielle's people. The following day it was reported that Mademoiselle Gabrielle had hired a coach and departed for Folkstone. A flurry of arrests completed matters. All this Michael learnt second hand, he was left idle at Harcourt's. He saw nothing of Elizabeth.

Michael took the opportunity of his idleness to visit his lawyer, Mister Rutherford. Rutherford, looking more bear like than ever, welcomed Michael into his gloomy office.

"Captain Roberts, a pleasure to see you again." Rutherford told the clerk who had brought Michael to get coffee for them both and then see that they weren't disturbed. "Tell me, Captain, how long are you with us for? Have you returned for good, or merely on leave?"

"Only a little leave, I fear, I have to be back in Portugal by the end of April."

Rutherford replied with a quiet "Hmm," and looked thoughtful. After a moment he began, slowly. "Captain, you will, I hope, accept that as your lawyer I must have your best interests at heart and that I must advise you accordingly?"

"Yes, of course." Michael wondered what this leading up to.

"I have heard from Senhor Furtado, a few days ago. He informed me that he has completed the sale of your quinta for what he considers to be a fair price. I have made a few enquiries and would agree with that assessment."

"I am pleased to hear it."

"Yes, and the money from the sale is now with your bank in Lisbon. Senhor Furtado was good enough to inform me of how that account now stands." He reached for a sheet of paper and perused it quickly. "I, as your lawyer, know the state of your account with your bank here. This is a summary of your financial position, leaving aside your military pay, which is, to say the least, irregular." He handed the sheet of paper to Michael and went on. As he did so Michael read it, saw the figures and was surprised. "You will see, that you are a man with a comfortable level of capital. The figure at the bottom is what I believe your income from that capital might be."

"Oh," was all Michael could manage.

"I have seen this situation coming for a while, Captain, as has Senhor Furtado. We have, forgive us, discussed it. We, ah, correspond quite regularly, you know. We found that we have a common interest. Apart, that is, from your good self."

"Do you?"

"Yes, err, we both keep bees."

It was so unexpected that Michael could barely suppress a chuckle. Rutherford and Furtado, bee keepers!

"Quite, it is a little unusual, but we both find it a relaxing pastime, calming even. Leaving that aside, however, and I trust you will take the revelation as a confidence?" Michael nodded. "Leaving that aside, I am duty bound to advise you that are in a position to live a comfortable life as an independent gentleman of moderate wealth. There is no reason, no financial reason, that is, for you to continue in the army."

"Ah!"

Rutherford went on, staring up at the ceiling as he did. "You are a young man, Captain, and in an ideal position to settle down to a comfortable life. Take a wife, raise a family. Forgive me if I am presumptuous, but these things are possible and I am bound to tell you." He dropped his eyes from the ceiling and looked directly at Michael. "There, I have said what I needed to. You may like to give the matter some thought before you return to Portugal."

Michael met his gaze and thought, but not for long. For a brief moment he was tempted, perhaps Elizabeth? Then he realised that he simply could not do it, not while the war continued. It was something he would have to see though to the end, there was unfinished business. He also thought he might get bored. No, when the war was over, then, perhaps, he might take Rutherford's advice.

"Thank you, Mister Rutherford, but I have no intention of leaving the army, not while the war continues."

"I can't say you surprise me, Captain. Now, let us discuss how you might make the most of your capital."

On his return to Harcourt House he was rather taken aback and concerned to find a letter from Horse Guards waiting for him. It was a peremptory command to attend at his earliest convenience. There was no explanation. Harcourt was not at home, but Michael left a message with Markham. Michael changed into his uniform, the new one, and set off in a hackney for Horse Guards. At Horse Guards his enquiries as to why he was wanted received no answer. He was simply put in a waiting room by a porter and told to wait. He heard the clock above chiming. After it had struck the quarter hours twice and the hour once, the door opened and a young Guards' Lieutenant appeared.

"Captain Roberts?"

Michael rose to his feet. "Yes. Can you tell me..."

"If you would just be so good as to follow me, sir"

The Lieutenant led him along corridors and upstairs before showing him into a more comfortably furnished waiting room. Michael's heart sank.

"If you would be so good as to wait here, sir?" The Lieutenant disappeared before Michael could answer. He put his shako, with its tall plume, that he had been carrying tucked under his arm, on the chair next to him and tried to make himself comfortable. The clock struck another quarter hour.

The door suddenly opened and another Guards' Lieutenant appeared. "Captain Roberts?"

"Yes, can you tell me..."

"This way, sir, His Royal Highness will see you now."

His mind in a turmoil of speculation, Michael picked up his shako and followed the Lieutenant to a large room with officers and clerks busy at desks. He recognised it. The Lieutenant strode to a door on the other side, knocked briefly and opened it, announcing as he went through, "Captain Roberts, your Royal Highness."

He stepped to one side and Michael followed him in. Seated at a desk on the far side of the room was the Duke of York. Michael marched smartly forward and stood to attention in front of him. The Duke gave him an appraising look.

"Roberts, I want an explanation."

"Your Royal Highness?"

"Don't Royal Highness me, Roberts. I have heard about the incident at Petersham's, about the public argument between you and a former officer of your Regiment," he glanced at a paper in front of him, "a Mister van Hagen. An argument that, according to witnesses, resulted in a challenge being issued, by you, sir, by you. I also understand, from Colonel Gordon, that at a dinner at Earl Harcourt's you expressed views of a very disparaging nature about the Marquess of Wellington, his conduct in Spain and the state of the army. Views that were subsequently published in that damn rag, the Morning Chronicle. What do you have to say, sir?"

"That I was acting under orders from the Marquess of Wellington, sir. It is an intelligence matter."

"What? It is, is it."

"Yes, sir."

The Duke of York gave him a long hard stare. "Musgrave involved, is he?"

"Yes, sir."

"And he'll bear witness to anything you say?"

"I believe so, sir, and Earl Harcourt."

"And Gordon?"

"No, sir. Perhaps, sir, if I might tell you the whole story from the beginning?"

"Damn it, I suppose you had better. Take a seat Captain. Arnold, coffee, there's a good fellow."

While Michael told the whole story to the Duke, he heard the clock strike the hour before he had finished. When he finished his story, Michael fell silent.

The Duke asked, "And you say Musgrave and Harcourt will confirm what you say?"

"Yes, sir."

"And Gordon has no idea?"

"No, sir."

"Hmm, probably for the best. What could he do anyway? He'd look a fool."

"Yes, sir."

The Duke looked sharply at him and frowned. "Be careful, Captain." He toyed with a pen on his desk. "Very well, be off with you. You'll be leaving for Portugal soon?"

"Yes, sir, Lord Wellington said I should be back by the end of April."

"Then enjoy the rest of your time in England, Captain. Good day to you."

Michael rose, bowed, and with a "Thank you, your Royal Highness," he made for the door where the Lieutenant was already standing ready.

He got back to Harcourt House just in time for dinner and had to tell the Earl the whole story. The Earl's sole comment was, "Harumph, I expect he'll want the whole story from me at some point."

At last, a note arrived from Musgrave, it merely informed him that Mademoiselle Gabrielle had reached home safely. Michael shared it with Harcourt, who was delighted. "That is splendid news. Wellington will be well pleased with you when he hears all about this. Reflects very well on you and the Regiment. We must celebrate. A small dinner, perhaps? Discreet, of course. Nothing formal. Mister Musgrave and Miss Elizabeth, and her aunt to keep the numbers even. Aunt Mary can gossip with my lady wife. Yes, six, that sounds right. I shall arrange it. Tomorrow evening, I think? No, the day after, Lady Harcourt has some engagement or other tomorrow evening."

Musgrave arrived first in his carriage, followed moments later by the Misses Trelawney in theirs. Markham was able to show all three into the drawing room together. "Miss Trelawney, Miss Elizabeth Trelawney, Mister Musgrave."

The Earl had been standing in front of the fire, his wife was seated on a comfortable sofa, Michael was at the sideboard, pouring them all sherries. Harcourt strode forward to meet his guests.

"Good evening, good evening, Miss Trelawney, Elizabeth, Musgrave, you'll all take a glass of sherry? Course you will. Roberts, three more!"

Elizabeth's aunt took a seat next to her friend, Lady Harcourt and the two were soon deep in conversation. Harcourt took Musgrave's arm.

"A word if I may, Musgrave," and led him to a quiet corner where the two talked with their backs to the room.

Michael handed Elizabeth a glass of sherry and glanced around. Then he spoke. "Miss Trelawney, will you allow me to congratulate you?"

Elizabeth raised her eyebrows inquisitively. "Congratulate me, Captain? Why should you do that?"

"Because the soirée  was your idea, you identified L'Ange Bleu as Mademoiselle Gabrielle and it was your suggestion to allow her to escape to Paris. Our success is due to you."

Elizabeth coloured slightly. "But you brought Faucher to us and without him we would still be looking for a man. You also performed brilliantly with Mister van Hagen and managed Colonel Gordon very well."

"Well, yes, but..."

"No buts, Captain!" She smiled, "Or perhaps I may call you Michael once more? Privately, of course."

"Certainly you may."

"Then I think you may call me Elizabeth." They smiled at each other and raised their glasses in salute.

Across the room aunt Mary and Lady Harcourt exchanged meaningful glances.

Dinner was a pleasant and convivial affair, they were seated together, but Elizabeth had Harcourt to her left at the head of the table and Michael had Lady Harcourt to his right at the foot of the table. He was opposite aunt Mary while Musgrave was opposite Elizabeth. The seating and the intimacy of the gathering gave Michael and Elizabeth no opportunity for anything other than polite conversation. Eventually the dinner ended and the ladies rose to retire. Michael moved up to sit opposite Musgrave. Markham poured the men glasses of port and then withdrew.

"Sorry to abandon you like that, earlier, Roberts, but I needed a word with Musgrave."

"Yes, My Lord?"

"Yes, seems I was right. York asked Musgrave, or rather he sent an aide to ask, about the truth of this whole affair."

"Oh!"

"Yes, and where do you think I was yesterday afternoon? With the Duke. Interrogated me like some damned subaltern." He chuckled. "Said he supposed you were to be congratulated. Looks forward to hearing you are back in Spain."

Musgrave laughed at the expression on Michael's face. "Come now, Captain, take the compliment, ignore the jibe."

"Thank you, sir, but surely it is Miss Trelawney who deserves the plaudits."

"Ah," Musgrave looked serious, "arguably, yes, but for her own safety and future effectiveness as an agent, the less said about her the better." He caught Michael's fleeting reaction to the comment. "Have no fear, I shall take great care of her, she has a fine mind and is valuable to me, and others." He had a twinkle in his eye and Michael felt his ears redden. Musgrave changed the subject and they talked of other things.

Harcourt emptied his glass. "Gentlemen, I think the ladies have had long enough, let us join them." So saying, he rose from the table and led the way back to the drawing room where coffee was served.

Michael managed to place himself in a chair next to Elizabeth and took advantage of the serving of the coffee to ask, quietly "Elizabeth, I wonder if I might see you, I have a week before I need to leave and..."

"Yes, you may, perhaps Hyde Park tomorrow morning? It will be easier to talk. Shall we say ten o'clock?"

Later that night, Harcourt and his wife were alone in their private drawing room. "William?"

"Yes, Mary?"

"What do you think of Captain Roberts?"

"What? Oh! Err, he's a very fine officer, everything I hear and see tells me so. And he has proven very adept in the less regular duties he has undertaken. He is well thought of by people who matter."

"Yes." She paused. "I think he is also well thought of by Elizabeth."

"You've noticed, have you?"

"William, you would have to be blind not to. And Mary tells me the same, she thinks Elizabeth is very taken, very."

"Serious do you think?"

"I do."

"Well, he's off back to Portugal in a week. Probably gone a long time." He looked thoughtfully at his wife. "Do you think I should write to her father? There's time, could take a twelve month to get a reply."

"I think perhaps you should."

At ten o'clock Michael was riding in Hye Park, slowly, looking out for Elizabeth. He caught sight of her, riding towards him, and his heart sank. He recognised the gentleman riding with her, it was Viscount Petersham. Then Petersham caught sight of him, said something to Elizabeth and pushed his horse forward to a trot. As he passed by Michael he raised the handle of his crop to the brim of his hat in salute.

"That was Petersham?" Michael asked as he swung his horse alongside Elizabeth's.

"Yes, yes it was. He was talking about the soirée the other day, said he gathered it had all worked well. I was just telling him that everything had worked out splendidly when he saw you, said he had to go, would leave us alone, and just rode off."

There was an awkward silence, neither wanting to address the implications of Petersham's comment. A gentleman in difficulty, clearly over horsed, provided a suitable distraction and change of subject.

"How is your black, what was his name, Johnny?"

"Very well, thank you, I had leave him in Lisbon. My groom, Bradley, has left me, he is marrying a Spanish woman."

"Oh dear. What will you do?"

"I already have a new groom." He started to tell her about Carlos and his friends and growing up in Lisbon. They talked happily until it started to rain. Then Michael insisted that Elizabeth should go home, despite her protestations that she had known worse out hunting. Eventually she agreed, but only when Michael said he would ride with her. Before finally parting they made arrangements to go to the theatre that night. Michael undertook to get tickets for something.

As it was, all he could manage at short notice was two tickets for The Grecian Daughter in Wyatt's new theatre on Drury Lane, with Sarah Bartley in the lead role of Euphrasia. It was not particularly light hearted and Michael promised to do better if Elizabeth would give him another chance. He managed Davy Jones Locker with a Miss Brown in the lead. This pantomime was far lighter and they emerged from the theatre smiling.

Elizabeth's carriage with her coachman Matthews and footman Varney in attendance, was waiting a little way down the street. They strolled slowly towards it. For early March it was a remarkably fine night.

"That, Michael, was much better. Thank you."

"And tomorrow?"

"Let me think. Meet me in the park, say at eleven? When do you have to leave?"

"My coach departs at half past seven in the evening the day after tomorrow."

"Oh, that soon? Then let me think, I shall see you tomorrow. Do you have any fixed engagements before you leave?" They reached the carriage where Varney was holding the door open. Michael helped her in, Varney closed the door and climbed up next to Matthews. Elizabeth leant out of the window.

"Do you?"

"I must dine with the Earl and Lady Harcourt on the day I leave, they are dining early and the Earl is sending me in his carriage to the coach inn." He smiled ruefully. "An officer has to obey his Colonel."

"So tomorrow is your last free night?"

"Yes,"

"Then I shall see you in the morning." She rapped on the carriage roof and it started to move. Elizabeth was barely visible in the carriage, but Michael heard her "Good night, Michael," as the carriage drove off.

At a quarter to eleven, Michael was impatiently walking his horse in the park. It was cold, the breath of horses and riders clear in the still air. There was a clear blue sky and there had been a frost. Then he saw Elizabeth entering the park and trotted over to her, falling in alongside.

"Good morning, Elizabeth, a fine winter morning."

She smiled at him, then looked a little downcast. "I suppose it will be warmer in Portugal?"

"Not so much, it's cold up in the mountains."

They rode along in silence. Michael thought Elizabeth looked a little nervous about something. Eventually she spoke. "Michael, I wonder, would you come to dinner at my house tonight? My aunt will be there, of course, but no one else. Well, Varney, of course, and my other servants, but they won't be dining with us." She smiled broadly.

"How is your aunt? The last time I came for dinner with you she was unwell." He was gratified to see a little colour appear in Elizabeth's cheeks.

"She is very well, as you know from dinner the other night, but we will just have to see." She paused. "It will be our last chance to talk before you return to the Peninsular and we do know each other much better now so I am sure there will much to talk about. Now, let us exercise these horses!"

Dinner was a relaxed affair. Aunt Mary was good company, intelligent, well educated and her views often forthright. Michael could see where Elizabeth got a lot of her character from, if all the Trelawney's were the same. Varney waited on them and the atmosphere was very much that of a small family dinner. Naturally, the two ladies were interested in the war in Portugal and Spain and particularly what he thought of Wellington, having served on his staff.

"But I do not spend that much time in his company!" He laughed. "I am a very junior staff officer. I spend more time with Don Julian Sanchez."

"Oh" said aunt Mary, "I have read of him, isn't he some sort of brigand?"

"No, not at all," answered Michael, and spent the next half hour regaling them with stories of Don Julian, Strenuwitz and their exciting break out from Ciudad Rodrigo. That led to Lloyd and his horse and from there to the new Mrs Lloyd.

Finally, Varney cleared the last plates and aunt Mary said, "Now, I am afraid I have a little bit of a headache coming on, so I will bid you good night, Captain, and thank you for the most diverting stories." And a moment later Michael and Elizabeth were alone.

"Elizabeth?"

"Yes?"

"I have been thinking."

"Oh dear." She smiled disarmingly.

"No, no, I have been thinking about your work, with Musgrave."

"Oh?" There was a warning note in Elizabeth's voice.

"Yes, and I have to say that I am, err, that is, I think you, err, you have impressed me, Elizabeth. I know I said that I thought it was no work for a woman, well, I was wrong. It is perfectly right for the right sort of woman, which, clearly, you are. It is, in some ways, no different from what I do."

"Perhaps not the soldiering, Michael, but your role in the other war, the secret war. And you are rather good at that, or so everyone tells me."

"Thank you, then we understand each other?"

"I believe we do, thank you."

"I only ask, if you will forgive me, that you take care, please."

"And do you care for me, Michael?" She could hardly believe what she had asked, it had come out spontaneously, without her thinking, it was too forward, she dreaded the answer, but realised that she wanted to know.

Michael looked her in the eye, "Yes, Elizabeth, I do, very much." He went on, hesitantly. "I should like to think, I hope that, perhaps..."

"Yes, Michael, I care for you as well."

Some unknown impulse drove them both to their feet and to stand together, face close to face, they took each other's hands.

"Elizabeth, would you do me the honour..."

She dropped his hand and placed a finger on his lips. "No, Michael, not that." He looked distraught. "Not now, not yet."

"But..."

"No, Michael, but you may ask me when this war is over. I hope you understand?"

"I,... I think so." He managed a weak smile. "A soldiers lot is nothing if not uncertain."

"Whichever war they fight."

"Whichever war. I love you, Elizabeth."

"And I you, Michael, just make sure you come back to me when the war is over."

They kissed.

At half past seven precisely the coach for Falmouth rolled out of the yard of the Swan With Two Necks. Michael had a seat inside while Hall was up on top. Apart from changes of horses there would be no halt until Exeter, at about three o'clock the following afternoon. There they would have a couple of hours, or less if the journey was slow, to get some dinner before the last leg to Falmouth where the coach was due in at around four in the morning. Michael glanced around at his fellow travellers and decided he would spend as much time as possible asleep. It would give him time to think, and he had much to think on.

Just after five in the morning, a day and a half later, he walked into the yard at the back of his uncle's house. As he had expected, there was a light in the kitchen window and he pushed open the backdoor and walked in. The servants were seated around the kitchen table having breakfast. Jenny, the maid, gave a little shriek at his sudden and unexpected appearance. Trevellick and Choak both started up to their feet while Mrs Trevellick cried out.

"Oh, Mister Michael, you gave me a fright, we weren't expecting you, sir, not at all."

Michael chuckled. "My apologies, Mrs Trevellick, I am just arrived on the coach from London. Hall is on his way with a porter and our baggage, Mister Trevellick, Mister Choak, would you be so kind as to go out and help him?"

"Right you are, sir," from Trevellick and "It's good to see 'e sir," from Choak, before they disappeared into the dark.

"Now, sir," said Mrs Trevellick, "ye'll be a wanting some breakfast, no doubt, sir. I'll get something for you right away, but there's no fire in the dining room as yet, sir. Your uncle and grandfather won't be a stirring for another hour or so, sir."

"Mrs Trevellick, if you will allow it, I shall be happy to eat here, and something for Hall as well, if you please."

Later there was a fire in the dining room and Michael stood before it as he heard footsteps hurrying towards the door. It flew open and his grandfather bustled in, still wearing his nightshirt with a quilted banyan for warmth.

"Michael, my boy, how are you, this is a surprise, I could hardly believe it when Trevellick told me you were here. Have you long? Are you staying? Tell me!" He shook Michael warmly by the hand, his face alight with pleasure.

As he finished, uncle Jocelyn also appeared, asked the same questions and shook Michael's hand just as warmly. Mrs Trevellick appeared with a pot of tea and Michael urged his relatives to sit down and eat while he explained things.

"I am afraid that I am only here until I can take the packet to Lisbon. That should be Saturday morning..."

"But Michael, it's Wednesday today!" His grandfather exclaimed. "That's no time at all, and you will have to be aboard on Friday evening!."

"Yes, I'm afraid so, but I am under orders. I must be at the Packet Office when it opens at ten to book our passages, and then I must see the customs people and make all the arrangements."

"Then we shall at least have your company for two nights, we must make the most of them." Michael's grandfather was philosophical about it.

Michael, accompanied by Hall, spent most of the rest of the day securing passage for them and sorting out customs clearance for their baggage. Michael had travelled in uniform and stayed in it to deal with their travel arrangements, it seemed to help a little. Dinner was a small affair, just the three of them, Michael, his grandfather and his uncle. They bemoaned the fact that they had seen so little of him during his visit to England. Uncle Jocelyn asked after Faucher and was reassured when Michael told him that he had proved very helpful and was certainly no supporter of Buonaparte. His grandfather asked after his old friend, Earl Harcourt, and was gratified when Michael passed on the Earl's very best wishes to him for a long retirement. He then asked after Elizabeth.

"Tell me Michael, did you see Miss Trelawney when you were in London?"

"Ah, um, yes, yes, I did."

"It was such a surprise and a great pleasure when she called on me. And when she particularly asked to be reminded to you. Were you able to see much of her?" He asked with an innocent expression.

"I, err, yes, we went to the theatre twice, and she was at a dinner Earl Harcourt gave."

"She struck me as a delightful and most appealing young lady."

"Yes, she is."

"Is there, perhaps, something you might wish to confide in us?"

"What? No, no, not at all, we are friends, that is all."

The Reverend Isles did not believe him for one moment, and he was quietly very pleased. He glanced at Jocelyn and saw that he had a slightly pleased twinkle in his eye. Michael determinedly changed the subject.

"How do you find it, living in Falmouth after all those years in your country parish?" As he listened to his grandfather and uncle chatting away about it, he realised that all was well. Indeed, he thought that both men seemed particularly lively.

Late on Friday afternoon, Michael and Hall went aboard the packet Duke of Kent, captained by Robert Cotesworth. He knew the captain a little and looked forward to a convivial voyage. At first light on Saturday, the winds being favourable, the packet slipped quietly out of the Carrick Roads and headed for Lisbon. They had a fast and uneventful passage. Some packets had been attacked by French and American privateers and a careful lookout was kept. Cotesworth admitted that he was glad to have on board two more men who could handle muskets. It took two and a half weeks and Michael and Hall stood at the ship's rail and watched as they sailed slowly up the Tagus to Lisbon. The weather was mild and dry, a hint of spring in the air, it was a welcome change from the cold and wet of the English winter.

"You'll be glad to be back, sir? Hall asked Michael.

"I am Hall, it is probably more home to me than Falmouth is."

"The weather's better, sir."

Michael laughed. "Indeed it is, Hall, now let's get ourselves ready to go ashore."

They walked up to the house from the docks, followed by mule drawn cart with all their baggage. Michael nearly led them in the back way, past the stables, but then he thought, no, damn it, I'm coming home and I'll come home through the front door. They walked up the steep street and he hammered on the door. There was a pause and then the door swung open to reveal White, whose face broke into a huge smile when he saw who was knocking. Within minutes all the baggage was in and Michael was surrounded by familiar faces. Bernardo greeted him, then rushed off to the stables to get Carlos.

"Duw, it's good to see you back safe, Captain."

"Thank you, Lloyd. Is everyone well?"

"Yes, sir, except Julietta has started teething."

Michael suddenly realised there was something different about the hallway and the open room off it. "Has this been painted?"

"Aye, sir, it has. Me, White, Bernardo and young Jacinto have been right busy, sir. Bernardo said as he couldn't do much in the garden because it's winter, so we decided to freshen up the house, sir. I hope that's alright, sir. Carlos and I have kept all the horses fit as well, Johnny is in the best condition I think he's ever been in." He chuckled. "Mrs Lloyd said what she thought wanted doing, and we just got on with it, sir."

Michael turned to Mrs Lloyd standing nearby, Julietta in her arms. "Have you indeed, Mrs Lloyd, well, good for you. When I think about it the house need sprucing up a bit. You had better show me what you've done, but first, coffee. I haven't had a decent cup of it since I left Lisbon."

The coffee was good, the work on the house had brightened it up and Michael was very happy with it. Mrs Lloyd informed him that Senhor Furtado had been a regular visitor and had made the funds available for the work. Michael asked for a cold lunch in the dining room and told Lloyd that he would have to go and report to General Peacock out at Belem. Then he wanted to see Sir Charles Stuart, the Ambassador.

"Lloyd, you come with me, best uniform, and I'll ride Johnny, I take it Rodrigo is well?"

"Oh, yes, sir. Good food and the right amount of exercise has done them all the power of good. You'd think they were different animals from how they were after Burgos, sir."

The visit to Belem was short and routine. The visit to Stuart was more interesting. The Ambassador greeted Michael and asked how things had gone in England. He was pleased with what he heard. They were sitting in Stuart's comfortably appointed office, in armchairs near the fire.

"You will be interested to hear what I have to tell you. I don't know how up to date you are with recent developments, but the French have left Madrid and marched north, Joseph has set himself up in Valladolid."

"Good Lord."

"Yes, the south of Spain is now free of the French. Since then, I have heard from Senora Ortega. Firstly, she tells me that Diego reappeared in Madrid, about three weeks after you sailed, from what I can tell. She's not sure what happened, but Diego is now working for Renard. Further, he appears to have told Renard about Faucher and Lucroy. So we may assume Renard thinks that you are in England, which may just be for the best." Stuart looked a little uncomfortable.

"Sir?"

"Yes, you see, Renard visited Ortega, told her that he knew she was a spy. Rather put the fear of God into the good lady. Then he told her that she was quite safe because Joseph thought so highly of her. There was, however, something she could do for him."

"Oh!"

"Yes. He, err, asked her to see that a message reached you."

"Me, sir?"

"Yes. He wanted you to know that it didn't matter where you were, you could run away to England, it would make no difference, he wasn't frightened by your threats, but he was going to see you dead."

"Ah." Michael chuckled. "I suppose he is only doing what I did."

"Yes, I suppose so, but it is just as well he doesn't know where you are and that you are joining the army again. You must consider, however, that with the French concentrated in the north and Joseph in

Valladolid, it will be much easier for intelligence to be exchanged with Paris. I suspect that, somehow or other, he will soon know where you are."

"Yes, sir, but I also know where he is."

The next few days were spent preparing to travel to Freineda. The pack saddles were carefully fitted to the mules and everything checked. All the equipment was gone over closely to check for any problems or weaknesses. Hall spent time putting a razor edge on the sabres. Pistols were checked and then Michael opened the small crate from Baker. Hall whistled when he saw the two rifled carbines and Lloyd muttered softly, "Duw, there's lovely."

"I thought they might be more useful than the Pagets," observed Michael, "I know they will be a little slower to load, but I think accuracy might be more useful, particularly if we are off on our own somewhere. I've tried them myself and I think you will like them."

They were a few inches longer than the Paget carbines they had been carrying, but fitted easily enough to the saddles in the same way.

"We can have few trials with them on the way up to Freineda," Michael said, "you'll have to make up some cartridges, but there's a good supply of balls and a mould to make more. The Pagets can be handed in to the Regiment as soon as we come across them."

Lloyd and Hall grinned with delight.

Three weeks later, Michael led his party into Freineda. As they rode into the little square in front of Wellington's headquarters, the first person he saw was the Marquess of Wellington himself, walking up and down, arm in arm with Don Julian Sanchez. Sanchez saw him and drew Wellington's attention to him. Michael saluted and dismounted from Johnny.

Wellington hailed him. "Captain Roberts, returned from your success in London!"

"Thank you, My Lord."

"Get your party organised and come and see me."

Don Julian gave Michael a friendly wave and then the two men fell to walking and talking again.

Nothing much had changed in Michael's absence, except for the welcome return of Murray to his role as Quartermaster General. He was in Wellington's room when Michael knocked on the door and entered in response to a gruff "Come!"

Wellington expressed his pleasure at Michael's efforts in London, then asked, "Tell me, how the Devil did you get that information into the Chronicle? It was perfection, Captain, perfection."

Michael told the story of the dinner at Earl Harcourt's, which caused Wellington to laugh aloud and Murray to smile. He also told him about his interview with the Duke of York. As Murray observed, "His Royal Highness can't have minded, or you would be under arrest awaiting your court martial." Wellington laughed again.

"Now, Captain, getting the intelligence to Paris, how did that go?"

Michael told the story of L'Ange Bleu, how Musgrave and his people had helped, how Petersham had helped.

Wellington clapped his hands in pleasure. "Well done, sir, very well done."

"Thank you My Lord. I called on Sir Charles Stuart in Lisbon. He told me about the French giving up Madrid and moving to Valladolid, Renard with him, sir."

Wellington grew serious. "Yes, that damned Renard. I gather he is busy trying to discover what we are about, which he mustn't discover. Why he can't be satisfied with the Chronicle I don't know. I also know about the message he sent for you." He looked at Michael for a moment. "I believe I have said this before, Captain. This had become personal for Renard. He will come after you until he is stopped. He will have to be taken care of."

Also by

David J Blackmore

Published by Brindle Books Ltd.

## To The Douro

### Wellington's Dragoon; Book One

A young man's decision to fight leads to a war within
a war…

To love…

To loss…

…and a quest for vengeance, as he plays a vital role
for the future Duke of Wellington.


## Secret Lines

### Wellington's Dragoon; Book Two

From the battlefield of Talavera,
by way of the guerrilla's merciless war,
to the back streets of Lisbon,
our hero fights to keep Wellington's great secret.
Can Michael gain the revenge he seeks and protect
the Secret Lines?

# Behind The Lines

## Wellington's Dragoon Book Three

From Buçaco to the fortified lines where the French
are finally stopped,
Behind the lines in Lisbon where the secret war
continues,
Through the devastated Portuguese countryside,
Michael Roberts continues his war, has a chance for
love, kills, and becomes a changed man.

# A Different Kind of War

## Wellington's Dragoon Book Four

An unhappy and angry Michael Roberts returns to
England expecting to be wasting his time at the
Regimental depot instead of fighting the French. He
soon discovers that the war is also being waged in
England, although it is a different kind of war.

# The Road To Madrid

## Wellington's Dragoon Book Five

Returning to the Peninsular, Michael Roberts finds himself plunged back into the intelligence war in Lisbon.
Joining the army in Spain he meets old friends, fights at Villagarcia, and, with Don Julian Sanchez, scours the road to Madrid, finding romance on the way.
He is present at the great victory of Salamanca and marches with Wellington to Madrid, where his success in the intelligence war comes at a price.